THEN THERE WAS YOU

ALEXA RIVERS

To you, dear reader,
for giving me the chance to do what I love.

PROLOGUE

Proposed conditions of sale:

1. Purchase of land is to the value of two million dollars.

2. The existing lodge cannot be demolished within ten years of sale.

3. No more than twenty people may be accommodated on the property at any time.

4. The waterfall trail must be maintained for visitor access.

5. The cabin may continue to be tenanted by Tione Kingi and his dogs (Trevor, Zee, Bella, and Pixie) for as long as they wish to stay.

6. The purchaser accepts responsibility for the care and feeding of the cat that lives beneath the lodge for the remainder of its natural life.

7. Any attractive male guest may be required, upon invitation from the Bridge Club, to attend one of their weekly gatherings (shirt optional, but not recommended).

STERLING KNIGHT SCANNED the ridiculous list of demands he'd received from Katarina Hopa, who owned the beach-front lodge his company wanted to acquire, and returned to

1

item seven, arching a brow. He wondered who was responsible for determining whether a man met the criteria for being "attractive"—and also what drug Mrs. Hopa had been under the influence of when she'd penned this letter.

If he agreed to her conditions of sale, the property would be rendered useless. His boss wouldn't be able to develop it, and Sterling wouldn't be able to prove how worthy he was of the great responsibility bestowed upon him. He shifted in the seat of his car, took a pen from his shirt pocket, and tapped each item in turn. Were there any he could accept?

For starters, the market value of the land was only a quarter of what she'd requested. He'd stopped by the place on the way to the cafe where he was scheduled to meet her in five minutes, and the building wasn't in great condition. He couldn't leave it standing because it would be an eyesore to the wealthy clientele he intended to attract.

Number three, he could work with. Keeping a resort on the smaller side would add to its perceived exclusivity. Number four was also a possibility, although he hadn't seen the trail, so he didn't know what he'd be working with. Still, having private access to a waterfall would be another drawcard for guests. Demand number five was impossible, as was six. If they demolished the lodge, the cat would be homeless. He'd do the right thing, though, and have someone catch the creature and take it to a shelter. Maybe this Tione guy. He sounded like he'd know how to deal with a cat.

He eyed the seventh request, rapping the pen against the paper as he thought. Who were the Bridge Club, and why did they want access to handsome guests? The whole thing sounded shady to him. Quite possibly illegal. He put a strike through the words, then tucked the paper into his pocket, adjusted his suit, grabbed his briefcase, and climbed out of the company car, locking it behind him. Haven Bay seemed like a safe little town, but hundreds of tourists passed through each day, and he wasn't taking any chances.

He made his way into the town square, a cobblestoned area speckled with old-fashioned streetlamps like something out of a quaint English village, and searched for Cafe Oasis, where Mrs. Hopa had asked to meet him. Spotting it on the opposite side of the square, he made his way past a statue and pushed his way in.

A doorbell chimed as he entered, and he only just managed not to flinch in surprise—it had been a long time since he'd heard anything of the kind since they weren't popular in busier Auckland stores. The cafe's interior was charming, he supposed, if you liked wooden floors and patterned wallpaper. He didn't see anyone who looked like he believed Mrs. Hopa would, and he was debating whether to order coffee when the table nearest him fell silent, six gray-haired ladies turning to stare with expressions ranging from curious to hostile.

One of them, a cherub-cheeked biddy in a pink tracksuit, slowly rose and shuffled over. She was less than five feet tall, but her piercing blue eyes skewered him, threatening all kinds of harm that should have made him laugh, but oddly sent a cold shiver down his spine.

"Good afternoon, Mr. Knight," she said in a tone that wouldn't have been out of place in a face-off from an old western movie. He half expected a tumbleweed to blow by.

"Mrs. Hopa?" he asked, surprised. He'd assumed the Katarina Hopa he'd be meeting was the same one who'd risen to fame in the women's rally circuit—it wasn't a common name, after all—but perhaps he'd been mistaken.

"No." The old woman's voice was steely, her apricot lips pursed together. "I'm Betty. I represent Mrs. Hopa."

"Oh." He glanced back over at the table she'd come from. "Is she here?"

"I'm afraid not." Betty crossed her arms, scowling up at him. "You'll be dealing with us today."

"No offense, ma'am, but I prefer to deal directly with my business contacts rather than an intermediary."

"Too bad." Her eyes narrowed. "If I've learned anything in all my years, it's that we don't always get what we want. As far as you're concerned, today we *are* Mrs. Hopa. We have her best interests at heart, and to be blunt, she doesn't want or need to speak to you." Then she took him by the arm, led him to her cronies, and claimed the last proper chair, leaving him with a stool that had no back and was half a foot shorter than the others.

He suppressed a laugh. The wily woman was trying Psychology 101 tricks to put him at a disadvantage. "Nice to meet you all," he said, nodding to each person in turn. "I'm Sterling Knight, and I represent Lockwood Holdings."

"We know who you are," one of them snapped, leaning across to glare at him. The set of her jaw and folds of her face reminded him of a bull terrier. "Tell us what you want."

He sat back. "Aren't you going to introduce yourselves to me?"

"No," the old bulldog growled. "That's not pertinent to this conversation. Tell us why you want Kat's property."

Judging from the determined expressions around the table, he wouldn't be making any ground until he gave them something to work with. That was fine by him. All negotiations required a bit of give on both sides.

"My employer would like to purchase Mrs. Hopa's property for a competitive price to redevelop the site into a five-star resort."

There was a collective gasp, then something thumped him in the chest, knocking the air from his lungs. He folded, clutching his ribs and hauling in oxygen to replenish what he'd lost. Once he'd recovered enough to straighten, he searched for whatever it was that had struck him.

A purple purse sat on his lap. Someone had thrown it at him with enough force to wind him. He rubbed his chest, wincing. Damn, these women were stronger than they appeared.

"Who did that?" No one so much as fidgeted in their seat. He held the purse up. "I'll ask again. Who does this belong to?"

Betty snatched the purse from him and passed it to the woman on her other side, staring at him as though he were a rattlesnake. "Dear God," she said, appalled. "First you say you want to tear down Sanctuary, then you hold poor Nell's purse hostage. What sort of monster are you?"

"I wouldn't have damaged anything," he said in his own defense, not that any of them believed him. No matter. He knew the truth. He may be ruthless when the situation called for it, but he'd never harmed a senior citizen, and he wasn't about to start now.

"You actually want to demolish our beautiful Sanctuary?" another lady asked, her lower lip quivering.

Sanctuary, he'd learned, was what Mrs. Hopa had named her partially renovated lodge. It was obscure and strange, in his opinion. Not at all a good marketing tactic. He kept his mouth shut, knowing it wouldn't be wise to voice his thoughts.

"Not necessarily. The building could be relocated to another site, but we'd construct the new resort from scratch."

"Move Sanctuary?" the bulldog demanded. "Just how do you expect anyone to do that?"

"It's quite straightforward these days." He ran a finger along the edge of his tie and adjusted his collar. The conversation was veering dangerously off topic. "I'd really prefer to speak to Katarina about this directly."

Betty puffed up like an angry poodle. "There's no need for you to bother her with your crazy plans. Darling Kat has enough on her plate, and luckily she has us to keep the likes of you away from her."

He tried a different tack. "Let's be reasonable. I can see

that Sanctuary means a lot to you, but it must be a drain on Katarina's resources. With the money she'd get from selling the property, she'd be able to start over elsewhere, and my company can help Haven Bay the way I'd like to."

"*Help* us?" a plump lady with a silver buzz cut demanded. "How on earth would you be doing that? We're overrun with tourists as it is. At least the ones we have are friendly. If you bring snobs into town, you'll ruin what makes the bay special."

Would he?

He dismissed the thought. Of course not. Things would change, but change meant progress, and progress was a good thing, even if it took people a while to realize it. Just look at what had happened with Eli's development in Itirangi. Everybody had hated the idea at first, but now it was a stunning success.

"I think you're being shortsight—ouch!" A heavy coin purse bounced off his shoulder onto the floor.

Betty scrambled to return it to the bulldog across the table before Sterling could get his hands on it. "Nice shot, Mavis," she said, lobbing it back.

Sterling stood and kicked his stool away. He battled the urge to yell at them, or throw something. They were frail and more than twice his age—it wouldn't be fair to retaliate. That didn't stop his body from heating with frustration. He picked up his briefcase and gripped the handle tightly enough to cut into his palm. He couldn't believe he'd driven all the way from Auckland only to be treated like scum by these abominable ladies.

"You're all being incredibly rude," he huffed, shoving his free hand in his pocket so he didn't strangle someone with it. As the chief operating officer of a multi-million-dollar corporation, he didn't have the luxury of wasting hours on fools' errands. His heart sank at the thought of the mountain of work waiting back in his office, and his throat constricted.

He closed his eyes until he'd regained his composure. "You should know better than to behave so poorly at your age." Then he swung on his heel and made for the door.

Something hit him in the back. He stopped, and turned around ever so slowly, scanning the floor until his gaze fell on a pink purse.

"It's impolite to mention a woman's age!" one of the she-devils yelled.

He wanted to stomp the purse into the ground. To scoop up the remains and set fire to them. It would serve them right. But he prided himself on taking the high road, so he gritted his teeth, nudged the purse with his foot, and stomped out.

The old ladies had won this round, but he'd be back, and next time he wouldn't be leaving without Katarina Hopa's signature on a dotted line.

FOUR MONTHS LATER

STERLING KNIGHT EXITED the southbound highway, following the sign toward Haven Bay, determined that this visit to the township would end differently than his previous one. This time, he'd done his research on Katarina Hopa and he wouldn't be dissuaded by a bunch of cantankerous old ladies.

He rehearsed his verbal offer under his breath. "Mrs. Hopa, I'm prepared to pay above market value for your property. The lodge itself is worth nothing to me. You may have it relocated elsewhere, should you wish to."

No, that wasn't right. Something told him the woman wouldn't enjoy hearing he considered her lodge worthless. Even if it was, objectively speaking. While he hadn't managed to get a hold of her financial records, based on the way the place looked, it couldn't possibly be operating at a profit. No, the lodge was irrelevant. It was the property he wanted. A large block of land sandwiched between the beach and the forest. Prime real estate.

Navigating around the edge of the township, located on the northwestern coast of New Zealand, he pulled onto Marine Parade, which ran parallel to the beach. He passed a surf school, an ice cream parlor, and a seafood restaurant clustered together around a pavilion with dozens of cars parked nearby. A few more buildings spotted the coast, and beyond them, grass gave way to an area of native flaxes and trees, with tents nestled between.

The road ended at a parking area on the other side of a bridge over a small stream. Bush rose up to his left, lush and green, and birds twittered in the trees. He wound down the window and listened to the waves lap at the shore in the distance. Paradise, just as he'd remembered it. In his boss's hands, this place had the potential to be a real moneymaker.

Beside the graveled parking lot, a lawn sprawled before a 1900s era building. A sign in front read, "Sanctuary." Coming to a stop beside a muddy four-wheel drive, he turned the engine off and took a moment to collect his thoughts.

Four months ago, he'd been railroaded, but now he wouldn't be put off. He'd driven all the way from Auckland to talk to Mrs. Hopa, and he wouldn't be leaving until she heard him out. No number of manipulative white-haired grannies were going to send him on his way with his tail between his legs. Not again. He wouldn't stand for it.

Stepping out of the car, he straightened his business suit, which had become crumpled during the drive and, with the press of a button, locked the car and headed to the lodge. He let himself into the foyer, a rectangular room with gray carpet and fold-out glass doors on the opposite wall that opened onto a garden. No one was around. Sterling checked his watch. Early afternoon, as he'd thought—time for guests to begin checking in. So why was no one here?

With a sense of foreboding, he crossed the room and went out into the garden, stopping abruptly when he noticed half a dozen old ladies kneeling in the flowerbeds that criss-crossed the sloping lawn as far as the cabin on the border of the forest. One of the ladies, whom he recognized from his previous visit, caught sight of him and her smile morphed instantly into a scowl.

Rising to her feet, she peeled off her gardening gloves and croaked out, "You again."

Sterling held his ground, refusing to be intimidated. "Me, again."

The woman, who had a deceptively sweet face and mischievous eyes, reminded him of Betty White, although maybe that was because they shared a name.

"Miss Betty," he said, beginning as he intended to continue, polite but firm. "I'm here to speak with Mrs. Hopa. Where can I find her?"

"That's *Mrs.* Betty to you," she corrected him, as two of her cronies joined her, standing one at each shoulder as though the three of them—with an average height of five-one and a combined age of over 200—could frighten him into leaving.

To be fair, they had managed to get rid of him last time. But it had been a strategic retreat. He'd regrouped, and this time, he was ready for them.

He obliged her. "*Mrs.* Betty, your friend will want to hear what I have to say, and I'd very much appreciate it if you could steer me to her."

Her eyes glinted. "Why would we let you anywhere near her, Mr. Knight? We have so much fun dealing with you ourselves." She turned to her friends. "Ladies."

The two women by her side moved forward, one gliding like a wizened ballet dancer, the other hobbling, both with their arms outstretched and lips puckered. Sterling stumbled backward, gasping in horror. This, he hadn't expected.

"Where are you going, handsome?" the hobbler cackled.

Reinforcing his spine, he planted his feet and refused to be cowed. They wouldn't *actually* kiss him, surely. It was a bluff. The more graceful of the women reached him and he clenched his fists but held very still, right up until she went onto her tiptoes and smacked a moist kiss onto his cheek.

That did it. He was waiting in his car, and locking the door. He spun around and strode back to the foyer but as he reached the exit to the parking lot, the door swung inward and he had to leap out of the way. All dignity lost, he clutched a hand to his chest, looked up, and came face-to-face with the most breathtaking woman he'd ever seen. Katarina Hopa.

Photographs of her had been plastered through the papers a few years ago when she'd scaled the international rankings in women's rally racing, but they didn't do her justice. Her skin was creamy brown and flawless, her dark eyes had a lively spark, and the hair spilling over her shoulders down to her waist was a lustrous inky black. His heart beat a rapid tattoo against his ribcage, so forcefully he worried he might go into cardiac arrest. When his eyes watered, he realized he'd forgotten to blink.

"Hello," he said, his voice dropping an octave.

"Hi." She smiled, and he could have sworn his heart gave an extra thump. Dear God, could attraction be fatal?

Then Katarina Hopa tucked her silky hair behind her left ear and all of the breath whooshed from his lungs. In a haze of lust, he'd failed to notice the pale scar stretching from her earlobe, along her jawline, and down the side of her neck. A souvenir of the crash that killed her husband. His gut twisted with sympathy. How awful would it be to look in the mirror every morning and see a reminder of one of the worst days of her life?

It's not your business.

He was here to negotiate a deal, and nothing more. Katarina Hopa, with her pretty smile and tragic scar, was none of his concern.

KAT'S SMILE weakened as long seconds stretched out and the blond man she'd almost knocked over stared at her like she was an exhibit in a curiosity museum. While it was awkward, she was accustomed to being ogled by strangers with either horror, pity, or a combination of the two.

"Were you leaving?" she asked, hoping to draw his attention to the fact that he'd blocked the entrance and she had an armful of shopping bags she'd like to put down.

"No." He shook his head, as though clearing cobwebs from his mind, then backed away to let her in. She couldn't help but notice that his cheeks were red and his breath was coming quickly. What was up with that? "I was looking for you, as a matter of fact."

"For me?" she asked, surprised. Brooke should have been taking care of guests while Kat was gone. She looked around, seeing no sign of her friend. "Did you want to book a room for the night? I think we're nearly full, but I should be able to find a place for you somewhere."

She mentally ran through the rooms, starting at the distant end of the east wing and working her way toward the foyer, which occupied the center space between the two wings. The rooms on the end were full, but the third along may be free if the elderly chap who'd been staying there for his niece's wedding had checked out.

But then her new guest spoke again. "I'm not interested in checking in."

Kat's eyes jerked up to his. The words were a little too abrupt.

"Oh, Katarina! There you are, dear." Betty, the president of the local Bridge Club, and her fellow club member, Mavis, hurried in, both ruffled and out of breath. Mavis still wore her gardening gloves. The stranger shrank away from them, placing Kat between him and the women, like a human shield.

Something was fishy here. Kat looked from Betty to

Mavis to the blond man and her eyes narrowed. "Someone better explain what's going on. Fast."

The man stuck out his hand. "I'm Sterling Knight from Lockwood Holdings." He looked at her as though she were supposed to know what that meant.

"Never heard of it."

His jaw dropped and he raised an eyebrow at Betty, who put her hands on her hips and lifted her chin in a gesture of defiance. Kat was both intrigued and exasperated. It wouldn't be the first time Betty had gotten herself into more trouble than she could handle.

"You haven't?" he asked. "Fancy that."

"Betty," Kat said sternly. "Explain."

Betty squirmed and studied the floor. "We were only looking out for you, dear."

"Mavis?" Kat asked.

"This gentleman wants to buy Sanctuary, bowl it down, and replace it with a five-star resort," Mavis said bluntly.

Kat choked, her throat seizing in horror. Demolish Sanctuary? *Her* Sanctuary? The home she'd made livable with her own hands? Over her dead body.

"Mavis!" Betty gasped, clasping a hand to her heart as though she'd been personally betrayed. "You've done it now. She's going to pass out."

Mavis shrugged. "She would have found out the minute this scoundrel opened his mouth."

Kat closed her eyes, hauled in a deep breath, and circled over to stand next to Betty and Mavis, reminding herself that no one could take Sanctuary away from her. She owned it outright.

"I take it you didn't know," Sterling Knight said, cool and unaffected by her display of emotion.

Kat swallowed, her throat tightening dangerously. "No."

"I emailed, and when you didn't reply, I wrote several letters, and arranged a meeting with you."

Kat nodded. The emails had probably gone straight to the trash folder. She tended to delete anything that wasn't clearly related to her accommodation business, especially if it looked like someone trying to sell her something. She didn't have the mental capacity to deal with them.

Sterling glanced at Betty. "At least I thought I had. Betty met with me instead and said that she was your representative and you weren't interested."

Despite herself, Kat chuckled. "Oh she did, did she?" She leveled a look at her friend, who blushed.

"Well, it's true," Betty muttered. "You're not interested."

"Mavis, were you involved in this, too?"

Mavis held Kat's gaze like the little bull terrier she was. "Yes, and I don't regret it. You've got enough on your mind. The last thing you need is to deal with someone like him, so we took care of it."

Kat's lips twitched, but she flattened them into a line. Best not to give Betty and Mavis any sign that she appreciated their support or was amused by their efforts on her behalf. They'd never behave if she encouraged them.

"But you didn't take care of it, did you?" she asked gently. "Because Mr. Knight came back. I suppose you've been stealing my mail as well."

Both women ducked their heads.

"Only the ones from him," Betty mumbled.

"Glad to hear it. I expect to see them all on my desk by the end of the day. Understood?"

They nodded and shuffled their feet like naughty school children.

"I know you meant well."

"You may as well know," Mavis began without raising her eyes, "that we sent letters in reply and put your name on them."

Kat's lips twitched again. "Oh, dear. And what did these letters say?"

"They included a ridiculous list of demands and conditions of sale," Sterling interjected. "Which I now suspect was intended to stop me pressing the matter. Fortunately, I'm not put off so easily."

Curiosity got the better of her. "What kind of demands?"

"Things like maintaining the building in its current condition, keeping the long-term tenants—"

"Feeding the stray cat," Betty added with a cheeky grin. "I thought that was a particularly nice touch."

Kat chuckled. "You two are terrible."

"We just didn't want you to worry," Mavis said. "You're too busy to fight off corporate leeches who want to suck out your soul."

"Don't you think you're being a bit overdramatic?" Sterling asked.

Kat ignored him. Though Betty, Mavis and their friends had been completely out of line, their concern warmed her on the inside. "You didn't need to do that. I can handle these things. You don't have to wrap me in cotton wool."

"We love you, Kat," Betty said. "That's all."

"And I love you, you crazy old bats." She thought she heard Sterling Knight scoff as she bent to kiss each of them on the cheek. "Now, be off with you. I think I hear the garden calling your names."

"No, that's Nell," Mavis said smartly.

Kat raised an eyebrow and they obediently trotted away, casting hateful glares back over their shoulders at Sterling Knight from Lockwood Holdings. She gave him a once-over herself. He was tall and lean, with tidy blond hair, vivid blue eyes, and sharp cheekbones. His face was unlined, as though he rarely laughed or smiled, which made it difficult to determine his age. She'd hazard a guess at early thirties, but wouldn't be surprised to find out he was a few years older or younger than that.

He was undoubtedly handsome, though in a distant way.

Like a model on a runway who you could look at but not touch. He gave off "stay away" vibes, and if she came within two feet of him, he'd probably move back to maintain the space between them. He seemed like a man who appreciated his personal bubble.

"Nice to meet you, Mr. Knight. I'm Kat."

2

STERLING SHOOK the hand Kat Hopa offered, wondering if she, too, felt the sizzle of attraction as their palms connected. A Maori tattoo snaked from the top of her wrist to her elbow, the swirls of dark ink surprisingly pretty. He took a moment to study it, wondering at the hidden meaning, but then she withdrew her hand and tucked it into the pocket of her high-waisted cream shorts. He couldn't help but be disappointed by the loss of contact.

"I know who you are," he said. "Katarina Hopa, thirty-two years old, business owner, former professional rally driver, no children, no university education." He softened his tone. "A widow, with a good head on her shoulders." Someone he could bargain with.

"What, did you read my C.V. or something?" she asked, her expression not giving anything away. "Do you have a whole file about me in that briefcase?"

"No, just the basics. It always pays to know your potential business partners."

"I'm not one of your business partners, Sterling." She watched him steadily. "Sanctuary is not for sale. Not now, probably not ever." She shrugged. "Sorry you came all this way for nothing."

Sterling fought off dismay. He wouldn't be deterred so easily. He eyed the contents of the shopping bags she'd laid on the floor, which included a couple of rolls of wallpaper, a bucket of paint and a box of nails.

"Fixing this place will require a lot of funds," he told her. "More than you have."

Last time he was here, he'd taken the opportunity to look around. While the east wing and communal rooms had been renovated, the west wing was in dire need of repairs. Broken windows were covered by cardboard, the wallpaper was peeling, and the floors were slumped. None of it was usable as accommodation.

"I'm willing to make you a very generous offer."

"I'm not selling," she repeated, shaking her head in disbelief. "Of all the crazy ideas I've heard today, that one takes the cake. And besides, you must know it wouldn't be a good investment. I cover my costs here and earn enough to pay the bills, but nothing more."

Just as he'd guessed. He didn't smile. Didn't let her see how much this news pleased him. A struggling business was easier to purchase than a booming one.

"At least consider our offer, Kat." He liked the way her name tasted on his tongue. He planned to say it many more times during the course of this negotiation. "We're prepared to pay you…" He mulled over the figure he'd come up with earlier, then decreased it by a small margin, and spoke it aloud.

Her eyes widened and her lips parted, but she didn't reply immediately. Those lips were full and deeply colored, although he didn't think she was wearing lipstick. Finally, she said, "That's very generous, but Sanctuary isn't for sale at any price. Sorry to disappoint you, that's just how it is."

Sterling stiffened. While he'd expected to have to work to get her agreement, he hadn't thought she'd reject his offer outright. Dismay settled in his gut, but then a thought occurred to him. She couldn't possibly *mean* it. Any intelligent person would at least try to barter with him. For God's sake, half the building was uninhabitable, old ladies were running rampant, and from here, he could see a dog the size of a small horse on the back lawn. The place was crazy. Out of control. Kat must know that, but she was trying to drive the price up by playing hard to get.

He voiced the original offer.

Annoyance flashed in her eyes. "Excuse me?"

He repeated it, and watched her jaw work.

"I'm prepared to bargain with you," he said. "How can I sweeten the deal?"

"You can't," she snapped. "This isn't about money. Sanctuary is my home, and you're not getting it."

He tried a new tactic. "With the profit from the sale, you can buy a new home. One in much better condition."

She gaped. "I love this place exactly the way it is. I'm not fishing for more money. You can offer me as much as you like, but it won't make a difference."

"Everyone has a price," he replied, and in his experience, that was true. Anything could be attained if someone had enough hundred-dollar bills in the bank. Even life could be bought. Something squeezed in his chest and his throat constricted.

Not now. He forced himself to think more pleasant thoughts. To imagine the luxurious five-star resort that could replace this chaotic mishmash of a building. Tourists would flock here because of the view out over the beach, the forest behind the property, and the dozens of winding trails that ran through the trees. They'd come for the picture-perfect scenery and balmy summers. Then, when they came, his boss would be raking in the cash, and he'd wonder what on earth he'd do without Sterling.

Kat Hopa watched him, her eyes softening with sympathy. "I'm sorry you believe that."

He scoffed. He didn't want or need her pity. "Explain to me why you won't consider selling. You've done a reasonable job of renovating parts of this place, but from what I can discover, it's taken a long time and you have a lot left to do. Allowing my employer to start from scratch would be a sensible business decision."

Her cheeks paled. "By 'start from scratch', I assume you mean flatten Sanctuary and build a soulless tourist trap in its place?"

He ignored her provocative language. "If you sell, you can start fresh somewhere else."

"Forget it. I'm. Not. Selling." She crossed her arms over her chest and tilted her head, her curtain of black hair swaying across her body. "I like the history of Sanctuary. I like putting it back together with my own hands. You seem to think you know everything about me, Sterling. Did you know I was in a wheelchair when I moved here? That every piece of Sanctuary I fix feels like putting a piece of myself back together?"

"No, I didn't." For once, he wished he had a better grasp of what made people tick. Unfortunately, human psychology had never been a strength of his, which was why he preferred to oversee projects from the safety of his office. He couldn't fathom her attachment to this place, and discussing it made him uncomfortably aware of his own emotional shortcomings. But he had to persist. Eli had given him this job as a test run, and Sterling needed to prove his boss's faith wasn't misplaced. To do that, he had to convince Kat to sell.

KAT DIDN'T KNOW how anyone could think to bowl over her beautiful Sanctuary and replace it with a corporate money-generator. Sure, the west wing needed repairs, but everything else was in great shape, largely because of the work she'd put in.

She studied Sterling Knight, who had a determined set to his jaw. "Look, I painted those skirting boards myself when I was still in a wheelchair." She'd cried tears for Teddy as she worked. "It took weeks to recover enough to use a roller to paint the walls, but I managed. See the carpet? I cut it myself." She didn't know why she was explaining this to him. Why would he care that just inside the garden door were a few flecks of paint on the carpet where she'd messed up as she was tidying things away. To him, this was an old building like any other. To Kat, who knew its every quirk and imperfection, Sanctuary meant everything.

"That must have been difficult for you," he allowed, his expression losing its hard edges, making him even more handsome, and a strange fizzing sensation began in the pit of her stomach, working its way upward. "I can see how you'd grow attached, but you're better now. You're capable of more."

Her lips pursed. He didn't get it, not at all. But the man had clearly had a bad day, and she could sympathize with that. She knew more than most people about bad days. He'd driven all the way here—not once, but twice—only to be harassed by Betty and the Bridge Club. If nothing else, he deserved a hot drink and a listening ear.

"Come to my office," she said, adding quickly, "I don't agree with you, and have no intention of selling, but I'll make you a cup of tea and we can talk."

He nodded and gestured for her to lead the way. She led him down the hall to her office.

"Go on in." She motioned him through the door. "I'll get those drinks."

Before she could go, Sterling spun around to face her. "How do you find anything in here?"

Kat glanced at her desk and the pile of loose paperwork, some of which had fallen to the floor. She was struck by the overwhelming urge to grab Sterling by the arm, yank him back out of her office and slam the door so he stopped looking at her in that unnerving way he had. It wasn't her fault she couldn't concentrate on paperwork for longer than an hour without feeling sick or getting a headache. Everyone healed from brain injuries at their own pace, and she may never be able to keep up with someone like him.

"I manage just fine," she snapped. "I don't need a fancy filing system. I know where everything is." A blatant lie, but she'd rather he think her inefficient than incompetent.

Sterling's expression didn't change. "I'll have a coffee, thanks."

She nodded, and unclenched her teeth. "How do you like it?"

"Black. No sugar."

Of course he did. Already she could tell he wasn't the type to sweeten anything. She backed away, reluctant to leave him alone, but what damage could he do? *You're being ridiculous.*

She headed to the kitchen, where she greeted Tione, the in-house cook and one of her best friends, with a smile and a kiss on his bearded cheek as she brushed past to flick the kettle on. Tione was preparing lunch for her guests, a selection of sandwiches, fruit, salad and cold meat. Kat stole a bunch of grapes and popped one into her mouth.

"Hey, I saw that," he grumbled. "Keep your sticky fingers to yourself."

"You saw nothing," she replied with a grin. "Is everything going all right in here?"

The side of his mouth lifted, about as close as he came to smiling, and his brown eyes twinkled. "Except for the grape thief who keeps sneaking into my kitchen, everything is fine."

Unabashed, she ate another grape. He rolled his eyes, and

she dropped the grapes onto a saucer and fixed a mug of coffee and one of mint tea.

Back in her office, Sterling Knight was sitting on the guest chair in front of her desk, holding a wooden photo frame that had previously stood atop the bookcase. The cheerful words she'd been about to utter died on her lips, and she blinked rapidly against stinging tears.

Kat knew the photograph in his hands better than she knew her own face. It had been taken the day of the World Rally Championship in Sweden. In it, she wore a jacket with her sponsor's logo and had just popped the cork from a bottle of champagne. She was grinning like she'd never been happier, and Teddy's arm was around her shoulders, his face lit with the contagious verve for life he'd always had. The photo always reminded her how cruel it was that he'd always squeezed the most from life and yet she'd outlived him.

She swallowed, then shook herself, and pretended not to notice as Sterling placed the frame back on the bookshelf. Instead, she made a show of clearing space for the mugs, dragged her chair around to join him, and blew on the surface of her tea before sipping cautiously.

"I'm listening," she said.

Sterling raised the mug to his lips, which were surprisingly sensual, with a defined Cupid's bow, but his shoulders remained square. Her mother would say he had good posture, but Kat saw it for what it was: tension. The man was wound tight. Now that she thought about it, he hadn't slouched or leaned or done anything to make himself comfortable since they'd met. His knees were bent at neat ninety-degree angles, his feet were on the floor, pointing forward, and his spare hand rested on the arm of the chair. When was the last time this guy relaxed?

Just like that, she itched to swap his coffee for a beer, strip off his starched suit and replace it with track pants and a t-shirt. The man desperately needed to unwind. If he was one of her guests, that's exactly what she would have done. Sanctuary wasn't just a hotel. It was a place to relax, discover yourself, and heal. But even though his soul was screaming for a little downtime, Sterling hadn't asked to be healed.

He nodded. "Thank you. I have a presentation outlining the benefits of selling and my employer's plans for the site. There are many positives beyond making a profit. If you wait a moment, I'll get it from my car."

Kat shook her head. "Don't bother. None of those benefits could justify shutting down Sanctuary."

If possible, he stiffened further, and she winced. That must be hell on his back. If she could dig her thumbs into the knotted muscles, perhaps the scowl would transform into a smile. She'd met plenty of people like Sterling before—all work and no play. He probably had no idea there was a different way of living, but she could show him. She was good at that. Teddy had said she could talk anyone into anything if she believed in her argument strongly enough, and she firmly believed that Sterling Knight needed a time out.

Then, like lightning, she was struck by a brilliant idea.

She considered how to phrase the suggestion. "You're stressed out, Mr. Knight. Anyone could see that."

His expression didn't change. "I'd be less stressed if you agreed to listen to my presentation."

"Or," she held up a finger, indicating for him to stop and listen, "you could stay here for a couple weeks and avail yourself of the perks of Sanctuary. Try out a different pace of life, and see how you like it. I think you might surprise yourself."

Two weeks would be enough time to ease his tension and lessen the shadows behind his unfathomable blue eyes. Enough time to bring him around to her way of seeing things. Sanctuary was a place to heal, and he was a prime candidate.

"During those two weeks, you can do your best to convince me to sell." She wasn't risking anything, because there was no way on earth he could possibly tempt her. "What do you say?"

She waited for him to agree. If the acquisition of her land meant as much to him as he said it did, a few weeks of his time wouldn't be too high a price to pay.

He was frowning. "I appreciate you trying to meet me part way, but that doesn't suit me. I can't take two weeks off work."

So she was right. He was a chronic workaholic. *Knew it.* Still, she was disappointed not to have the opportunity to steer him in the right direction. She swallowed a mouthful of tea, along with her regret, and set the mug down.

"Then I'm sorry, but our business together is done." She stood. "Feel free to stay until you finish your coffee, but I have things to do." She left without looking back, reminding herself that she couldn't save someone who didn't want to be saved.

3

"STAY FOR TWO WEEKS?" Sterling muttered as he drove over the bridge and away from Sanctuary. "That's even more ridiculous than the other demands." As if he could take a couple weeks away from his job on a whim because Katarina Hopa disapproved of his lifestyle and *might* listen to him if he indulged her crazy idea. It wasn't possible. Not with his boss, Eli Lockwood, having moved from central Auckland to the lakeside town of Itirangi in the South Island to be with the woman he loved. Someone needed to keep the employees under control.

Sterling swerved into a parking lot near the beachside pavilion and wandered across the road, where he sat on a wooden bench. He withdrew his phone from his pocket and dialed Eli's number.

"How's it going?" his boss asked, upon answering.

Sterling scowled. "It's a bust, unless we want to take drastic action. The woman won't sell. She won't even listen to my full proposal unless I agree to stay at the lodge for two weeks with her."

Eli chuckled. "Are you saying she propositioned you?"

"*No,*" he replied sharply. "Of course not." Although the idea appealed more than it should. Kat was a striking woman.

"Then what?"

"I think she got it in her head that I need saving from myself, and that she's the woman for the job. She's strikes me as a do-gooder."

Eli made a noise in the back of his throat like he was thinking. "Is she a sweet old lady?"

"Hardly."

"A pretty young lady?" Now Eli definitely sounded interested.

Sterling stifled a groan. Ever since Eli had put a ring on the finger of a lovely woman, he'd been seeing happily ever afters everywhere he looked. "It doesn't matter. I can't take two weeks off work without any warning."

He expected Eli to agree immediately, but his boss hesitated. "Actually, you have several months' worth of leave you've never taken. Perhaps some time away would do you good."

Sterling couldn't believe what he was hearing. "But what about the staff? The projects I'm managing?"

"I'm sure you've kept a detailed log of everything you're working on."

"I have." But no one else was equipped to deal with it.

"I'm due to spend some time at headquarters," Eli told him. "Aria, Lauren and I can come up for a while. Aria wants to try bonding with my parents again. They've been getting along better since the baby came."

Sterling cringed. This was not going according to plan. He'd wanted to prove he could handle everything himself, and now Eli was going to have to leave his home to hold things together. "I'd hate to put you out."

"You won't be. Take the time off and do what you need to

convince her to sell. If you're successful, we can talk about attributing some of your hours to work. If you're not, you can take it all as leave."

Sterling considered it. If anyone could take care of things in the office, it was Eli, and he'd packed an overnight bag before he left Auckland in case the negotiations took longer than expected, so he could easily stay a while. But in that madhouse?

You could handle it. For job security and a good sum in the bank, he could handle anything.

"Okay, I will." Thankfully, he sounded more certain than he felt. "But I'll take the entire time as leave regardless of the outcome. I'm never going to use it otherwise."

"All right. Now go convince that woman to sell." Eli paused, then added, "But keep an open heart."

Keep an open heart? What did that mean? Sterling ignored the cryptic advice, said goodbye and ended the call. He stared out at the waves rolling onto the sand until the churning in his stomach eased, then went back the way he'd come.

Though he'd been gone less than half an hour, Sanctuary had been thrown into chaos. Half a dozen people loitered in the foyer, lined up to speak to a petite blonde who looked completely overwhelmed, and Kat was nowhere in sight. He skirted around the group and made his way to her office, rapping on the door. No answer. He tried the handle. Unlocked. Easing it open, he peered inside, but she wasn't there. Then one of the hall doors swung out and she strode into the corridor like a woman on a mission.

"Katarina," he said as she drew near and gave him a distracted smile. "Can I talk to you?"

"Not now," she replied, passing by him and into the foyer.

He hurried after her, and found her exchanging words with the blonde, but before he could reach her side, she took off again, through an open doorway that led to the dining hall.

"I'd like to discuss making a deal," he called as she powered through the room.

"I don't have time right now," she said, without glancing back.

"When will you?"

She didn't answer, vanishing through a white door at the far end of the dining hall, beside a window that was probably used to pass drinks and meals through from the kitchen. A sign on the door read "Staff Only." He considered knocking, but supposed that wouldn't endear her to him, so he took a chair at one of the tables and waited for her to re-emerge.

Ten minutes passed. He checked the emails on his phone. Twenty unread, seven of which he needed to deal with. He switched on his email auto-responder to redirect new queries to Eli, then forwarded on the non-urgent emails and set about responding to the others. He was replying to an architect who'd significantly exceeded his budget when Kat marched back into the dining hall.

Sterling stood and matched his pace to hers. She was tall for a woman, but he was taller. "Does now suit?" he asked.

"Not really," she said, having the decency to look apologetic as well as harried.

"When will? Tell me and I'll wait until then." He could find a quiet corner and keep himself occupied.

"At this point, I really couldn't say. Maybe in a couple of hours. Could be longer." She paused, turning to face him. "I'm having one of those days where everything that can go wrong *is* going wrong. I can't judge how long it will take to get things under control. Sorry."

Then she flicked her hair over her shoulder and raced off.

"What can I do to help?" he called after her, but she'd already turned a corner into the foyer and disappeared from sight. Sterling sighed, pocketed his phone, and went after her.

――――

KAT ANNOUNCED herself outside one of the guest bedrooms. When no one answered, she selected a key from her chain and let herself in, scanning the room for damage. Everything seemed in order. She checked the en suite bathroom. Except for a couple of towels on the floor, nothing was out of place. Trevor hadn't gotten in here. She moved on to the next room and called out to Tina, the guest who was staying there.

Tina opened the door with a smile and the smell of fresh paint wafted out. "Hi, Kat."

"*Kia ora*," Kat replied. "Please tell me your room hasn't been trashed by a big, chocolate-colored mastiff."

Tina laughed. "It hasn't. He came up to the outside door while I was painting, but I shooed him away."

Thank God for small mercies. Kat shuddered to imagine the damage Trevor could cause if he stepped in Tina's oil paints. "Glad to hear it. If he comes back, can you give me a yell?"

"Sure thing. Bye, now." Tina closed the door. Kat didn't take offense at the dismissal. Tina visited regularly to get alone time to paint. Once she got going, she could stand behind her canvas for hours without stopping.

The next room was Brooke's, who hadn't gotten so lucky. Muddy paw prints splotched the pale gray carpet, and papers had been knocked off the desk and strewn about the floor. Ducking into the bathroom, she hoped to find Trevor and put an end to his spree of destruction, but it was empty. Streaks of mud lined the interior of the bathtub, as if he'd leapt into it and struggled to get out again. If it weren't so damned frustrating, she'd laugh. Trust the crazy dog to choose today, when her cleaner was away sick, to go on a rampage. When she found him…

"Whoa, what happened in here?"

Glancing over her shoulder, she saw that the immaculate Sterling Knight had followed her and was staring at the bathtub, eyes wide with horror.

"This is a private room," she said.

He shrugged. "The door was open. So, what happened?"

"My employee's bull mastiff got a little overexcited and thought he'd share his excitement with us."

Sterling's eyes slid to the side and his expression pinched nervously. "Where is it now?"

"*He* is somewhere around here. That's what I'm trying to figure out." She brushed past him and knocked on the next door, then let herself in. No muddy footprints in this room, but the outside door stood ajar, a breeze ruffling the net curtains, and the duvet had been dragged onto the floor, one corner touching the grass outside as though Trevor had started to make off with it before he'd been distracted by something else. Kat bundled the blanket under one arm, trudged up the hall to the linen cupboard, and chose a clean one to replace it.

Sterling stayed on her heels while she checked the remaining bedrooms which, thankfully, were undamaged and Trevor-free. Then she headed into the west wing, where renovations were ongoing. She crossed her fingers and prayed that whichever of the guests had been working in there last had shut all the doors.

She cheered aloud when the only sign of the mastiff was two dirty prints on a glass door. Wherever he was, he wasn't in the lodge. He'd probably run off into the bush, in which case, he'd find his own way back. In the meantime, she needed to clean the floor and bathtub in Brooke's room. Unfortunately, she couldn't clean properly without hot water, and four guests had reported the hot water hadn't been working.

"Damn," she muttered.

"What is it?" Sterling asked from behind her.

She turned. "You're still here?"

"Never left. What's the problem?"

Kat rubbed her eyes with the heels of her palms. "My cleaner is sick and I need to tidy up Brooke's room but there's no hot water."

"Kat!" a voice hollered from down the corridor. Tione. Maybe he'd found Trevor. She could hope.

"Yeah?" She hurried down the hall toward him.

He was in the foyer, tattooed arms crossed over his chest, his mouth curled in a dark scowl. "There's more people for dinner than I expected. I'm short six portions of everything."

Ugh! Could this afternoon get any worse?

She sucked a breath through her teeth and tried to cool her temper. A throbbing had started behind her right temple and she knew that if she got any more frustrated, it would explode into a full-blown mind-fogging headache and she'd have no choice but to retreat to her bedroom and sleep through it. Then who would clean, and fix the water, and buy groceries?

She addressed Tione. "Make a list of everything you need, and I'll bike down to the shop and pick it up."

"Give me two minutes and I'll get you a list. The sooner you can head to the shop, the better. I'm making slow-cooked pork tonight and it needs as much cooking time as I can get."

No pressure then. "I'll do what I can."

"You're the best." Tione strode back to the kitchen.

The best. Yeah, that's what she'd be if there were another two of her so she could somehow do everything that needed to be done.

"I can see you're busy," Sterling said. "If there's anything I can do…"

Kat flinched. She'd forgotten about him. "Yes, I am. I doubt I'll have time to sit down with you until after dinner. As you can see, it's a little crazy."

Turning away, effectively dismissing him, she dialed the plumber's number on her cell phone. "Hi, Phil," she said. "The hot water is on the fritz. Any chance you could spare an hour to come and fix it?"

"I'll be there in twenty," Phil replied in his booming voice. "I'm unblocking the pipes at The Den. Again. Should be done soon."

She breathed a sigh of relief. "You're a lifesaver. I hope Logan's paying you extra for doing his dirty work."

He chuckled. "Yeah, right. He's the biggest tight-ass I ever met. For a laid-back guy, he sure pinches his pennies."

"That's how he runs two businesses."

"Too right. See you soon, Kat."

Hanging up, she took two steps forward and nearly collided with Sterling. Was he *still* there? Could the man not take a hint? She couldn't deal with him right now. She opened her mouth to ask him more firmly to leave, but he cut her off.

"How can I help?"

Her mouth dropped open, his offer completely unexpected. "Um…"

He shifted his feet impatiently. "The sooner everything is sorted out, the sooner we can talk, yes?"

"Yes."

"So tell me what you need me to do."

"You're serious?" He nodded, and she wasn't about to look a gift horse in the mouth, so she said, "If you could pick up the groceries, that would be amazing."

"Consider it done."

"Fantastic." She beamed, and he took a step backward.

She cringed. She hadn't thought her smile was that awful, but sometimes she forgot her scar could take a while to get used to. "Wait here and take the list from Tione when he comes back. Tell him you're running an errand for me."

"Tione is the cook?"

"Yeah." Acting on impulse, she reached out and squeezed his hand. "Thanks. You're doing me a massive favor."

4

Once Sterling had received the shopping list from the cook, Tione, who seemed reluctant to have anything to do with him, he strolled to the gravel parking lot. On the way inside earlier, he'd noticed that the parking space beside the door was reserved for the owner. It was currently occupied by a yellow bicycle with a plastic basket on the handlebars.

Was that Katarina's primary mode of transportation? Surely not. Perhaps her car was at a workshop for repairs. That would make sense, based on what he'd seen of her. The woman had bitten off more than she could chew, but she would run out of motivation or cash before long. She'd be better off selling to him and buying a small, modern bed and breakfast that didn't need extensive work to make it habitable.

He drove into town, taking directions from a GPS navigator with a robotic English accent. When he reached his destination, a minimart in the cobbled town square, he parked and got out. Dozens of people milled about the courtyard, eating ice creams or baked goods and chatting. Many of them had cameras slung over their shoulders, and some snapped photos of a bronze statue in the center of the square.

The minimart was to his left, a blocky, whitewashed building with square windows through which he could see two cashiers serving customers. As he was about to head over, the knot of people surrounding the statue moved and he got a better look at it.

How strange. The subject of the statue wasn't a politician, military man or hero; it was a shirtless surfer, leaning on a surfboard, located on a raised platform in the middle of a fountain, with water spraying up from a number of small jets around him. Behind the statue, Sterling could see the local pub, with a sign hanging above the door that read *The Den*. He spun to check the signs of the other buildings that fronted onto the square: *The Book Trove, Cafe Oasis, The Hideaway, The Treasure Chest, Sea Glass Gallery, Seafaring Adventures.*

Charming names. How had he not noticed this during his research? His attention settled on the building beside the minimart. *The Hideaway.* The sign on the road frontage read "Gym and studio of Rebecca Cane, artist." He frowned. In what world did it make sense to combine an artist's studio and a gym? He closed his eyes, counted to twenty, and blinked the fuzziness away. The sign still proclaimed that The Hideaway was a gym and art studio.

Someone passed by and jostled his shoulder, bringing him out of his reverie and back to the task at hand. Groceries. He chose a small shopping cart and entered the fresh produce section, consulting the list to see what he needed from this part of the shop. He was selecting ripe avocados when someone tapped his shoulder from behind.

"I'll just be a moment," he said, privately thinking the person could stand to learn some patience. It wasn't like he was hogging the avocado bin. They could reach the other side if they wanted.

"Excuse me, son."

"Give me two minutes, and I'll get out of your way." If he sounded snappy, so be it. Finding the best avocados took effort.

"It's not the avocados I want, Mr. Knight."

Hearing his name, Sterling turned. The man had sparse white hair, hazel eyes and a creased face. He was perhaps in his sixties or seventies. While he was shorter than Sterling, his shoulders were straight, his posture good, and his white button-up shirt stretched tightly over his paunch.

Sterling didn't recognize him. "I'm sorry, do I know you?"

"No, but you will soon enough. I'm Hugh MacAllister, elected council representative for this fine town." He held out a hand and Sterling shook it. Hugh MacAllister had a surprisingly firm grip.

"Pleasure to meet you, Mr. MacAllister." Sterling stretched his lips into a rare smile. He'd learned from Eli's dealings down south that having the local powerhouses on-side mattered. "It doesn't sound like I need to introduce myself?"

Hugh MacAllister shook his head. "I know exactly who you are and why you're here, my boy."

How? He'd been in town for less than two hours and had hardly spoken to anyone during that time.

Hugh must have noticed his confusion, because he laughed, a deep booming sound, and said, "Everyone knows everyone's business around here. Usually before they know it themselves."

Sterling nodded. This day kept getting stranger. "Was there a reason you wanted to talk to me, Mr. MacAllister?"

"Hugh, please. I just wanted to welcome you to the community."

"Oh, I won't be staying."

Tapping his forefinger to his nose, Hugh said, "You might surprise yourself, Mr. Knight. The bay grows on people."

Sterling shook his head. He wouldn't give it a chance to grow on him. Hugh turned to leave, tipping his head in farewell, but Betty interrupted them both.

"Hugh," she exclaimed, kissing the cheek he offered, then glowered at Sterling. "I see you've met Mr. Knight. Did you know he's trying to convince Kat to sell Sanctuary?"

"Yes, I'd heard that, Betty. How are you, dear? Don't tell me you've gotten yourself worked into a dither. Kat has a good head on her shoulders. She won't sell."

Sterling stared at the two of them in disbelief. If Kat had a good head on her shoulders, of course she'd sell. Her lodge was a money-suck. Where was their common sense?

Betty sighed. "She's a good girl, but she's vulnerable, and I don't want to see the corporate vultures make a meal of her."

Corporate vulture? Him? Well, now he'd really heard it all.

Peering into his shopping cart, Betty asked, with what sounded like disappointment, "Are you staying? Is there a group of you here to pressure poor Kat?"

At first, he didn't understand her meaning, but when he followed her gaze to the mound of vegetables, he realized it was obvious he was shopping for more than one person. "This isn't for me," he explained. "It's for Kat. She had some unexpected guests and I got roped into helping."

Hugh chuckled and clapped him on the shoulder. "That's how it goes with Kat. You find yourself helping even when you never intended to, all because she's such a force of nature that it makes you feel like a no-good sloth in comparison." He turned to Betty. "I notice the Bridge Club still visit to help in the garden every week."

"It's no hardship lending a hand to that lovely girl." Betty's eyes narrowed at Sterling. "She's had a rough time of it. Besides, it's good for us old souls to take to the sunlight now and then."

"Never said it wasn't, Betty. Now let's leave this young

man to do his shopping." He nodded to Sterling. "Welcome to the bay. I'll be keeping my eye on you. Good day." He strolled off, and Betty—who offered a parting glare—trotted along at his side.

Sterling shook his head, bemused. What a bizarre conversation.

He finished his shopping, carried the bags to his car, and fired up the engine. He'd made it as far as Marine Parade when he spotted the stooped form of Betty on the opposite side of the road, a grocery bag in each hand. She was shuffling along, her progress incredibly slow. Sterling would rather not spend any more time with the difficult woman than necessary, but even watching her was painful. Did she not have a car, or someone who could drive her around?

Sighing, he pulled over. Then he wound down his window and called, "Betty, would you like a ride?"

She glanced over, eyes narrowing to slits. "No, thank you, Mr. Knight. I'm perfectly capable of walking."

He resisted the urge to roll his eyes. Of course she wouldn't make this easy. "Are you sure? I don't mind. It looks like those bags are heavy."

She positively bristled. "I'm visiting a friend, and I'd rather you didn't know where they live, in case you decide their home would make a nice resort, too."

He held up his hands. "My apologies. I was only trying to help."

"I don't need your variety of help."

No, it appeared she didn't. Or at least, she'd never accept it. So Sterling nodded politely, checked for traffic, and resumed the trip back to Sanctuary.

KAT WAS on her hands and knees, scrubbing muddy paw prints out of the carpet when Phil the plumber called to let her know he'd arrived. She tipped the remaining water onto the carpet, dabbed at it with a towel, then propped the external door open and switched on the dehumidifier, positioning it beside the wet carpet. Satisfied, she headed to the foyer and greeted Phil with a smile and a kiss on the cheek. The plumber was a stocky bald man with very little neck and bulging biceps. He was surprisingly sweet, despite a propensity for coarseness.

"How you doing, sweetheart?" he asked, giving her a one-armed hug.

"Been better. Trevor got inside again, then Tione threw a tantrum because he doesn't have enough ingredients, and now the hot water isn't working. Please tell me you can fix it."

"'Course I can." He grinned. "Is it working in some rooms, or is it out of action everywhere?"

"Everywhere." She glanced toward the kitchen. "I'm lucky Tee hasn't needed it yet."

"Is that grouchy bastard being difficult today?"

She rolled her eyes. "Always." The front door swung inward and she heard the rustle of shopping bags. Sterling was back. She gave a mental cheer. She'd half expected him to take the list and do a runner.

"Are you all right if I leave you to it?" she asked Phil. He nodded. "Give me a call if you need anything."

Sterling held up the bags. "I've got the food you wanted."

"Fantastic." She ignored the flashes of light dancing across her vision, the first sign of an impending migraine. "Take them through the dining room over there and knock on the door at the other end. Tione will be thrilled."

He strode in the direction she indicated, and she pressed her fingertips to her temples and squeezed her eyes shut. She counted to twenty and opened them. The flashes of light blinked again. *Damn.* She went to her office and rummaged in the desk, searching for the tablets her doctor had prescribed. She didn't like to take them, but sometimes it couldn't be helped. Swallowing one, she washed it down with a swig of water, then collapsed into her chair and rested her forehead on the edge of the desk. Paper poked her face. Why did there have to be so much paperwork involved in running a place like this?

She enjoyed the brief moment of peace and quiet. Then someone knocked on the office door. Groaning, she looked up to see Sterling hovering in the doorway. Of course. She should have known better than to think she could escape for a few seconds of respite.

"I really appreciate you helping out," she said, giving him a weary smile. "Thanks."

"You're welcome," he replied. "Have you got a couple of minutes free?"

She raised her hands and gestured at the piles of paper. "I'm always busy, but it's nothing that can't wait." Truth be told, she probably wouldn't be able to read in her current state, but knowing that didn't give her any more patience. She'd had a shorter fuse since the accident. "As I explained earlier," she said, willing herself not to snap, "I'm not interested in selling my home, but I'll listen to your argument if you give the bay lifestyle a chance."

"Have you honestly considered the possibility of selling?" he asked, sitting across from her, somehow managing to look crisp and fresh while she felt wilted. "You're in over your head. After a couple of hours, I can see that much. This place needs more work than you can afford, and from what I've read, you're a sportswoman, not a businesswoman. I admire what you're trying to do, but it's important to recognize your limitations before you burn yourself out."

At this, she scoffed. "You know about my limitations, eh? Tell me, what does a wealthy white guy know about limitations?" Before he could answer, she barreled on, "I bet you would have told me I couldn't earn a top place in the

World Rally Championships. Plenty of people did, and most of them meant well, but they were wrong. The only limitations a person has are the ones they impose on themselves."

He tilted his head curiously. "Do you really believe that?"

"I do. As the *whakatauki* says: *He iti hoki te mokoroa nana I kakati te kahikatea*. If a determined little grub can gnaw through a kahikatea tree, I can certainly do anything I set my mind to."

That *whakatauki,* or proverb, had been her mantra when she'd first moved here. As she'd dragged herself around and battled to do even the simplest tasks, she'd reminded herself that she had to take on the tree one bite at a time. It had worked. Here she was, years later, with a fully functioning body and a business that kept her afloat. She had friends, and people who cared for her. If she sometimes yearned for a man's arms to wrap around her as she slept, that was no less than she deserved. Loneliness was her penance for what she'd done to Teddy.

Sterling seemed unmoved. "That's an admirable perspective, but surely you can see how impractical it is when you're swamped with work and don't have enough time or money to handle it."

Picking up a pen, she doodled a *koru* on her left palm. This was another tactic she used to focus. "Not everything that's worthwhile is practical."

He stood, pushing the chair back. For a moment, she thought she'd finally gotten through to him, but then he said, "The deal you mentioned earlier still stands? If I stay for two weeks, you'll agree to let me pitch my plan and give it serious consideration?"

"Yeah, sure." Kat barely managed to conceal her smile. Getting him to agree had been easier than she'd expected. Sterling Knight would be singing Sanctuary's praises before the two weeks were up.

"Okay, then." He cleared his throat. "Is there a room I can book?"

She nodded. "I'll find you one."

Another person for dinner. Tione would threaten mutiny. But no doubt he'd produce a great meal and get over it, because that was what he did. Referring to the guest roster on her desk, she found an empty room midway up the hall. She fished in her drawer for a key with the corresponding door number and handed it over.

"Here you go. Up the hall, on the right."

"Thanks." He hesitated. "Will I see you again tonight?"

"Probably, but I won't have time to talk. Things should be a bit calmer tomorrow."

He nodded and withdrew. Kat's email pinged, and she scanned the new message that popped up. A reminder from her accountant that she might want to start getting things in order because the end of the financial year was only a couple months away.

"Kat?" Brooke stood in the doorway, her forehead furrowed in concern. "Everything all right?"

Too exhausted to explain, Kat just nodded.

"Can I borrow you for a few minutes, please?" Brooke asked.

"Sure. No problem."

Hours later, Kat finally collapsed onto her bed and fell asleep without undressing, or even getting under the covers.

5

At dawn the following day, Kat knocked on Sterling's door. Sanctuary was already bustling—many of the guests being early risers, especially on mornings when yoga classes were running. When there was no answer, she tried again. The door cracked open and a man's groggy face blinked at her. She double-checked the room number. Definitely the right one, but if she didn't know for sure that this man was the one she'd met yesterday, she wouldn't have recognized him. His blond hair was rumpled, there was a crease across his cheek, and his blue eyes were hazy and befuddled.

"Is there a fire?" he asked, his voice as sleepy as his expression suggested.

A strange feeling bloomed in Kat's stomach. A kind of unsettled fluttering sensation. At the same time, her heart squeezed that way it did when faced with a fluffy kitten or puppy and she became almost giddy. What was this? Was something the matter with her? Was she finally having a breakdown?

"Is there an earthquake?" he asked.

How did he know the world was shifting beneath her feet? She hadn't felt this way since… since…

Since Teddy had been alive.

Dear God, she was *attracted* to Sterling Knight.

She'd noticed yesterday that he was a good-looking man. Anyone would've. But beyond that, she hadn't felt a thing. It seemed she could resist the man when he wore a suit, but not when he dressed in ratty sweatpants and a t-shirt.

"A tsunami?" he pressed impatiently. "Is there a reason you woke me?"

Fine gold stubble dotted his jaw. How would it feel to run her fingertips over it?

"Kat?"

"Yes?"

"Why are you here?"

She blinked. "Because this is my home."

He sighed. "I mean, why are you at my door before six thirty in the morning?"

"It's time for yoga."

"No, thanks." With that, he pushed the door shut.

She knocked again.

"Go away," he groaned. "Let me sleep." But he opened the door, one forearm resting on the frame near her head, bringing him into closer proximity than she'd expected.

She gulped. Yeah, he was lean, but he looked *fine* with the muscle in his bicep flexing and a scowl curling his lip.

"We have a deal," she said, stepping back to put some distance between them and crossing her arms over her chest. "You have to embrace my lifestyle for a while, and I do yoga in the mornings. Grab a drink and let's go."

Muttering under his breath, he retreated into the room, leaving the door open a smidge so she knew he'd return. When he did, he'd combed his hair, changed his pants, spritzed with a subtle cologne and tucked a designer water bottle beneath his arm. She sighed. Getting Sterling to relax might be more difficult than she'd anticipated.

"A couple of ground rules," she said. "While you're here,

you don't wear a suit and you don't shave every night. Lower your standards. You're on holiday."

"Technically, I'm working."

She narrowed her eyes. "Then consider these my terms."

"You can't change the deal whenever it suits you."

"Watch me." He was the only one with anything material to gain out of this arrangement. All she had on the line was her ego. And while she saw something within him crying out for her help, nothing awful would happen if she failed in her mission. At least, not to her. Sterling was bound to burn out at some point.

He didn't respond and they walked down the hall to the foyer, where Rebecca Cane—Bex to her friends—had already set up in front of the glass doors leading to the garden. Bex owned the local gym and art studio, but she came to Sanctuary two mornings a week to lead classes. Five guests sat cross-legged on yoga mats opposite her.

"*Morena,*" Kat greeted them.

"Morning, Kat," Brooke chimed in with a sunny smile.

Kat blew her a kiss, then led Sterling to the front to meet the teacher. "Bex, this is Sterling. He arrived yesterday." She stepped to the side so Sterling and Bex could face each other. "Have you done yoga before, Sterling?"

"Never." He managed to look completely unenthusiastic and more than a little forbidding at the same time.

"You're in good hands, then," she told him. "Bex is the best yoga teacher on the west coast."

Bex laughed. "She only says that because none of the other yoga teachers live in the bay."

"And none of them are my friend." The two women bumped shoulders.

"Nice to meet you, Bex," Sterling said, reaching out to shake her hand.

Bex took it, a sly smile lifting the corners of her mouth. "The pleasure is all mine."

Sterling's cheeks flushed, but he didn't say anything, almost as if he realized she were flirting with him but didn't know how to respond. Interesting. Most men were smitten with Bex at first glance. She had dark eyes and brows, golden brown skin, a straight nose, and full lips that were permanently quirked in a mischievous smile, except for when she was painting or mothering. Then, she was the very image of concentration.

Bex gripped his hand for a moment longer than necessary, then released it and snapped the elastic band off her wrist to collect her ebony tresses at the nape of her neck.

"Let's get a mat and choose a spot," Kat said. She collected a yoga mat from the edge of the room and handed another to Sterling, who followed like an obedient puppy. She claimed the spot beside Brooke and sat, cross-legged, facing Bex. Sterling arranged his mat in an identical position on her other side. From here, she could sense the tension radiating from him.

It was the beginning of a brand new day. What did he have to be stressed about?

Is this a nightmare?

Sterling closed his eyes, counted to ten, and opened them. No, he was still in a room full of attractive women—and one athletic man—expected to do something he had no idea how to do. He was going to make a fool of himself in front of Kat, the cute instructor, and the pretty blonde who'd been booking in guests the previous day.

He'd be willing to bet everyone here would put him to shame. His jaw clenched. Yoga was something his friend Mark would do, but Sterling wouldn't dream of. He just wasn't wired to be comfortable manipulating his body into strange positions in front of an audience. Why had he let himself be persuaded to leave his room?

"All right," Bex said from the front. "I think that's everyone." She switched on a speaker and a soft, soothing melody started. "I want you to sit in whatever position is comfortable and keep your head high, shoulders relaxed, and breathe deeply with me. In and out through the nose." She counted breaths. When she reached five, she said, "Now move into a tabletop position, on your hands and knees. Hands beneath your shoulders, knees hip-width apart, spine in neutral."

Sterling followed her instructions, feeling utterly ridiculous. He hadn't knelt like this in years, except to look for something he'd dropped on the floor.

"As you breathe in, curve your spine down and lift your head into cow pose. When you exhale, round your spine and drop your head into cat pose. Inhale, exhale."

This was completely absurd. What good could it possibly do to bend his back up and down while breathing? His head began to spin.

"Stop hyperventilating," Kat hissed. "If you keep that up, you'll faint."

"She said to breathe deeply," he muttered.

"Just ease back a bit. You're too pale."

How embarrassing. They hadn't done anything challenging and he'd already gotten it wrong.

"Bring your toes together, knees wide," Bex instructed. "Lift your right arm towards the roof, then slide it under your body and thread the needle. Lower your ear and shoulder to the floor, and if you can, twist your left arm behind your lower back."

Sterling watched Bex do the movement and tried to copy it, but his shoulder didn't want to touch the ground. Instead, he ended up leaning on his head, his neck bent at an uncomfortable angle. He drew in a shaky breath. Then another. His left arm trembled. Thankfully, before he collapsed, Bex directed them to revert back to the tabletop position.

Okay, he could handle that. For the three breaths they held still, he almost enjoyed it—not that he'd admit to such a thing. Bex instructed them to lunge forward and come into a squat. He did so, feeling quite pleased with himself. But then, in a seemingly effortless movement, she twisted her body around and down, placing her palms on the floor and raising her feet off of it.

How the hell...?

Sterling peered over his shoulder at Kat, who mimicked the movement just as gracefully.

"How do I do that?" he whispered.

He couldn't see her face, since she was turned the other way, but he heard her when she said, "Just go as far as you can. Rest the inside of your knees on your elbows and try to lift off."

Taking stock of the other people in the room, he noted that the other man and the petite blonde had managed the move, while a redhead and a Chinese woman couldn't seem to get themselves off the floor. Knowing he wasn't alone in the struggle made him bold enough to give it a shot. He wiped his palms on his shirt then dropped them to the floor and shifted his weight as Kat had said.

For all of two seconds, his feet left the ground, then his arms gave way and he fell onto his ass. *Hard*. Pain jolted up his tailbone. It faded quickly, only to be replaced by embarrassment as he heard the unmistakable sound of a giggle. He looked around. The redhead was laughing at him. His cheeks heated. Why would anyone subject themselves to this for fun?

"Don't worry about it," Kat said. "We've all been there. You'll get it eventually."

Would he? He wasn't so sure, and he was over this. He'd

given it a try, and as far as he was concerned, that was that. "I'm going now."

"Hold up. We've barely started. Unless you hurt yourself…" She sounded concerned.

"No." Only his pride.

But then, he wasn't a gym-goer. He didn't lift weights or attend boot camp. The closest he'd come to yoga was when he'd slept with a pilates instructor in his second year of university. He was a runner. Occasionally, he ran with a partner, but usually he ran alone. He wasn't cut out for group fitness classes. All of these people watching him. Waiting to laugh if he failed.

"You're doing fine," the Chinese woman murmured as they moved into a plank, something he could do without screwing up since his core strength wasn't bad.

"Thanks." Was he supposed to tell her that she was, too? He didn't know the right etiquette.

From the plank, Bex explained how to step up into a standing fold. While Sterling was miles away from touching his forehead to his knees, he managed the transition just fine. When she instructed them to straighten and lift one foot from the floor, planting it on the inside of the opposite thigh, his sense of balance was challenged. He wobbled back and forth, trying to steady himself using the stable leg, determined not to give up. He wobbled again, but gritted his teeth and kept his feet where they were. Beside him, Kat stood completely still, her spine straight, palms pressed together in front of her chest. Her eyes were closed, long lashes fanning over her cheeks, inky hair spilling down her shoulders.

God, she was beautiful.

And just like that, he tipped, landing on his hands and knees with a thud. There was a collective intake of breath. He picked himself up, grabbed his drink bottle, and stalked from the room before anyone could say a word. His knees throbbed, but his pride stung worse.

"What a fucking great way to start the day," he muttered, his tongue curling around the curse word, as he didn't use them often.

Back in his room, he showered and shaved—because regardless of what Kat said, he was here for business, and businessmen presented themselves well—then retrieved his navy suit from the wardrobe, dressed, and went to find breakfast.

"WHAT'S HIS DEAL?" Bex asked as Kat rolled up her yoga mat and snapped a strap around it.

"Who, Sterling?"

"Yeah. Mr. Tall, Blond, and Cranky."

Kat sighed. The yoga session hadn't gone exactly as planned. She'd considered chasing him when he'd run off, but decided to let him lick his wounds in peace. Besides, he'd been rude to her friend, storming out of the class just because he'd lost his balance, as most beginner yogis did.

"He wants to buy Sanctuary," Kat said.

Bex whistled. "No shit."

"I think his plan is to flatten it and build a resort."

Bex winced. "Yeouch. Obviously you said no."

"I did, but I promised to hear him out if he stayed for a while."

The two women began to gather yoga mats and blocks to carry to Bex's car.

"Why?" Bex asked.

Kat flicked her hair out of her eyes and held the door open with one hand so Bex could pass through, then followed her to her Mum-mobile, a gray mini-van with toys strewn over the back seat.

"Have you seen the guy? He needs to unwind. It's not healthy to be so uptight, and you know Sanctuary is the perfect place for him to lie low and recover."

Bex unloaded her armful into the trunk and put a hand on her hip. "You're not worried about him talking you around while he's here?"

"Nope." Kat dropped her own load and straightened. "I'll just listen, tell him thanks but no thanks, and send him on his way, better for having been here."

Bex shook her head. "Saint Kat strikes again."

Kat snorted. "Not hardly."

A smile curled Bex's lips. "I don't suppose you conned him into staying because you wanted to stare at his cute tush in exercise shorts…"

The flippant comment caught Kat by surprise. "Bex," she warned, "you know I don't do that."

"What?" Bex asked, as though she had no idea what Kat meant, when in fact, she knew very well. "You mean you don't ogle sexy men? Because I beg to differ. You've been known to ogle a well-built guy a time or two."

Kat tried to tamp down the panicky feeling rising in her chest like a butterfly battering against the inside of her rib cage, and massaged the spot, drawing in a long, even breath. "Whatever."

Bex touched her shoulder. "You okay? You know I'm only teasing, right?"

"I know." Kat forced a smile. "Besides, I saw you checking out his butt just as much as I was. He's got a stable job and probably a bit of money in the bank. Dad candidate?"

"The guy can't even try yoga without getting pissed off," Bex replied. "He's not a great dad candidate. Parenting Izzy is a great big exercise in failure. Like, a contest to see how

54

many times I can get it wrong." She shrugged. "Not the place for someone like him."

"Don't you give me that, girlfriend. You rock the solo parenting gig."

Bex leaned over and kissed Kat's cheek. "Now tell me, why would I need a man in my life when I've got a kick-ass woman like you?"

"Oh, you sweet talker." Kat hugged her, then stepped back. "Go pick up that beautiful daughter of yours and give her a kiss from Aunty Kat."

"Will do. Bye, now."

As the Mum-mobile crunched over gravel on the way out of the parking lot, Kat headed back inside. In the foyer, she grabbed the sweater she'd stowed earlier and tugged it over her head, making her way to the dining hall, where she waved to each group she walked past, and breezed into the kitchen.

"*Morena*," she called to Tione, who was peering into the oven, wearing both a hair net and a beard cap.

"*Ata marie*," he returned, reaching in and sliding out a tray of breakfast muffins.

"Mm, smells great. Mind if I steal one?"

"I'd be disappointed if you didn't."

With deft fingers, she plucked a muffin and dropped it onto a plate before it could burn her. She split it open with a knife, scooped a dollop of butter into the middle, and was delighted when it immediately melted and soaked into the fluffy muffin. She pinched a small mouthful off the edge and tasted it, licking the butter from her fingers.

"You've outdone yourself," she announced. "The best so far. What's different today?"

"Added chives," he said.

"Nice."

Tione's breakfast muffins were an ongoing work in progress, and every now and them, he ditched the recipe completely and started over. For a while, the muffins had been variations on fruit, nuts and spices, but recently he'd been opting for savory flavors.

Plate in hand, Kat left the kitchen and returned to her office. She dropped the plate on her desk and switched on the laptop. When it came to life, she checked her emails for new bookings, and then turned to the bills.

An hour later, as her focus was waning, someone knocked on the door.

"Sterling." She greeted him with a smile, pleased for the opportunity to escape her paperwork. "Just the man I was hoping to see."

"Can we talk business?" he asked. Since leaving the yoga class, he'd showered and dressed in a dark suit that should have washed him out but somehow managed to emphasize the blue of his eyes instead. He'd shaved, too. Kat didn't know whether to laugh or groan. Getting this guy to loosen up was going to be a challenge.

"Not right now," she replied, both because her brain needed a break and because she had a better idea. "Come with me. There are some people I'd like you to meet."

"I really think our time would be best spent—"

She ignored him, sweeping through the exit and striding down the hall, her long legs eating up the distance quickly. She assumed he'd follow her, but turned and found him still in the doorway.

"With all due respect, Kat, it's your turn to listen to me."

She sighed. She obviously wasn't going to get any more participation from him without giving something in return. "Come with me now, and I promise I'll sit down with you later this afternoon."

He eyed her warily. "No excuses later on in the day? No 'emergencies' keeping you busy?"

"No," she promised. "Just you and me."

"Okay." He nodded, and made his way to her.

Releasing a breath, Kat led him to the first room in the west wing, which had been turned into a lounge. Comfortable leather sofas were spread throughout the large space, and a bookshelf occupied one corner. On the sofa directly in front of the garden window was Nancy Heath, a tiny birdlike woman with a head of steel-gray curls and full-moon reading glasses. She was making her way through one of the sexier volumes from the bookshelf, and slipped a bookmark into it as Kat and Sterling approached. Kat saw Sterling glance at the cover, his eyebrows shooting up at the sight of a naked male torso. Her lips twitched with mirth. Someone should tell the man that women were never too old to enjoy a steamy romance.

"Good morning, Nancy," she said, sitting on the arm of the sofa. "How's your book coming along?"

"Wonderful, dear. He finally got the guts to ask her on a proper date. It was terribly awkward, of course. What he doesn't realize is that she doesn't want to be wooed with expensive champagne." Her gaze settled on Sterling, over Kat's shoulder. "Who's your friend? Oh, don't tell me, you're going on a date!"

Nancy, the eternal optimist.

"No dates for me. This is Sterling Knight. He's staying here for a while. I thought you might like to meet him." She winked at Nancy, whose cheeks became splotchy and red. Kat sensed a crush coming on. Tione would be pleased if the older lady shifted her adoration from him to Sterling. The cook had mistakenly believed showing Nancy his tattoos would put her off, but if anything, she'd become more intrigued and taken to reading bad boy romances with inked heroes.

"Lovely to meet you, Sterling." Nancy fluttered her eyelashes at him. "Has anyone ever told you that with your name and the way you look, you could be someone's knight in shining silver armor?"

"Actually, yes." His lips twisted into a smile. The first sign of humor she'd seen on his handsome face. "My friend Mark likes to call me the company's Sterling Silver Knight. He thinks I should have my middle name changed to 'Silver' but I think 'John' is perfectly serviceable."

"Sterling John Knight." Nancy said it as though she was practicing introducing herself as *Mrs.* Sterling John Knight.

"We'll let you get back to your book," Kat said. "But don't be afraid to say hi to Sterling if you see him around. He's staying all by himself."

As they moved away, he murmured, "She's a sweet lady."

"She has cancer," Kat replied, blinking back the tears that threatened every time she thought of it. "Terminal. She's staying here to enjoy the last few months of her life until she needs to move somewhere with round-the-clock care."

Next, she stopped beside Tina, who'd finally emerged from her room and was piecing together a puzzle on the floor, legs crossed, a frown of concentration marring her brow. She glanced up to greet them, brushing aside a lock of ginger hair as it floated across her face.

"Hey, there."

"Hey." Kat sat next to her and sifted through the puzzle pieces, helping organize them according to color, which she knew was Tina's preferred method. "Did you finish another masterpiece?" Sterling stood behind her, apparently reluctant to dirty his suit by kneeling or sitting. "Tina is a fabulous artist. She paints landscapes. Usually in oil paints, but she's done some great watercolors, too. I've got one in the foyer, of the waterfall up one of the trails at the back of the garden."

"There you go, stroking my ego," Tina said with a laugh. Then she turned to Sterling, cupped her hand over her mouth as though confiding a secret and whispered, "I'm a terror when I'm working, but they tolerate me here because I pay them to."

"That's so not the truth," Kat objected, swatting her arm

playfully. "We tolerate you because of the mural you painted in Brooke's room."

Though it was a joke, both of their expressions softened as they thought of Brooke. Kat knew Sterling must be wondering what she was up to, but he didn't ask. Perhaps he wasn't comfortable prying.

She stood and brushed her palms together, businesslike. "Tina comes here when she needs to boost her creativity," she told him. "She gets blocked sometimes but staying at Sanctuary helps."

"Because no one is knocking on the door every two minutes and there's inspiration everywhere I look."

"Sterling is a new guest," Kat said, which wasn't technically an untruth. If she told all and sundry that he wanted to buy her out, they'd cast him out before she could say boo.

Tina cocked her head, sizing up his shiny black shoes and silk tie. "Let me guess," she said. "You're a corporate highflier, but you've burnt yourself out and need a break."

"Something like that," he murmured, expression inscrutable.

Damn, but Kat wished she could read him. She didn't know whether anything she said or did was having an effect on him.

"Well, you've come to the right place." Suddenly, Tina's eyes glazed over, and she dropped a puzzle piece, shot to her feet and rushed off, nearly tripping over the box on her way out.

"Her muse has visited," Kat said, by way of explanation. "Come over here and meet Arthur."

"I KNOW WHAT YOU'RE DOING," Sterling said as he and Kat walked away from an elderly man who was staying in the lodge while he recuperated from his third knee surgery and wrote the spy thriller novel he'd dreamed of for years. "You're trying to emotionally manipulate me, and you're not being very subtle about it."

He might not have noticed if she'd stopped after the first two people, but this cinched it. She'd started her crusade to convince him of the healing powers of Sanctuary in earnest.

Kat stopped walking and crossed her arms over her chest, lifting her t-shirt enough to reveal a sliver of skin at her hips. "Subtlety is overrated."

Sterling couldn't look away from that strip of bare skin. Then he noticed a pucker of paler skin at her left hip. Something in his expression must have given him away because she dropped her arms and tugged the t-shirt down. Had that been a scar? If so, it looked like a particularly painful one.

"Mr. Knight," she said coolly.

Oh, yes. What had she said?

"I tend to agree. Subtlety is overrated. But I need to set you straight about something before you drag me to meet Exemplar D. I sympathize with these people—I truly do—but I'm not like them. I don't need you to save me. And just think how much more you could do for them if you accepted my offer. With more money, you could improve the facilities to cater to a wider range of people and set up shop in a nice modern building."

"You don't understand," she growled, then muttered something under her breath in Te Reo. "The whole point is that the lodge isn't perfect. It's a work in progress, just like we are. *He waka eke noa.* Everyone here is in the same boat. They need something that only Sanctuary can give them. Peace and quiet, a place to heal. Or maybe they need to learn a new skill. Did you know we have DIY classes that run every weekend? My guests and I are fixing up Sanctuary ourselves. It's a journey we're on together. It means something to us."

"You're right," Sterling said, and for a moment, she stopped, caught unawares. A smile started to cross her face, but then he added, "I don't understand." Her smile vanished. "You could give them a place to heal, or to have some peace, in a fully equipped facility two minutes down the road. Your whole shtick is about this being a 'sanctuary', right? Nowhere has anyone said that 'sanctuary' needs to be run-down or in a state of disrepair."

Her expression shuttered, and he experienced a twinge of guilt, but tamped it down. In order to persuade her to sell, she needed to see the truth. Perhaps she had a personal connection to the lodge or the property, but that wasn't a reasonable basis for making business decisions. If she was thinking with her head rather than her heart, she'd know that.

"Spoken like someone without a sentimental bone in their body," she shot at him, eyes narrowed as though daring him to contradict her.

He shrugged. "You caught me. I confess, I've never loved a place like you obviously love this one, but you can't let that color your decision-making."

Her lips pursed and she pressed her palms together in front of her torso, interlacing her fingers. "I'm sorry for you. Everyone should have a home of their heart." Then, as if the conversation had never occurred, she spun and started toward the exit to the garden. "*Haere mai.* Come along."

Like a dog being called to heel, he followed, hypnotized by the swaying of her rounded hips. One thing he could say for Katarina Hopa: she had a way with people.

7

OUTSIDE, the morning air was mild, the scent of pollen heavy from the flowers that were blooming in the garden. Striding along the path that wound between the flowerbeds, Kat stepped over an abandoned trowel, dodged a pile of dog poop, and gestured for Sterling to do the same.

Tione's cabin was on a rise, nestled among the trees at the edge of the forest. Kat knocked on the door. It was between meal prep times, which meant he should be around.

"What's up?" Tione asked, resting one hand on the doorframe while the other held his Chihuahua, Pixie.

"I wanted to properly introduce you to Sterling," she said, stepping back so the two men were face-to-face. "He'll be here for the next two weeks."

Tione's chin jerked up. "Hey."

"Hi."

They sized each other up. Then, macho posturing completed, Sterling stared at the cat-sized dog curiously.

"Who's this?"

"Pixie," Tione replied. "She's a princess among dogs."

Kat laughed. "Only because you spoil her."

Sterling cocked his head. "She's cute. Will she mind if I pat her?"

Tione gave Kat a look that said, "Is he for real?", but shrugged. "Yeah, go on."

Kat sighed. Clearly, they weren't going to be best buddies, but perhaps they could find some common ground. Hesitantly, Sterling reached toward Pixie and let her sniff his hand, then scratched behind her ear. The tiny dog closed her eyes in bliss, and wagged her tail. Sterling's expression softened, and Kat's heart melted a little. Apparently, the corporate knight had a chink in his armor after all.

"Tione caters all of the meals we serve at Sanctuary," she explained. "He keeps us well fed." To Tione, she said, "Sterling is a businessman, down from Auckland. I'm hoping we can help him unwind a little."

She crossed her fingers that her friend noticed the subtle hint to be nice—not his default setting. Tione looked over their heads, into the distance, probably wondering if he could escape down to the beach without her noticing.

Finally, his gaze settled on Sterling and he asked, with reluctance, "What do you do for work?"

"I'm chief operating officer at a property development company."

He snorted. "Sounds like a glorified name for a paper-pusher."

Sterling bristled, and dropped his hand from Pixie's head. She huffed in protest. "These days, I'm responsible for the day-to-day running of the entire company."

"How do you feel about big dogs?"

The question gave Kat a chill of premonition. Looking around, her jaw dropped at the sight of Trevor bounding across the garden toward them, kicking up lumps of dirt with his massive paws, ears flapping, tongue hanging out.

"I'm not really—"

Kat saw the exact moment Sterling heard Trevor bark. It

was impossible to miss. An expression of horror passed over his face as he turned. His head recoiled, eyes wide. Then, Trevor sprung. His paws landed on Sterling's chest, smearing mud down the white fabric. Spittle flew from the corners of his mouth, spraying Sterling's face. The full force of fifty-five kilograms of dog transferred onto Sterling and his knees buckled. He went down, his butt hitting the ground, and Trevor pinned him, licking his cheeks and forehead, and sniffing his neck—where, presumably, he'd applied cologne. The entire scene was absurd. Kat exploded into laughter. She couldn't contain herself. The juxtaposition between dog and man was too fantastic.

"I'm sorry," she gasped, as Sterling shoved Trevor aside and climbed to his feet. She covered her mouth and suppressed another wave of laughter, her shoulders shaking with the effort. Tears pricked the corners of her eyes. God, she'd needed to laugh. It had been too long.

Sterling glared at her, his eyes like shards of ice, apparently unable to see the humor in the situation.

"Are you okay?" she asked.

"Fine." He brushed off his shirt to no avail, swung around and stalked away. She looked at Tione, who was patting Trevor's head and holding the dog's collar to prevent him from giving chase.

"Good boy," Tione cooed in a ridiculously high-pitched voice. "*Ka pai*, Trevor." He glanced at Kat and raised a black brow. "I reckon you should go after him."

"Probably." She jogged after Sterling's retreating back. "Hey, wait up!"

He didn't stop.

"I'm sorry," she called. "I didn't mean anything by it."

He looked over his shoulder, but didn't pause, making good time toward his bedroom, where she assumed he meant to lock himself for the foreseeable future. Unless, of course, he'd had enough and was leaving. She didn't want him to leave on these terms. Especially not when she suspected he needed Sanctuary more than ever. He strode through the foyer, down the hall, and reached the bedroom door.

"I really didn't mean anything by it," Kat repeated. "You look adorable. Please, let me help."

He unlocked the door, went inside, and shut it firmly behind him.

Guess that's that.

AFTER HE'D SHOWERED—AGAIN—STERLING perched on the edge of the bed and wondered how he'd managed to make such a fool of himself in a short amount of time. Not only that, but he was failing at his job. Miserably. Staying in the bay served only one purpose: to convince Kat to sell. So far, he was no closer to accomplishing that than he had been yesterday.

To make matters worse, she probably thought him a pompous idiot. He certainly hadn't done anything to persuade her otherwise, but for some reason, that grated. Perhaps because he wanted her to respect him enough to do business with him. *Or perhaps,* a little voice in the back of his mind whispered, *it has nothing to do with business and everything to do with your attraction to her.* Few women interested Sterling, which was how he preferred it. He'd dated when he was younger, but during recent years he'd been too focused on helping Eli grow the company for anything else. Romantic entanglements complicated life. He'd seen it with Eli. While his friend seemed happy, it had taken a lot of heartache to get to that point, as well as a drastic change of lifestyle.

But he wasn't opposed to relationships, on principle, and Kat interested him, both physically and mentally. She was good with people—something he could never claim to be—

and with her height, fit figure, and scars, she was striking. She wasn't a wilting violet or a young sprout that had yet to be challenged by the world. She was a hardy purple rose who'd survived the winter and emerged out the other side more beautiful for it.

God, listen to him wax poetic. Next, he'd be serenading her with a violin.

He fetched his laptop and googled dry cleaners in the area. The nearest was half an hour away, in a neighboring town. *Seriously? What kind of place doesn't have a dry cleaner?*

He packed his work suit into its plastic carry-case and took it to his car, then followed the GPS directions out of Haven Bay, relieved when the town disappeared in his rearview mirror. On his way along the coast, he brainstormed. He needed to take action. Not only had he looked like a fool today, but he hadn't made the smallest step toward accomplishing his goal. Being at Sanctuary wasn't working for him. He was too far out of his element. He needed to take Kat somewhere he was more comfortable. To get her into his element, and show her what she'd be missing out on if she didn't sell. Tempt her with the things she could have or places she could go if she had a healthy bank balance.

He pondered this. What kind of things would Kat miss out on by being completely absorbed by her business? Social time? From what he could see, she managed to center her social life around her guests and colleagues. Time to relax? Contrary to the advice she espoused, she'd been on the go constantly since he arrived. Dating? Based on Sterling's intel, her husband had died three years ago. She was still young. Surely she'd want to find another life partner.

His fingers drummed the steering wheel. Thinking, thinking… then it struck him. Two birds, one stone. He could give her an evening away from work and reintroduce her to the dating scene by taking her out for dinner at a top-notch restaurant. *Yes.* Excitement grew, and he assured himself it was because he had a plan and not because he wanted to take Kat out on a date.

AFTER TREVOR KNOCKED Sterling on his ass, Kat didn't see her guest for hours. At first, she thought he must be hiding in his room while he nursed his injured pride, but when she knocked with a tray of lunch, the door was locked and she couldn't hear any noise inside. She checked the parking lot and his car was gone. Had he left? For good? No, she decided. He couldn't have. No matter how wounded his ego, he'd have had to check out. Hopefully he'd headed into town to buy an ice cream and a pint of beer and take a load off.

She was explaining the layout of Haven Bay to an American couple when he walked into the foyer, wearing a pale blue t-shirt and dark jeans. Her mouth went dry. *Yowza*. If ruining his suit was what it took to get him into more casual attire, she didn't regret his misfortune quite as much as she had a minute ago. The shirt hugged his lean torso and brought out the color of his eyes like two pops of summer sky on a cloudless day.

Her tongue tripped over itself. She swallowed and repeated what she'd been saying to the couple, then she handed the map to the woman, and said, "Good luck. You can call me at the number on the bottom if you get lost or run into any trouble."

"Thank you, Kat."

"No problem." She shifted her attention to Sterling. "Have you been exploring?"

"I drove to the nearest dry cleaners and dropped off my suit."

She winced. "Oh." Not relaxing with ice cream and beer, then. And now that she took the time to look, his shoulders were stiff and his bearing upright, despite the casual clothes.

Not at all how someone on holiday ought to be holding himself. Damn. She had her work cut out for her. "What's the plan for the rest of the afternoon?"

He shrugged one shoulder. "I haven't decided yet, but while I've got you here, let's talk."

That sounded ominous, but also piqued her curiosity. "Okay, so talk."

"Have dinner with me at Figaro."

Kat had two thoughts simultaneously. One: how would going out for dinner help his cause? Two: hell *no*.

She addressed the first. "Why?"

"It doesn't matter why," he said, stuffing his hands into his pockets. "My reasons are my own. Will you join me?"

"Is this a date?" Because she flat-out didn't date. Ever.

His cheeks flamed red. "Of course not."

Well, he didn't have to sound so appalled by the idea. People wanted to date her. Occasionally. It wasn't unheard of.

"I can't, sorry. I can't leave Sanctuary for the evening. I'm needed here."

"I'm sure the guests and staff can manage on their own for a few hours," he replied, nostrils flaring as though he hadn't expected her to drag her heels and was frustrated by it. "Surely you've spent the evening away before and everything didn't blow up."

Probably far less frequently than he imagined. She'd hardly been away from Sanctuary since she moved here, and never overnight, except for when she ventured into the forest to camp, as she did when she desperately needed time away from distractions to mull over her thoughts. That was beside the point. She would not share her real reason for refusing to go to Figaro, which was a half-hour drive away. Some things were better off not shared with handsome strangers.

"I can't," she told him. "I'll go out for dinner with you anywhere within walking distance, but I won't go to Figaro."

Sterling's hands came out of his pockets and he smoothed them over his already immaculately groomed hair. "The point of going to Figaro is to show you that you could have much more than what's available in the bay. How am I supposed to convince you of anything when you throw up barriers?"

I'm not intentionally being difficult.

She didn't say the words. She didn't owe him an explanation. She had her issues, just as he had his, and on this, she wasn't budging. "You'll have to deal with it and modify the plan. Isn't that what business is all about these days?"

"Fine." He pivoted away from her. "I'll adapt. But I expect you to try to meet me halfway."

When he left, she exhaled shakily and leaned against the wall for support. It had been a long time since anyone questioned her choices, and it made her uncomfortable. Unfortunately, there was no changing the way she was.

8

DIFFICULT WOMAN.

How was Sterling supposed to bring her around to his way of thinking when she kept changing the rules? Was she intentionally making it harder for him to do his job? Or had she actually gotten so absorbed in her tiny world that she never ventured away? That level of obsession certainly couldn't be healthy, even he could recognize that.

Never mind. He could, and would, adapt. He shut himself in his bedroom, powered up his laptop and did an internet search for luxury activities in Haven Bay, scrolling through links until one caught his eye. *Beauty in the Bay: A Luxury Spa Experience.* Further investigation showed that the spa was less than three kilometers away—walking distance—and offered a variety of treatments.

Sterling wondered how long it had been since Kat had a spa day. Based on how hard she worked, he'd guess it hadn't been recently. Perhaps she was overdue for a little forced relaxation, exactly as she was trying to impose upon him. He thought on it. The two women he knew best, his friend Mark's sisters, raved about massages, manicures, pedicures, and other beauty therapies he didn't fully comprehend.

Hunching closer to the screen, he looked through each of the options. He recognized very few of the terms, but he persisted, selecting a package and booking it for the following morning. Then he set about answering work emails.

When he next looked up, dusk had fallen, and his laptop clock told him it was time for dinner. He righted his clothing, and wandered down the hall to the dining area. Whatever was cooking, it smelled good. Food had been laid out on the counter separating the dining hall from the kitchen, and guests were clustered around the tables, all wearing smiles. Tione stood behind the counter, most of his face covered by hairnets, and the sight of him brought on a flashback of the scene earlier. He shuddered. What kind of person kept a lion-sized animal for a pet?

Sterling dished himself spiced chicken, a green salad, and boiled potatoes, then investigated seating options. Kat sat with the slim blonde who'd been helping at reception the day before.

He made his way over. "Mind if I join you?"

Kat gestured at the empty spot across from her. "Go right ahead."

The blonde smiled at him. She was pretty, with straight brows, blue eyes that angled down at the corners, an upturned nose, and peach lips. He'd estimate her to be in her early twenties.

"I'm Brooke," she said, her voice as sweet as her appearance. "I saw you arrive yesterday."

"I'm Sterling," he told her. "I'm staying for a couple weeks." Provided he didn't convince Kat to sell first. "Do you work here?"

Brooke giggled, a high-pitched, airy sound that enchanted him. "Not technically. I live here, and part of my board is helping out when Kat needs it."

He frowned. He must have heard wrong. He'd assumed

Kat and the cook were the only people who lived on-site. "You live here?"

She nodded and glanced at Kat under her lashes. "As long as I keep paying rent and Kat doesn't get sick of having me around."

At this, Kat said, "As if I could ever get sick of you, sweetheart." She met Sterling's eyes. "I didn't introduce you to Brooke earlier because I didn't want to interrupt her. She's working on her PhD in art history."

"Aw, Kat, you act like such a proud mama sometimes," Brooke teased.

"I feel that way, too."

"You're less than ten years older than me, so unless you were a really young mother..."

Kat laughed. "You're good for my ego, kid."

The conversation lulled while they ate. Then Sterling finished his potatoes, placed his cutlery on the edge of his plate, and said, "I've booked you a half-day session at *Beauty in the Bay* tomorrow."

"*What?*" Kat's knife clinked against the plate as her hands slipped. Her neck snapped up, and she stared at him with the force of a laser beam. "I can't leave for half a day. I'm needed here. Why would you do that? I thought after our talk earlier, you'd check with me before you made any plans."

Sterling stared back, cool and unfazed. He'd expected this reaction. "The spa is within walking distance," he said. "And I'm sure that everything won't fall apart if you're gone for four hours. You shot me down without a decent explanation last time, so I think you owe me the courtesy of considering it."

Beside Kat, Brooke's eyes widened. "You should go," she urged. "That kind of offer doesn't come around every day. I can keep everything here running smoothly for a while, just like I do when you go camping. I'm perfectly capable, and you deserve some personal time."

Some of the tension left Kat's shoulders and they slumped. "I know you are, but you need to work on your thesis."

"I can spare half a day."

"But—"

"If I fail to graduate, I think it will be for a more serious reason than not putting in four hours of work."

"Sounds like it's settled," Sterling said, pleased with how the conversation had gone. He hadn't even needed to argue her into submission because Brooke had done it for him.

Then he noticed something he hadn't before. Brooke was sending meaningful glances in Kat's direction, mouthing something he couldn't make out. When she saw him watching, she stopped and scooped up a forkful of pasta.

"Why did you book me a spa day?" Kat's question drew his attention away from her friend's odd behavior.

This, at least, he could answer. "Because you seem overworked and if you sell to me, you'd have the time and money to visit the spa more often."

"Ah." She nodded. "You're showing me what I'm missing out on."

He didn't respond. She wasn't wrong.

"Okay, I'll go to the spa, but you have to make me a promise in return."

"That hardly seems fair. I played your introductions game this morning."

She smiled tightly. "Humor me. For the rest of your stay here, ditch the suits. You're on holiday."

Considering the cook's horse of a dog had ruined his suit and it wouldn't be ready for a few days, agreeing wasn't a hardship. "Fine, I can do that."

THE FOLLOWING MORNING, a warm breeze stirred Kat's hair as she walked to *Beauty in the Bay*. Birds sang from trees, and in the distance, she could hear waves rolling onto the beach. She closed her eyes for a moment and smiled. Haven Bay on a summer morning was one of her favorite experiences, closely followed by spring, when the flowers were blooming, and autumn, when the leaves turned hues of orange, red and yellow and littered the ground. Winter, she could do without. Although there was something to be said for long days spent inside while rain drummed on the roof.

She passed the glamping pods and waved to a couple who were eating breakfast at a picnic table. Outside the local primary school, half a dozen cars were parked while parents accompanied their children to the gate.

"Hi, Shane," she said cheerfully to the teacher manning the road crossing, his preschool-age son hanging off his leg.

"Morning, Kat," he replied, nodding to her. His son, Hunter, waved shyly, his face half-hidden behind Shane's thigh.

She waved back and called out, "*Morena*, Hunter. Are you helping your papa today?"

"Yes, Mrs. Hopa."

"*Ka pai.* You're doing good." She gave him a thumbs up and picked up the pace as a pair of mums approached, both looking far better than anyone ought to at this time of day, and both wearing predatory smiles. Shane beseeched her with his eyes not to leave, but she just laughed and carried on.

When she reached the spa, she paused outside and wondered if Anica and Harriet Rubis-Staats, the owners, would be particularly bothered if she turned around and went back to Sanctuary. It had been an enjoyable walk, but she couldn't really spare four hours away from work.

But she *had* agreed to give Sterling a chance to persuade her to the dark side. While she may not have the slightest

74

intention of changing her mind, she should at least make it look like she was open to the idea. She dithered on the doorstep, then a light flickered on, prompting her to action. She'd gone five steps in the opposite direction when a woman yelled after her.

"Kat? We're opening up. Where are you going?"

Kat bit into her lip, swung around and pasted on a false smile. "Harriet! It's been ages. How are you? You look great."

Harriet raised a pierced brow and put a hand on her hip. "Girl, I know you were *not* just doing what it looks like you were doing, because most people would kill for a massage from my Anica. She has magic hands and you're going to go inside and act like there's nowhere you'd rather be and neither of us will mention this—" with two fingers, she gestured back and forth between them "—*interlude*. Hear me?"

"Loud and clear." Kat's cheeks heated in a guilty flush and she mumbled a quick prayer of gratitude that it was Harriet who'd caught her fleeing and not her wife, Anica, who'd most likely have watched her go, and then wondered whether she was somehow to blame.

Inside the waiting room, where soft piano music played and a water feature bubbled beside the desk, Anica greeted her with a welcoming smile. "Good morning, gorgeous."

Coming around the desk, she put a hand on Kat's shoulder and kissed her cheek, bringing with her the scent of vanilla. Kat kissed her cheek in return and hoped Anica would use that body lotion on her during their session.

"Hi, lovely," Kat replied. "I hear I have you all to myself for the morning."

"That's right." Anica beamed, revealing teeth that were perfectly straight, courtesy of the braces she'd worn as a teenager. The expression transformed her from merely pretty to captivating, especially when combined with her flawless complexion, courtesy of her Lithuanian mother.

"We'll start off with a massage, then an exfoliating back scrub, a facial, and finish with a manicure and pedicure. Does that sound great, or what? This mystery man of yours sure knows how to pamper a girl."

It sounded like a long time to sit still and dwell on whatever was happening at Sanctuary.

"Looking forward to it," she said, not wanting to disappoint Anica or dent her ego by being unenthusiastic. "And there's no mystery man."

Anica blinked at her expectantly. "Oh, so you're openly dating him?"

Harriet snorted with laughter. "I don't think that's what she meant, babe."

"It's business-related," Kat explained. "He's trying to sweeten me up so I'll do a deal with him."

Harriet became thoughtful. "Is this the guy who wants to buy Sanctuary?"

"The very one."

"No!" Anica clapped her hand to her chest. "You're not selling, are you?" Her eyes widened, then narrowed on her wife, who was immediately preoccupied with booting up the computer. "Why didn't I hear about this, Harry?"

Harriet squirmed. "I knew it would only upset you, babe. You know how I hate that."

Anica pointed a finger at her. "We'll talk later."

Kat decided to intervene. "I'm not selling. That's crazy talk. I've told him as much but he thinks he can butter me up and I said I'd let him try."

"Suddenly I feel like I'm doing the devil's work," Anica muttered as she selected a bottle of massage oil from the cupboard and tucked a packet of green gunk under one arm.

"That doesn't mean she'll put on a half-assed performance," Harriet said. "My girl won't ever do less than her best."

"Come and pick a polish." Anica led Kat to a shelf upon

which dozens of nail polishes were arranged, from dark purple at one end to bright yellow at the other, with all of the colors of the rainbow between, and a number of glitter and confetti options.

Kat eyed the choices, picking up a highlighter orange bottle. "People actually go for this?"

"I take it that's not your color?"

"Not quite." She picked up a few more bottles, studied the contents, and returned them to the shelf, settling on a pale peach color because it would be less obvious if she chipped it, as she was bound to do.

"Strip off and lie face down," Anica instructed, once she'd led her into the adjoining room. "Cover yourself with a towel. I'll be back shortly."

Kat waited for the door to click into the jamb, then undressed and piled her clothes on a stool in the corner. She shuffled awkwardly onto the massage table, beneath the towel, and rolled onto her stomach. A crease pressed into her cheek, and she tried to adjust herself but only succeeded in shifting it to her forehead. Anica knocked softly, then let herself in. Kat could hear her moving around the room. After a moment, she laid a hand on Kat's back.

"Are we going to work over everything today? Do you have any injuries I should know about?"

"Everything sounds good." Kat's voice was muffled by tissue paper. "No injuries." She recalled the latticework of scars up her torso, including a vicious one on her thigh. "Except old scars. They don't hurt, so don't worry about them."

It wasn't a complete lie. The scars didn't usually hurt. Sometimes, though, they pulled tight and made moving uncomfortable. She'd become accustomed to the pain. It was her penance for losing Teddy.

Something warm splashed onto her skin and Anica rubbed it in. Before long, Kat lost herself in the pleasure of being touched, having the aches massaged out of her muscles, and the knots of scar tissue loosened. Okay, so maybe she'd needed this. She could admit it. She'd even thank Sterling later.

By the time the massage finished, she was half asleep, eyelids heavy, and her mind very much outside her body. She was vaguely aware of noise in the background, and then Anica began to apply something to her back that wasn't oil. Something that felt like thick, gunky moisturizing lotion.

"Whassat?" Kat mumbled sleepily.

"This is the exfoliating cream," Anica explained. "In a few minutes, we'll move you to the shower to rinse it off."

"Mmkay."

As she waited for the shower, without the distraction of a massage, reality started to creep in. What was she doing? She should be at home, plowing through paperwork as she typically did in the morning, while her mind was fresh. Or she could be walking Tione's dogs along the beach so they didn't run rampant through the grounds. Or greeting new guests and helping them settle in. Or laying the last of the floorboards in the room she was currently working on so the group of DIY-ers who came on the weekend could paint the walls and lay the carpet. The list went on.

The lotion on her back itched. She fidgeted, trying to ease the tickling sensation, but only made it worse. The itch traveled up her back and across her shoulder, like the scratchy little feet of a mouse. She jerked back and heard a splat as some of the exfoliant fell to the floor. Whoops. Resigned to suffer the itch, she lay still.

"Okay." The voice came from far closer than she'd expected, and she flinched. "Sorry, love. Didn't mean to frighten you. I've turned the shower on. It's through the door to your right. I'm going to wait in reception. You wash off, dry yourself and get me when you're ready."

"Yep, sure."

Kat washed quickly, toweled off and met Anica in the waiting room, eager to get their session over with. They returned to the room for her facial, which seemed far more thorough than warranted. By the time Anica began painting her fingernails, she could barely sit still.

Anica's brow furrowed in concentration and she hovered inches above Kat's hand, painstakingly varnishing her nails. Kat swallowed a sigh. The whole exercise was pointless. She'd only chip them later, when she was doing the dishes or hammering timber. They probably wouldn't survive the hour undamaged. But she kept her frustrations to herself. There was no reason to air them to Anica, who was only doing her job. The problem was Kat. She wasn't used to idleness, and felt ready to burst out of her skin.

Finally, *finally*, she was finished, and Anica released her. Kat gave her a hug, and trotted out the door as quickly as she could do so politely. Her stomach growled as she power-walked back toward the lodge. It was nearly lunch and she usually ate a mid-morning snack. She'd have to raid the kitchen and see if Tione had any breakfast muffins left over.

When she got home, she hurried inside, and found chaos. A family of four waited in the foyer with Brooke, who looked on edge, her jaw clenching and lips pressing together. Other guests milled around, restless and unhappy. Her stomach sank to her sneakers.

"What's going on?" she asked.

Brooke's face sagged with relief at the sight of her. "The MacFarlanes would like to check in, but I can't work out which room is available."

"Room two is empty as of this morning," Kat told her. "Susan should have cleaned it out by now, but it might pay to check, just in case." Mrs. MacFarlane combed a hand through her hair while restraining her toddler with the other, and looked to be at the end of her tether. "Welcome to Sanctuary. Why don't you take a seat while Brooke checks the room for you? Help yourself to a chocolate." She gestured to the jar of wrapped chocolates atop the small counter.

"Thank you," the woman said, visibly grateful.

Brooke left and Kat noticed Tina loitering by the garden door. She went to her and touched her shoulder. Tina's eyes were rimmed red.

"What's wrong?"

"The sprinklers went off inside," she said, tearful. "I don't know why. There's no fire. But the canvas I was working on is ruined."

Oh, no.

If the sprinklers had gone off, they'd need to air out every room in the building. Kat scrubbed a hand down her face and tried not to cry. Her eyes watered, but she blinked rapidly and rolled up her metaphorical sleeves. She had a lot of work to do.

9

AFTER THE SMOKE alarm blared and the sprinklers started, Sterling took his laptop and went to the local library. At five, he got kicked out so they could close, so he went to the cafe next door to buy a slice of pie, then sat beside the fountain to eat.

It had been a pleasant day. Though he'd been annoyed by the interruption earlier, he'd enjoyed people-watching while he worked at the library, which overlooked the town square. When the pie was gone, he stood, and the seagulls that had been circling at a cautious distance swooped for the crumbs left behind.

He strolled back to the car, a block away, and drove to Sanctuary, watching the increasingly familiar scenery pass by. No one was in sight as he entered the foyer, so he returned to his room and worked for another few hours. When he felt like he'd done enough, he stretched, his back groaning in protest, and closed the laptop.

He hadn't seen Kat all day. He knew she must have gone to the spa as per their agreement because she hadn't been around that morning, but he'd hoped she'd come and see him after, so he could gauge how effective it had been at softening her toward his proposal.

He padded down the hall and knocked on her office door. No answer. He tried the handle and it opened, but the room was dark. Kat had a bedroom on the premises, but he wasn't sure where, so instead he looked for her in the foyer, and the dining hall, where Brooke and Tione sat across from each other with steaming mugs.

"Join us," Brooke offered. Tione looked decidedly less welcoming.

"No, thanks," he replied. "I'm looking for Kat. Have you seen her?"

"Try the living room," she suggested.

"Thanks. Goodnight."

The communal living area was dark, too. He switched on the light and spotted her immediately, slumped on a sofa, head tilted to the side, mouth open, eyes closed. Asleep? He tiptoed closer, and her eyes cracked open.

"Hey, there," she murmured, the words slurring together. She looked exhausted. Dark shadows circled her eyes and the pink slash along the side of her face seemed particularly bright in contrast to her ashen cheeks. Wisps of long, dark hair fell across her forehead, casting shadows.

Something tugged in his chest. A deeply emotional yearning he'd never experienced before. He wanted to wrap her in his arms and provide whatever support and comfort he could. But he hadn't held a woman in a very long time, especially not to reassure her, and he was bound to mess it up, so he stuffed his hands into his pockets and resisted the urge.

"Hi." His face flamed at how breathy the word was. Thank God she was too tired to notice. "How was your morning?"

She tucked the loose tendrils of hair behind an ear. "It was all right. The massage was lovely, thank you."

Warmth oozed into the cavity around his heart. He felt

inordinately pleased, but also something more. Something he didn't care to define, but which certainly didn't have anything to do with his job here. "You're welcome."

She heaved a sigh, her chest rising and falling. "Unfortunately, when I got back, it was Armageddon. Clearly, I can never take a morning off again."

Another unfamiliar impulse unfurled within him. The desire to make her laugh. To wipe the weariness from her brow and tilt the corners of her mouth with amusement.

"Perhaps you need a holiday," he prompted.

She propped her elbow on the arm of the sofa and rested her chin on her palm. "As if that could ever happen."

"You know," he said, injecting his voice with every bit of slyness he could muster, "if you sold Sanctuary, you could run away to the islands, find a cave by the beach and survive by spearing fish and living off the land."

She stared at him for a long moment as though he were a heretofore unidentified alien species. Then she threw her head back and roared with laughter. The delicate skin of her throat pulsed and the tension faded from her face. He was transfixed.

"You never let up, do you?" she demanded, gulping for air.

He shrugged and pretended to yawn so he could hide his smile.

"Thank you," she said, wiping her eyes on her sleeve. "I needed that."

"No problem."

She sat upright. "I'll fix us both a cup of tea. What would you like?"

"Oh, no, you won't." She looked wiped out. "You stay here, and I'll make the tea."

She nibbled her bottom lip. "Are you sure? I'm the host, I should do that."

"And I'm the guest," he reminded her, "so you should let me do what I want. And I want to make you a cup of tea."

She relaxed against the pillows. "Chamomile, then. Cheers."

He went to the dining hall, nodding to Tione and Brooke as he entered. "I found her, thanks."

Then he flicked the kettle on, and searched for chamomile tea among the selection on the counter. He filled the mugs and watched the herbal blend diffuse, wondering how strong Kat liked her tea. Should he leave the teabags in, or remove them? He dithered for a minute, then opted to take them out because drinking around teabags was a nuisance.

He returned to the living room, and offered a mug to Kat. She blew steam from the surface, her lips curved into a soft smile.

"Thank you," she said. "I really needed this."

Heat radiated throughout his insides. Strange how she seemed more grateful for a simple cup of tea than she had for the expensive spa package he'd treated her to. Perhaps he needed to change tack.

"Why don't you employ more people to help around here?" he asked, genuinely curious.

Her smile faded, but he couldn't regret the question.

"The budget doesn't stretch that far," she replied. "Besides, I can manage everything myself."

WHAT A DOWNER.

Kat made a conscious effort to smile and perk up. Despite the weight of the responsibility sitting on her shoulders, she'd been enjoying her conversation with Sterling. When he wasn't hyper-focused, he was actually quite pleasant. Awkward, but well-intentioned.

"Enough of the doom and gloom," she said. "Tell me about

yourself. Who is Sterling Knight and where does he come from?"

He laughed, which lightened his face and made him devilishly handsome. He was a good-looking man. Everyone had noticed. Even Tione, who was used to being everyone's eye candy—a fact he'd bemoaned until he risked being replaced.

"I'm a chief operating officer from Auckland," he said, shrugging one shoulder. "That's really all there is to know about me."

"Now that can't be true." She patted the space beside her. "Come. Sit." He sat. She wrapped her fingers around the warm mug and sipped, observing him over the rim. She liked him like this. More relaxed, fewer barriers between them. "Have you always lived in Auckland?"

"Yes. For as long as I can remember, anyway."

"Do you have a house or an apartment?"

"I own a lovely apartment in the city center, near the office. I've been there for three years. Before that, I lived on the fringe of town, and earlier on, I was in student housing."

"You studied at Auckland University." *Obviously.* Kat hadn't had much of an education. None of her *whanau* had gone on to university or polytechnic, and with her love of rally, there seemed to be no point. She'd thought she'd race professionally until the day she croaked. Turned out she'd raced until the day *Teddy* croaked. Back then, she'd wished it had been her. Sometimes, she still did.

"Bachelor of Commerce," he said, bringing her back to the present.

"Nice work, champ." She raised her knuckles to bump his. He frowned but mimicked the gesture. Had no one ever treated the guy with casual camaraderie? "So, you live where you work. You have a degree. What else? Tell me about your family."

His shoulders hunched and his whole body stiffened. If someone searched Google for "back off vibes" they'd find a

85

picture of him at this very moment. "There's not much to tell," he said woodenly. "I don't have any."

No *whanau*? Incomprehensible.

"You must have parents. You didn't just spring from the ground."

"My mum is dead and I don't know who donated the sperm. Frankly, I don't care. No siblings, no aunts or uncles, no grandparents." His knuckles whitened around the handle of his cup. "It's just me."

"I'm sorry. *Aroha mai.*" She laid a hand on his forearm and felt the muscle leap beneath her touch.

"Can't mourn what you've never had."

She didn't buy into that way of thinking, but if it comforted him, she wouldn't judge. "I'm sorry you lost your mum."

"It was years ago."

"Doesn't mean it doesn't hurt. You're talking to the voice of experience here." His chin jerked up in acknowledgment but he didn't say anything. She took that as a hint to drop the subject. "Okay, so family is a no-go. What do you do for fun?"

His lips pressed together. He sighed, then raised his palms to the ceiling, and looked stumped.

Huh?

Did he not have any hobbies? Play any sports? Collect stamps, for God's sake?

Her heart weighed heavily in her chest, brimming with sadness for a man who was all alone in the world and didn't have time for fun. Her fingers tightened on his arm. She'd have to help him figure out what he enjoyed. Before he left Sanctuary, he'd have found a source of joy. She'd make sure of it. She may not be a miracle worker, but she could manage that much.

"What about you?" he asked.

She leaned back onto the sofa, confused. "What about me?"

86

"Do you have much family? Do you see them often?"

She wondered whether this was his way of angling for more information he could use in his quest to convince her to sell her home, or if he genuinely wanted to know. Whichever option was true, he could easily find out her back story with an internet search, or by asking around, so there was no point being evasive.

"Mum and Dad are still alive. So are my grandparents. I'm an only child." She took a breath to fortify herself. "And a widow."

"Yes, I'd heard that." He reached across and touched her hand. "You still wear your wedding ring."

She glanced at the simple *pounamu* band with a gold inlay. "I still love him."

"I'm sorry." For some people, "sorry" was a throwaway word, but he seemed to truly mean it. "What was he like?"

Kat shook her head. How had the conversation taken this turn? She supposed she could only push him so far before he pushed back. A bittersweet smile twisted her lips. "Teddy was… vibrant. Larger than life, you know. But he was kind and supportive, too." She swallowed against the rising tide of emotion. "We met at a race and shared a passion for rally. Together, we were magic on the track. He died three years ago." She swallowed again, blinking rapidly to keep the tears at bay. "Feels like yesterday."

"Strange how life continues even when you think it shouldn't." He sounded like he was the one speaking from experience now. His cobalt gaze was distant. He was somewhere else. They sat together in silence for a long moment, then he said, "Can I take up an hour of your time tomorrow?"

It seemed they wouldn't be sharing any more sad stories. "That should be fine."

"Thank you."

She lifted her mug and realized it was empty. "Guess that means it's time for bed."

"For me, too." They stood and walked down the hall. "Which room is yours?"

"Up the end on the left," she told him. "My suite is a little larger than the others."

"As it should be. It's your home. I'll walk you to your door."

"Oh, you don't have to do that." They'd literally walk past his room on the way to hers.

"Let me."

Something in the way he said it gave her pause, and she stepped sideways so they could fit two abreast in the corridor. When they came to her door, she turned to him and discovered she was strangely breathless. It felt like they were teenagers and he was walking her to her parents' doorstep after a first date. They were awkward with each other, not quite sure how to act. She fidgeted with the hem of her shirt and studied the carpet.

"Kat."

She looked up and met his laser-beam eyes. Her stomach flipped over and her skin tingled everywhere.

"Sweet dreams."

She watched his lips move and her innards clenched. How she wished they were moving over hers.

"Goodnight!" she squawked, her voice breaking. Then she twisted the handle, slipped inside and shut the door.

That had been a close call.

10

STERLING ROLLED out of bed feeling refreshed. He showered, but didn't shave, instead rubbing a palm over one cheek so his stubble rasped against the skin. He couldn't remember the last time he'd been anything other than clean-shaven and he itched to go back to the bathroom and fix himself, but he had something to prove. In order for Kat to make concessions, he'd need to make some, too. That said, one concession didn't mean he was completely caving to her demands. He paired a collared shirt with designer jeans for a tidy-casual look.

Ready to face the day, he wandered down the hall to collect a breakfast muffin, then headed for the garden, but encountered Kat along the way.

"Is that a suit?" she asked, nose crinkling.

"Jeans," he explained, pinching the fabric to demonstrate how stiff it was.

Her hands went to her hips. "Are they tailored?" She said the word like it was dirty.

"No, they just fit well."

"I'll say." She cocked her head and looked him in the eye. "You didn't shave."

He hoped she appreciated it. "Feels unnatural."

"Funny, because it suits you."

His heart stuttered, and he told it to behave. There was no need to get excited because a striking woman complimented him. "It's scruffy. Unprofessional."

"I disagree. If I saw you with that facial hair across a boardroom table, you wouldn't look any less professional to me. But you do look edgier." She grinned. "Sexier."

Below his belt, something stirred. While his brain knew that he needed to focus on business, his body had missed the memo. Seeing Kat's luscious plum-colored lips form that word, and knowing she found him attractive, was almost too much. Hell, if she liked the way he looked with a little stubble, maybe he'd let his scruff grow wild and free for as long as he was here. There was no office dress code to adhere to. No underlings to maintain appearances for. And who knew? Maybe once it stopped itching, he'd like it.

"Are you going outside?" she asked, because he'd been staring at her mutely for the better part of a minute.

"Yes."

"Well, enjoy yourself." She touched his shoulder as she scooted past. "It's a beautiful morning."

It was. The sun had risen over the hills and golden light bathed the garden. He breathed in the perfume emanating from dozens of flowers, and studied the array of vegetation —a veritable rainbow. Pausing by a pink rose, he bent to sniff a bloom.

"Lovely, aren't they?"

His eyes cut to Brooke, who sat cross-legged on the grass opposite him, wearing gardening gloves that came halfway to her elbows. She was pulling out weeds with cheerful vigor.

"Yes." He nodded to the chrysanthemums and the pansies. "It's an eclectic garden."

"That's because it wasn't planted by one person."

"Not Kat?"

Brooke laughed, and peeled off a glove to wipe the corner of her eye, which was red-rimmed and watery. "Definitely not. Kat isn't much of a gardener. She planted a few shrubs, because that's all she could keep alive. I planted some." She pointed to the pansies and marigolds. "Tione planted the ones nearer his cabin, and the Bridge Club planted the rest."

"The Bridge Club?" It wasn't the first time he'd heard of this club.

"Betty runs it. I think there are ten members. They live at The Refuge, which is the local retirement community. It's mostly wealthy, single, older folk. They're good sorts, but they like to meddle."

He wondered if the Bridge Club had been the collection of women who'd chased him away from the bay when he'd first come. "I've met Betty."

"You know what I mean, then." Brooke resumed yanking weeds, carefully shaking off the loose dirt and setting them aside on a growing mound beside her. "She's a force to be reckoned with. Best I can understand, she and the ladies decided to make a project out of Kat when she moved here. They weren't sure what to think of her for a while, but now they're her staunchest supporters. They turn up every Saturday to help out and sometimes a few of them will drop by during the week."

"How neighborly of them."

A strange expression came over Brooke's face, as if she was frozen. She rocked back and forth once, twice, then sneezed an almighty sneeze, cupping the gloves around her face so she didn't spray him.

"Ugh, gross," she muttered. "Sorry about that."

Sterling hoped he didn't look as disturbed as he felt. Germs and dirt had bothered him ever since his mother had been ill and he'd had to fight to keep her in sterile conditions without the tools to do so properly. "Do you have hay fever?"

She nodded, eyes still leaking down her cheeks. "And a thousand other maladies."

"Then why are you in the garden?" he asked.

"Can't let a silly thing like sneezing hold me back." She glanced over his shoulder and her attention caught. "Hi, Betty," she said. "We were just talking about you."

Dread crawled up Sterling's spine and he turned slowly, coming face-to-face—or more accurately, chest-to-face—with his nemesis.

"Good morning," he said.

"Likewise, Mr. Knight." Betty's cheeks were rouged with pink, and she was arm-in-arm with a rounded woman who had short pink hair. "Let me introduce Edith Partridge. Edie, this is the man I was telling you about."

His stomach tightened, and he wiped his palms on his jeans. The old biddies made him nervous, but with good reason.

"My pleasure," Sterling said, offering Edith Partridge his hand.

She didn't take it. "From what I hear, it'll be a pleasure when you leave."

And another burn from an old lady. "Give me a chance, Mrs. Partridge. You might be surprised."

She blinked hawkishly behind glasses. "I'll reserve judgment."

"That's your right."

"Oh, lay off the new guy," Brooke chirped. "He's not so bad."

Sterling's lips parted. She'd defended him. Mildly, but still. He couldn't recall the last time someone stood up for him. He was perfectly capable of doing it himself, so his friends and acquaintances had never bothered.

"Uh, thank you," he croaked, throat dry.

"We need to speak with you," Betty interrupted, jabbing his chest with one wrinkled finger.

"About what?"

"Consider this a warning," Edith continued, picking up where Betty had left off. "If you upset Kat, we'll run you out of town."

He should have laughed. Most men would, when threatened by two octogenarians, but he could see their determination to protect Kat from harm and respected that enough to hold his tongue.

"I don't want to upset Kat," he told them. "That's not why I'm here. I want to find a way for us both to win, and I genuinely believe we can."

Edith peered up at him, then her mouth pursed. "I can see that you do believe that."

"Don't disappoint us," Betty added, removing her finger and backing off. "Good day, Brooke. Mr. Knight."

"DOES NOW suit for me to take up some of your time?"

Kat raised her forehead from the desk to see Sterling in her doorway, arms crossed over his chest, the top two buttons of his shirt undone to reveal a vee-shaped patch of pale skin. Eminently lickable. *Where did that thought come from?*

She must be overly tired, her mental barriers lowered by drowsiness. Yeah, that was it. With difficulty, she shifted her focus from his chest to his face. Much safer.

"Sure thing. Have a seat."

He didn't move. "Actually, I'd like to take you for a walk."

Her forehead scrunched. Perhaps she'd dozed off and was dreaming. "A walk?"

"Yes." He moved his weight from one foot to the other, and appeared to mistake her confusion for reluctance. "It won't take long. An hour, tops."

"Just let me grab a sweater."

"You won't need one," he told her. "It's sunny out."

"Okay, then." She followed him outside, her sneakers crunching on the gravel, sun beating down on the top of her head. One of the downsides of having black hair was that it attracted heat like no one's business and her scalp burned easily. She reached up and mussed it so there was no exposed skin down the center part to burn.

They strolled side by side in silence, except for the sound of gulls crying and the Tasman Sea rolling onto the beach. Kat snuck a peek at him out of the corner of her eye. His profile was tall and lean. He could be called lanky, but he moved with the grace of a big cat. She wondered whether he'd purr if she petted him. He glanced over and caught her checking him out, and she flushed but didn't look away. That would make her seem even guiltier.

"Not that I don't love a good walk, but where are we going?" she asked, as if she'd only been looking his way in order to speak to him. *Smooth, girl. Super smooth.*

"It's a surprise."

Her eyes narrowed. "I'm not a fan of surprises."

"Neither am I. But don't worry, it's nothing bad."

"'Bad' is relative."

He led her, with surprising confidence, past the beachside pavilion and into the residential section of town bordering the coast. Pulling a flier from his pocket, he checked something and came to a stop outside of a large white-stone house with a "for sale" sign beside the mailbox. Something prodded at the back of Kat's mind as he opened the mailbox and extracted a key. Some thought or idea about what he was up to, but she couldn't quite grasp it.

"We're going in?"

"Yes." He slotted the key into the door and it swung inward with a shushing sound, passing over thick, gray carpet.

Kat slipped off her shoes, because God forbid she track

dirt onto that gorgeously lush carpet. She stepped inside, her eyelids fluttering shut at the soft sensation beneath her bare feet. Sterling entered and passed her, rounding the corner. She stayed on his heels as they moved into an airy, open lounge, big enough to rival the one at Sanctuary. French doors on the opposite side were ajar, and beyond, a small lawn merged into the beach. She could have jogged over the sand and been at the water in less than a minute.

"What are we doing here?" she asked.

He held a finger to his lips. "Save the questions until after I've shown you around. Come through here." He paced to a doorway and gestured for her to enter. "This is the kitchen. It's registered as a commercial kitchen and meets the requirements of the Food Safety Act."

Kat blinked. Tione would be in heaven with all of the gadgets in here. They were color-coordinated, and even the same brand.

"The laundry is through the door over there." He pointed to the other side of the kitchen. "And if you follow me this way—" he backtracked into the lounge and through another door "—we're in the dining room." A long rectangular table occupied the center of a narrow room running parallel to the beach.

"Very nice," she said, since he appeared to expect a response.

He nodded. "The bedrooms are off the hall, on the other side of the lounge."

They went through each bedroom. There were six, all painted cream with beige drapes and gray carpet. All spacious and comfortable. All lacking any kind of personality.

"Well, what do you think?" he asked, once they'd returned to the lounge and sat on a sofa.

She shrugged. "It's a nice house."

His smile turned upside down. "Just nice?"

"Great location, nice view." No personality.

"Better than Sanctuary?"

She laughed. "Nothing is better than Sanctuary."

"But imagine what you could do with a place like this. It doesn't need any work, so you could put all of your time and money into your guests and turn it into a spectacular bed and breakfast."

Ah, so that's the angle he was taking. Finding her an alternative he viewed as better than what she currently had. Except it wasn't better because this place had no soul. She'd put money on it being no more than five years old and built from a catalog. There were probably a dozen others like it.

"If this place is so much better than Sanctuary, then why doesn't your company buy it instead?"

"My employer has the money to invest in your property to make the most of it. You're trying to patch up the leaks in a sinking ship. Lockwood Holdings could build a new ship." She started to talk, but he powered over her. "Think about it. You could still make this a retreat where people come for downtime or to indulge their artistic streak. It's in Haven Bay, so you wouldn't lose your connection to the community, and you'd have more time to yourself. Don't you think you deserve a break?"

No, she didn't. She had too much to make amends for. Furthermore, she couldn't afford to be selfish. She didn't *deserve* to be selfish. But she wouldn't verbalize those feelings.

Besides, he was totally missing the point. She'd explained it to him, but apparently he hadn't paid attention. Sanctuary was a work in progress, the same as she was, and the same as many of her guests were. It was symbolic. It gave her a mission to work toward. If she could repair Sanctuary, and in doing so, help others through their difficult times, perhaps one day she could do the same for herself. But she wasn't there yet, not by a long shot.

"This place is nice, but it isn't what I need," she said. "I don't expect you to understand that, although I wish you could. It makes me sad that you can't see the value of a place beyond dollar signs. I'm done looking. I'll wait outside." She swung on her heel and stalked away.

"That's it?" he called after her. "That's all I get?"

She heard his footfalls behind her.

"You agreed to consider my proposition fairly."

"I considered it," she snapped over her shoulder.

"Did you really? Because it seems like your mind was made up from the beginning. I agreed to your two-week condition on good faith, believing you'd give me a chance."

She stopped walking, a twinge of guilt twisting her gut. She had no intention of selling Sanctuary, but she'd never deceived him about that. "I am giving you a chance."

"But you haven't told me why this place won't meet your needs. How can I find what you need if you won't explain it to me?"

She turned to face him, arms folded. "I already have. You didn't listen."

"So tell me again." He sounded so reasonable, and his cobalt eyes pleaded with hers. He scratched the back of his neck, ruffling his hair, and it formed a cowlick on top of his head. Her stomach lurched, the way it used to when she was racing and flew over a dip in the road at breakneck speed. Why did he have to be so freaking gorgeous? And why did it have to be *him* who made her realize that her ability to be attracted to a man hadn't died with Teddy? She wasn't in a position to get into a relationship, and even if she was, Sterling wouldn't want her. Not tragic, scarred Katarina. This man could have any woman he wanted. Heck, he might even have a girlfriend waiting in Auckland. She hadn't asked, and he hadn't shared.

Her shoulders slumped. "Maybe later."

She couldn't get into this now. Not while she was feeling

raw and exposed, as though he could see how she felt about him in her eyes, or hear it in the tone of her voice. For all she knew, he could. She hadn't been so drawn to a man in years, and she didn't know how to conceal it.

Damage control. Switch topics. Evade and distract.

"How would you like to go for an ice cream?" she asked. "Faith experiments with the most creative flavors."

"Okay," he agreed.

He was letting her get away that easily? She wanted to question it, but feared he'd change his mind. They made their way back into town, and she pointed out sights as they went. At the pavilion beside the beach, a large wooden deck occupied the center, with a seafood restaurant on one side and Faith's ice cream parlor, The Shack, on the other.

Kat pushed The Shack's glass door open and held it for Sterling, then followed him in. The parlor was small and well-lit, with a bar along the wall where people could sit while they ate. Tubs of ice cream were arrayed behind a glass screen, with little gold name plates in the front.

"Hi, Faith," Kat called to get the attention of the redhead behind the counter, who was washing a collection of metal scoops in a sink of soapy water.

Faith glanced over her shoulder, her hazel eyes magnified by thick-framed glasses. Her red-hued lips parted in a crooked smile and she spun around, the skirt of her 50s era polka-dot dress swishing around her calves.

"Kitty-Kat!" she exclaimed, startling the tourists who were browsing options. Faith didn't have volume control, and she'd never heard of an inside voice. She was either on or off. "What brings you to my shack of sin on this fine day?" Her gaze alighted on Sterling. "You've brought me fresh blood." She rubbed her palms together and Kat could have sworn Sterling whimpered in terror. Faith could be a tad overwhelming, at first. "What's your poison, sugar?" She sauntered over to the ice cream and waved at the customers who were observing her with varying degrees of fascination.

Kat stood back and let Sterling look over the flavors.

"Coconut curry," she heard him mutter to himself. "Pear and blue cheese? Roasted strawberry and buttermilk?"

He was scanning the gourmet section, beside which were the Kiwi classics, with flavors such as pineapple lumps, pavlova, and feijoa and ginger.

"What's it going to be, Alexander?" Faith asked.

Sterling frowned. "My name is—"

"I know you're not Alexander, sugar. Let a gal dream. So?"

"Feijoa and ginger, please."

"Ah, a man of good taste. One scoop or two? Cone or cup?"

"One scoop in a cone."

They exchanged ice cream for cash and Kat stepped forward to eyeball the experimental flavors. She was one of Faith's favorite guinea pigs because she was willing to try anything. "I'll take a single scoop of carrot cake and cream cheese."

"Anything for you, love." Faith scooped a healthy portion into a cone and handed it over with a wink. "Tell me how you like it."

As they left, Sterling ducked his head and asked, "Why did she call me Alexander?"

Kat licked her ice cream. Mm. A little sweet, a little spicy. "She likes to name people after the celebrities she thinks they most resemble."

"Strange."

Kat shrugged. She didn't consider it strange anymore. Faith had quirks, just like Kat did. She looked him up and down. "In your case, I'd say she was thinking of Alexander Skarsgård from *True Blood*."

He sampled his ice cream, his tongue flicking out and

licking droplets before they melted down the cone. "This is good."

"Of course it is. I wouldn't lead you astray."

They started walking. "Should I be flattered to be compared to this Alexander guy, or insulted?"

"Definitely flattered. I think she's into you."

He coughed and spluttered as though he'd sucked ice cream into his windpipe. "*What?*"

She smiled and patted his back, enjoying the banter that seemed to come more easily between them with each passing moment. "I'm teasing, Sterling. Unwind a little."

He stopped walking. "I'm going to go and ask for her number."

Now it was Kat's turn to choke on shock. Red hot needles of jealousy stabbed into her gut. Faith was fun and curvaceous and whole. Any man would be interested in her. Not like Kat, who was used goods, both physically and emotionally.

"You—uh—"

Sterling chuckled, the sound deep and full of amusement, like music to her ears. "You should see the look on your face."

She gaped.

"Unwind a little, Kat. I was only teasing."

Oh. My. God. He was having her on.

She didn't think he had it in him. She thumped his arm. "You jerk! You really had me going."

He rubbed the spot she'd hit and grinned, his eyes alive with humor. They didn't seem like chips of ice anymore. They were more like the endless blue of the sky on a clear summer day. Kat stared into them, unable to look away. Unable to breathe. Then she felt something cold ooze over her hand.

"Ugh, ew." She licked the melted ice cream from her skin and was afraid to raise her head in case her cheeks were blazing. She'd been ogling him like a silly girl with a crush, and now she looked like a fool.

When she did dare to glance up, his eyes had darkened and he was watching her with parted lips and intense focus. Though the sun was beating down overhead, she shivered. He broke away first, switching his focus to the ice cream.

"How's yours?" he asked, and it took her a few seconds to realize he meant the food.

"It's good. You want a try?"

She thought he'd refuse, but he surprised her once again, leaning over to swipe his tongue across the top of her cone. Whoa, that felt more intimate than she'd expected.

He savored it. A blob of ice cream remained at the corner of his mouth. "I like it. You want to try mine?"

"No, but thanks. I've tried all of the regular flavors before."

"I'm not surprised," he said. "If I had that place nearby, I'd be there every day. I'd need to double my run to stay in shape."

The fleck of ice cream was still on his face, and Kat itched to draw him down and lick it away.

That was a problem.

She wasn't supposed to want anything from Sterling.

She was helping him. That was what she'd decided the day they'd met, so instead of giving in to her insane urges, she gestured for him to wipe it off with his sleeve and kept her hands firmly to herself.

11

"Good morning."

The polite greeting came as a surprise. Considering how Sterling had reacted the last time Kat had woken him for yoga, she'd half expected him to slam the door in her face. As it happened, he seemed to have already been up and about. He was dressed in shorts that revealed muscular calves dusted with gold and had clearly run a brush through his hair.

She paused on the threshold. "Are you going somewhere?"

He nodded. "I like to run in the morning."

She'd just bet he did. His gorgeous legs attested to that. "Yoga is starting soon," she said. "I'd hoped you might join in again."

A scowl darkened his face. "That didn't go very well last time. What makes you think it'd be different today?"

She fidgeted. What had made her think things would be different? Perhaps because she'd believed they were bordering on a friendship of sorts. "Won't you just give it another chance? You can go for your run after and I won't pester you again today. Promise."

He studied her so intensely she couldn't help but squirm. Finally, he gave a curt nod. "Okay. But then you don't bother me about yoga again."

She grinned and offered her hand. "Deal."

They shook on it, his palm warm against hers. She sent him what she hoped was a supportive smile, then led him to the foyer, where they claimed mats next to each other in the rear of the class. A few more people arrived, then Bex called the group to order. She started a gentle soundtrack and demonstrated warm-up stretches. Kat watched out of the corner of her eye as Sterling bent his head one way, then the other, his chest rising and falling with even breaths. He managed to pull off a convincing downward dog, though she noticed him panting through it.

When they had to lower themselves to their stomachs to shift into cobra pose, he hit the first snag. He was halfway down when his arms buckled and he flopped onto his stomach like a landed fish. She held her breath and waited for the fireworks. Bex had also stilled, ready for anything. But then he shook his head, picked himself up and rearranged himself into the correct position. A collective breath was released.

He next encountered difficulty with tree pose, wobbling dangerously as he struggled to balance on his right leg with his left foot pressed into his thigh. Teetering back and forth, he had to drop his foot to regain balance more than once, but he only rolled his eyes and tried again. She had to admit, persistence was a very attractive trait in a man. As was the willingness to risk looking like a fool when giving something a second try.

Kat watched him so single-mindedly that she lost her own balance and tripped forward, knocking into Tione.

"Oy, watch it," he grunted, hitting the floor with a thump.

"Sorry." She backed off, pleased she didn't have the kind of complexion where it was obvious when she blushed. She met Bex's eyes, and Bex waggled her eyebrows suggestively, shooting a glance at Sterling. Damn, her friend knew what had been on her mind. Talk about embarrassing.

A hand touched her waist and she flinched. It was Sterling, helping her to right herself. And damned if he didn't smell as good as he looked. He must be wearing cologne because no man naturally smelled this good in the morning.

"Thanks," she murmured, then tried to give her attention to their teacher.

Everyone moved into chair pose. Of their own volition, her eyes were drawn like a magnet back to Sterling, only to find him looking straight at her. Their gazes clashed and held. Unspoken messages flew between them.

I'm attracted to you.

The feeling is mutual.

What are we going to do about it?

Nothing. They couldn't do anything. Kat closed her eyes, severing the connection. *Remember who you are*, she told herself. *You don't deserve to share an attraction with an interesting man. You don't deserve happiness. You don't deserve love.*

For the rest of the session, she pretended there was a brick wall dividing her from him. For all intents and purposes, there might as well have been.

After a quick shower, Kat grabbed a notebook from her office and headed to the kitchen, where Tione was preparing breakfast.

"Meal planning," she announced. "Next week. What are you thinking?"

"I'm thinking," he said, as he whisked omelet mixture, "that I'd like to know what you're doing with the suit."

The pen slipped from her fingers and she bent to pick it up, her hands trembling. "What do you mean?" Had she been that easy to read? "I'm helping him loosen up."

He laid the whisk down, poured mixture into a skillet and raised an eyebrow dubiously. "I think you'd like to do more than loosen him up, Kat."

She swallowed. "I would?"

"Yeah." He bobbed his head, skewering her with sharp brown eyes, not letting her off the hook. "I've never seen you look at a man that way. Gotta say, I don't think it's a good idea."

She tried for breezy. "Pssh. It's all in your head. Nothing is going on."

"Doesn't look like nothing." He crossed his arms. "All I'm saying is, be careful. A guy like that will walk all over you if you give him the chance."

She stiffened. After all the time she'd spent with Sterling, she didn't think Tione was giving him enough credit. "He's a better man than he seems."

His jaw tightened. "I don't see it, but I know you're not stupid." He heaved a sigh. "It's great you've remembered you're a woman, but couldn't your first crush be on someone better for you?" He shifted, looking uncomfortable. It wasn't in his nature to pry, or talk about relationships and feelings. He was saying what he was for the sake of their friendship and her happiness. She needed to remember that. "What about Shane? He's a good guy."

She barked with laughter, unable to help herself, and wiped moisture from the corner of her eye. "Oh, man. You should know better than anyone, you can't choose who you think is hot. Shane is a nice guy, but there's nothing there. Less than nothing. I'd date *you* before I dated him." Panic flashed into Tione's expression, and she gurgled. "Oh, please. As if I'd go there." She straightened and kissed his cheek. "I appreciate you looking out for me. Now, do you think we could stop having this conversation and focus on the menu?"

He looked up at the ceiling, his lips moving silently. Then he said, "You have no idea how happy that would make me."

FREE TIME WAS a new concept for Sterling, and he found he didn't quite know what to do with it. Stuffing his keys and phone into his pocket, he left Sanctuary and crunched across the parking lot, then past the flax and native grasses of the sand dunes to the beach. He'd decided to invest in this place based on photographs and testimonials. It had seemed to have the best of everything. Near a town, but not within it. On the edge of the forest but with modern conveniences, and a short jaunt from the beach.

Now, he decided he may as well explore the area and see its pros and cons firsthand. He had the time. He already knew he could hear the ocean from inside the lodge at night, when everything else was silent. It was something he'd never experienced before. At first, the constant sound had annoyed him, but after a while, it lulled him to sleep. Reaching the sand, he untied his shoelaces and continued on in bare feet. He didn't want to ruin his expensive leather shoes, and he hadn't walked barefoot on a beach in, oh, fifteen years or so. People who lounged about on beaches were idle. He had more productive ways to spend his time.

As he picked his way along the foreshore, sand squished between his toes, soft as powdered sugar. Further down, he could see the silhouettes of children playing, but the wind carried their voices away. Gulls dived overhead and other seabirds skimmed the surface of the sea, past the breakwater. White-tipped waves rolled onto shore, and a strange sense of calm descended on him. He lowered himself to the ground, his toes burrowing into the warm sand, and leaned back, tilting his face up to catch the sun. Something rustled in the dunes. There was a splash as a bird caught a fish and soared off with it. The summer rays caressed his cheeks, and his lips curved.

Serene. Carefree. At peace. This was exactly how he wanted the guests at Eli's future hotel to feel.

The creak of a rusty hinge disrupted his tranquility, and his eyes flickered open.

"And here, you'll find the wet suits, paddleboards, surfboards, and sea kayaks."

Kat's voice. He tried to tune her out by focusing on the rhythmic sound of the ocean.

"The shed is unlocked at six every morning and locked again after dark. No one should be on the water overnight, but otherwise, you can borrow equipment any time you want."

He sighed. It seemed his peace was at an end.

"Awesome-sauce. Thank you," an American-accented woman said.

"No worries. Make yourself at home. I'll see you later on."

Sterling's hands interlaced behind his head, but he straightened when footfalls approached.

"*Kia ora.* Beautiful day, isn't it?" Kat sat beside him, tucking her legs beneath her butt. Her waterfall of hair cascaded down her back, shimmering blue-black in the harsh sunlight. Her hands rested in her lap, and he studied the *koru* tattoo wrapped around her wrist. He'd never had thought he'd find tattoos sexy, but on her, it was feminine and intriguing. He wanted to trace the outline of the ink while she explained what each elegant swirl meant.

"It is," he agreed. "I've been enjoying the peace and quiet."

"I hope you sun-screened."

His brow quirked up in question.

She shrugged. "Looks like you'd burn easily."

"I do." He took his eyes from her and watched a figure in the distance jog into the waves with a surfboard.

"You ever surfed?" she asked.

"No." Eli had invited him out on a couple of occasions, but he'd always declined. He wasn't athletically gifted—or particularly coordinated—which was why he stuck to running.

"You know what? That won't do. I'll have to teach you."

He jerked around, looking at her incredulously. Was she yanking his chain? He'd given yoga a second try, and even enjoyed himself doing it—not that the words would ever cross his lips—but surfing? Nothing good could come of that.

Maybe that was what she was hoping for. Maybe she wanted to laugh at him.

No, Kat wasn't like that. She'd laugh, certainly, but then she'd help him do better.

He hesitated. If ever there was an opportunity to venture outside his comfort zone, this was it. But did he want to? There was nothing wrong with his comfort zone.

"Give it a go," she urged. "We can't let it be said that you came to Haven Bay and didn't surf."

"I really don't think—"

"Don't think." She laughed. "Just do."

He sighed and ran a hand through his hair. "What happened to no more pestering me today?"

Her smile fell and she deflated. "Sorry, you're right. I totally forgot." She backed away. "I'll leave you to enjoy yourself."

She took a few more steps, and he mulled over his options. He liked her too much to let her leave when he'd clearly hurt her feelings.

"Kat, wait." She paused, but didn't turn. "You can try to teach me, but I can't promise I'll enjoy it, or that I'll be any good. Also, I'm not doing it alone. You're coming with me."

She swung around and strode back, grin in place. "You're on, Donkey Kong." Reaching down, she pulled him to his feet. "Don't suppose you brought your swimsuit with you?"

"No. I wasn't planning a holiday."

"Thought as much." She walked to the storage shed and

called back over her shoulder, "There are a couple of spare pairs of board shorts in our lost and found."

She emerged with a laundry basket full of odds and ends, and searched it, then tossed something his way. He caught it, and shook it out. They were red shorts, possibly a little broad for him, but they had laces and could be tightened.

He looked around. "Is there anywhere to change?"

She lifted one shoulder. "If you're worried about preserving your modesty, you can use the shed."

He did. As expected, the shorts were too big, but he could make do. He checked out the array of water sports equipment, which was impressive, then found a bottle of sunscreen and covered the parts of himself that he hadn't done earlier. When he let Kat know he was decent, she sized him up and chose a massive surfboard for him, then a smaller one for herself.

Out on the sand, she laid her board down with the bit that looked like a shark fin facing the sand.

"Before we get out there, we're going to practice the movements," she told him. "First off, when you carry the board into the water, you lift the end above the waves, otherwise it'll be much harder work to drag it out there."

"Got it."

"Once you see a wave you want to catch, you turn your board around to face the beach, jump on and start paddling." She dropped onto her belly on the board and made wide, arcing movements with her arms. "Like this. It's important that you're moving, otherwise the wave will just pass beneath you." She raised herself up, kneeling on the board. "Go on, show me how you paddle."

He cringed. Was she actually going to make him run through the whole process like a little kid learning to swim? He made some half-hearted swinging motions then folded his arms over his chest.

"Nah-uh. That won't cut it, buddy. You paddle like that

out there and you won't be riding any waves."

"I feel silly," he muttered.

She rolled her eyes. "Everyone feels like that when they're starting out. Look around you. What do you see?"

"I see the beach, the lodge, a couple of people out on the waves."

"And no audience," she said meaningfully. "No one is watching. It doesn't matter if you look a little silly."

He sighed, realizing they wouldn't progress with the lesson until she was satisfied. With a furtive glance over his shoulder to make sure no one was looking, he lay down fully and worked his arms the same way she had.

"Good," she exclaimed. "But wiggle down the board a bit more. You want your toes to be almost touching the end."

He adjusted his position.

"*Ka pai.* That's more like it. Okay, so now pretend we're out in the waves. You've seen a good one coming. You've started paddling. Next thing is to get upright."

"That seems like the hard part."

"It is, but less so than you might think. There are two ways you can get onto your feet. The first, which is best if you've got good balance, is to jump straight from a lying position to a squatting position, like this." She lay flat, then brought her palms up under her shoulders and with one fluid movement, leapt to her feet, her knees bent. "When you're standing, you want your feet to be parallel to the rails, which is what we call the sides of the board. Try to keep a low center of gravity, arms stretched towards the nose, and head aligned with your front shoulder." She jumped to the sand and nodded to him. "Your turn."

He tried to mimic her actions. It was harder than it looked. Bringing his palms to the correct place, he pushed up, but then wobbled precariously as he tried to position his body as she'd instructed.

"Am I doing this right?" he asked. "It feels awkward."

"Can I touch you?"

He nodded, swallowing hard as her competent hands landed on him and she adjusted his stance. It was one of the first times she'd touched him without it being a mere brush of their bodies in passing, and he wanted to close his eyes and drink in the sensation.

"You don't want to lean forward or you'll take a dive off the nose," she warned.

"Am I going to hurt myself doing this?" With all the precautions she kept mentioning, it seemed inevitable.

"Nah, probably not. If you fall, the water cushions your landing."

"Okay." He wasn't sure he believed her. "What's the second way to get upright, because I doubt I'll pull the jump off." He'd probably end up somersaulting head-over-heels through the waves.

"Option two," she said, lying down again. "You push to your knees, bring your right foot level with your right hand, on the inside of your arm, then stand up."

Option two looked more awkward than the first, but also more doable. He copied her movements.

"That's right. Do it again."

Reluctantly, he did. And again, and again, and *again*, until she was satisfied.

"I think you're ready to try for real," she said with a grin, and started toward the water, leaving her surfboard behind.

"Aren't you forgetting something?" he called, pointing to it.

She waved a hand dismissively. "I'll come back for it once you've got the knack."

She was going to supervise him? What if he was terrible? What if he humiliated himself in front of her?

"Don't look so worried." She laughed. "You'll be just fine."

He ducked his head, afraid he was blushing because of how easily she'd been able to read him, and jogged into the shallow surf. The water was cool against his skin—refreshingly so—but despite the early hour of the day, it was warm enough that he didn't flinch. Kat waded in up to her thighs, then turned and walked backward so she could see him. He made sure to lift the end of the board—the *nose*—above the waves, as she'd instructed.

"All right, this is far enough," she said, when they were in water up to his waist. It was a little higher on her, soaking her tank top up to the bottom of her breasts. Why hadn't she changed into a swimsuit? He hadn't thought to ask until now, when he could clearly see the outline of her bra through the fabric.

"Turn the board around," she said. He did. "See that wave?" She pointed to a faint crest forming a hundred yards away. "We're going to aim for that one. Jump on the board and start paddling. I'll give you a push to get you going."

Jumping on the board wasn't as easy as she made it sound. He gripped the sides and awkwardly belly-flopped onto it, cringing when his balls smacked the hard surface. There had to be a way to do it that didn't involve flattening his testicles. He'd just opened his mouth to ask when, without warning, she shoved the board forward. He started paddling and tried unsuccessfully to look back over his shoulder and see where the wave was.

All of a sudden, like someone had attached a jet pack to him, he was motoring across the water, speeding toward land. Glancing down, he realized he'd caught the wave. This was how it felt to be carried to shore by the power of the sea. Unreal.

He came onto his knees, dragged his right foot up and placed it inside his right arm, then he was tumbling forward, hitting the water with a splash, bumping his hip and rolling to a stop. He surfaced, spluttering.

"Nice work!" Kat yelled.

Was she mocking him? He mopped the water from his

eyes and blinked in her direction. She seemed sincere. But he'd failed. Fallen on his ass. How could that be considered "nice work"?

"Pick yourself up and get back out here," she called.

He did. Over and over, until, on his fifteenth or twentieth attempt, he finally got to his feet and rode a wave. The feeling was incredible. He flew over the surface of the water like he was weightless, divorced from the usual problems that dragged him down. Like nothing existed except him, the water, the board beneath his feet, and the endless stretch of sand he was hurtling toward. Adrenaline danced in his veins, and the hairs on his arms prickled. What a rush. A crazy, surreal rush.

He wanted to laugh. He wanted to leap into the air and somersault.

When he reached the shallows, he jumped off the board and jogged onto the sand, dropping onto his bum. His eyes watered and his nose was running but he'd never been more exhilarated in his life.

Why had he never done this with Eli? How had he lived for more than thirty years without discovering what it was like to walk on water?

Kat whooped, and he looked at her across the waves. She was grinning wildly, like she was as thrilled by his success as he was. A sudden pang squeezed his heart. Was this what it felt like to have a romantic partner? He'd often wondered what he was missing out on, and for the first time, he had an inkling.

She gave him a thumbs-up. She was soaked, her hair plastered to the side of her face and her eyes red-rimmed. Appreciation for her welled within him. She'd taught him something about himself. He liked to surf. What else could he learn from her? And more importantly, when could he find out if she was as playful and passionate in *all* aspects of her life?

Dayum boy.

Okay, so when Kat suggested she teach Sterling how to surf, she hadn't had an ulterior motive. That didn't mean she wouldn't take advantage of the opportunity to get an eyeful of his toned torso and legs. He got to his feet, still grinning like a loony, and waded back out to her.

"Did you see me?" he asked, eyes lit with the same excitement as some of the boys she'd seen at the surf school.

"I did. You rocked it." They high-fived. "You're good to go solo. I'll grab my board and join you."

His grin stretched wider and he strode past her. She watched him, her gaze slipping down to the tight buns beneath his borrowed shorts, and drew in a deep breath. For some reason, seeing him play in the waves and finally let go of his inhibitions made her unaccountably hot for him. And man, she loved that grin. She suspected it didn't come out very often because there were no smile-lines around his eyes, or brackets around his mouth. It made her giddy with pleasure that he was enjoying himself so much with her.

She trudged up the sand, wringing the water from her shorts and tank, to fetch her own surfboard. She didn't wear bikinis. Partly because she hated the scars decorating her body—they reminded her of what she'd lost—and partly because she wasn't eighteen anymore. The beach babe look wasn't her style.

She grabbed the board and dragged it to the water. As the sea lapped at her feet, she saw Sterling catch the beginnings of a wave and clamber upright. He was leaning too far forward. But then he corrected himself and rode the wave for a full ten seconds before tumbling off, his head vanishing underwater. She hurried over, but he popped up right in front of her and she stumbled, losing her footing.

Sterling's body saved her from going under. She grabbed ahold of his chest to right herself, and then their limbs entangled as they both struggled to reach the shallower water, where they collapsed, breathless and laughing. Her head rested on his shoulder and one of her legs threaded between his. They locked eyes, his rivaling the sky above them as they blazed into hers. His free hand came up to grasp her chin, ever so gently.

"Kat," he breathed. "I really, really like surfing."

Her smile trembled. Her nerves were all alight. She was too wired by his proximity to do anything more than say, "I'm glad."

His hand curved around her cheek. "I also really, really like you."

Her heart stuttered. "I… umm… God, I like you, too."

Slowly, slowly, his lips descended toward hers. She had plenty of time to pull away. Plenty of opportunity to escape. But though she knew she didn't deserve this wonderful, isolated moment with a man who looked at her as though she'd unraveled the secrets of the universe, she couldn't resist. It had been such a long time since a man held her close, since she'd been able to smell the salt in his hair or feel the rapid thud of his heartbeat.

Their lips connected. Clung for a moment. Then her

breath eased out as they drew apart. Sterling's hand slid down the arch of her neck and cupped the back of her head. He looked at her with a question in his eyes. She leaned forward, wrapping both of her arms around his neck, and kissed him.

The kiss started out as an exploration. Soft, inquiring. When neither of them drew away, it deepened. His tongue traced the seam of her lips, then delved into her mouth. The tips of their tongues touched. She exhaled shakily and he shifted, his free hand curving around her lower back and drawing her closer. She complied, shimmying onto his lap, only breaking the kiss for a second.

They were deaf to everything around them. Blind to anything except each other.

He trailed kisses across her cheek and down the side of her neck. She shivered when he licked the skin at the base of her throat, and a noise rumbled in his chest. Heat pooled low in her belly, and tugs of wanting corresponded to the kisses he dropped on her damp, yearning skin.

Just when she thought she might go up in flames, water slammed her full in the face and shoved her onto her back.

Shit.

She coughed, and dragged herself off his lap and further up the beach until she reached dry sand. She mopped her sopping wet hair out of her face, then lay back and stared up at the sky.

Well, that was unexpected.

A laugh burst from her at the absurdity of the thought. She wasn't even sure if she'd meant the kiss or the face-full of wave.

"You okay?" Sterling asked, reaching her side.

"Who the hell knows?" she asked, not expecting an answer. Only one thing was clear: she'd crossed a line, and there was no going back.

IF ASKED when he woke this morning whether he'd be kissing Kat before midday, Sterling would have laughed and answered in the negative. Yet here he was. Lying beside her on the beach after they'd shared an exquisite, meaningful moment. He could scarcely believe it. This was the woman who'd been occupying his dreams, as well as a good portion of his waking thoughts. He'd hardly dared to imagine she might return his interest, although their connection during yoga had given him some degree of hope.

"That kiss…" he began, unsure how to finish the sentence.

"It was pretty good, wasn't it?" Kat said.

"Better than good." How about amazing? Mind-blowing? Momentous?

It may have come out of left field, but he was hooked on her. Wanted to spend more time with her. To get to know her better. Turning, he smiled, meeting her warm, brown gaze. His heart flipped over. Did she feel the same way? He was afraid to ask.

She sighed and rose up on her elbows. "I'd better get back to work. There are more guests arriving soon."

He tried not to let his disappointment show. "I'll walk you to the lodge."

"Sounds good." She got to her feet, and he followed. Together, they packed the surfing equipment away.

As they strolled over the dunes toward Sanctuary, the sun heated his back, and he had a spring in his step. Pausing outside the foyer, he touched her arm.

"I had a great time just now. Thank you."

She beamed. "You're very welcome." And then she dropped a light kiss on his lips and gestured for him to enter. As he did so, she swatted his backside, and he jumped in surprise. He glanced back at her and saw her eyes dance with mischief. "I'll see you later, Sterling."

While she headed into the dining hall, he made his way along the east wing, grinning like an idiot. He felt gooey inside, but buzzed with excitement for the future. Most of all, he felt *alive*.

That is, until he reached his bedroom door and spotted the burly cook lurking outside, tattooed arms crossed over his chest, scowling darkly enough to make Sterling reevaluate his life choices.

"Hello," he said cautiously.

Tione's chin jerked up. "Hey." He unfolded his arms and they swung at his sides as he stalked toward Sterling. "I saw you."

"Okay." He wasn't sure where this was going.

"Outside," Tione explained, as though he was a dumbass. "With Kat."

"*Oh.*"

Tione took another step forward; he wasn't tall enough to tower over Sterling, but he was broad enough to give him pause. "*Kissing* Kat."

Oh, shit. He hadn't picked up on any romantic vibes between Kat and Tione, but maybe he'd been wrong. He wasn't exactly known for his proficiency with body language or nonverbal cues.

"Is that a problem?" he asked.

Tione didn't answer, just studied him from beneath thick black brows, standing between Sterling and his door. Then he said, "What are your intentions toward Kat?"

Sterling blanched. "Excuse me?"

"It was a straightforward question."

"I beg to differ." He winced, realizing he sounded like a pretentious prick.

"Let me put it in a way you'll understand." Tione's hands went to his hips and he leaned forward. "Kat is more fragile than she seems, and if you hurt her or in any way interfere with her happiness, I'll personally make sure you regret it. You get me?"

Sterling cleared his throat and nodded. "I get you. But from where I'm standing, you're not giving her enough credit. She's stronger than you think."

Tione tilted his head. "Maybe. But less so than you think."

Sterling pursed his lips. The fierce gleam in Tione's eyes, combined with the wide-legged stance that was no doubt intended to intimidate, made him wonder whether there was more between Tione and Kat than friendship. Or, at least, if Tione would like there to be more.

"Do you love Kat?" he asked curiously. "Are the two of you involved?"

Tione spluttered and covered his mouth so he didn't spray Sterling. "Hell, no. I mean, I love her. But like a sister. Her and me," he shuddered, "it'd be practically incestuous. Jesus, man, where'd you get that idea?"

"You're awfully protective of her."

"Like I'd be if I had a sister," he insisted. "I don't want to see her get used and tossed aside by some city slicker who thinks she's easy pickings."

Sterling saw red. "I'd *never* do that to her. She's an amazing woman, and I'm not a total asshole."

"Just a cold fish."

The words stung, but he couldn't disagree. It was what he'd been accused of his whole life, and he'd never given people a reason to think differently. The fact was, he used his brain as a compass rather than his heart, and a lot of people couldn't understand that.

"I won't hurt Kat," he promised, his good mood well and truly gone. "I care about her, more than I'm comfortable saying. Can I go into my room now?"

Tione glared but stepped aside, and Sterling brushed past him, closed the door, then sank against it, his heart pounding like he'd just finished a four-hundred-meter sprint. Dozens of thoughts whirred through his mind, and he couldn't focus on any of them. If this was how most people felt on a daily basis, he wasn't sure emotions were all they were cracked up to be.

13

THE BREEZE DRIED Sterling's shower-damp hair more effectively than a hair dryer as he strolled into town, passing The Hideaway and waving to Bex, who was standing in the window. She waved back. He continued across the road to the pub, The Den, and went inside, blinking as his eyes readjusted to the dim lighting. When his vision sharpened, he looked around.

The Den was just as he imagined classic small-town pubs ought to be. A massive bar occupied the far wall, and behind that, liquor bottles lined an old-fashioned wooden cabinet. The walls were painted lichen-green and two blackboards took up much of the space to each side of the liquor cabinet. One was a drinks menu and the other listed bar snacks. A surfboard had the specials of the day scrawled across it. A number of long, narrow tables occupied the space between Sterling and the bar.

The atmosphere was different from that of the places Sterling occasionally visited in Auckland, which were well-lit with monochromatic surfaces. Feeling like a fish that had been picked up by a seabird and dropped onto dry land, he cautiously approached the bar. There was no one in sight.

No staff, no customers. He cleared his throat. How was he supposed to order a whiskey if no one was here? He searched the bar for a bell or button and came up short.

"Excuse me," he called. "Is anyone around?"

Something thudded behind a door he hadn't noticed to the left of the bar, and a masculine curse followed.

"Be with you in a minute!" a male voice yelled back.

Sterling waited. A full two minutes later, a man shoved the door open and emerged into the room. The first thing Sterling noticed about him was the quantity of bare skin on display. A hairless golden chest and ropy arms, with board shorts that dripped on the navy carpet.

The man reached up and shoved sopping hair off his forehead. "What can I do you for?"

Sterling stared. The guy was working half-naked and soaked? He glanced back at the door. Yes, it definitely said the pub was open.

"Uh, mate? Can I help you?" the guy persisted.

Sterling's mouth dropped open. He snapped it shut. "Whiskey, neat."

The bartender checked his watch. "Bad day?" he asked, retrieving a bottle of Jack Daniels from a shelf and measuring out a single shot, which he slid across the counter.

"Just the opposite." For the most part.

"Ah, we're celebrating, are we?"

"Sort of." Not in the way he'd expected, but then, he could never have predicted the turn today had taken. He'd shared something truly special with Kat, and while he didn't know where they were going, he knew it wasn't to be taken lightly. There was a connection between them. One he couldn't understand, much less explain.

"Not much of a talker, eh?"

"No." He sipped the whiskey, letting it roll over his tongue. He never drank to excess, but he didn't waste his time with weak drinks, either.

"You mind if I do some work while you drink?" the bartender asked.

"Not at all."

The man retreated through the side door and returned a moment later, wearing a dry t-shirt, with a shoebox in his hands. He removed the lid and started sifting through papers. From where Sterling stood, he could see receipts, handwritten notes, and a few printed invoices. The bartender grabbed a pen and spread papers across the counter, jotting notes in the margins. Then he double-checked something he'd previously written, set the pen down, cupped his face in his hands and groaned.

Sterling drank his whiskey and wondered whether he should ignore the man's distress. This whole tightknit community thing was still new to him, and while he knew Kat would have jumped in and asked what was wrong straight away, he wasn't like Kat, and he didn't want to over-step. He'd never been one to make small talk with those around him. He wasn't even sure he knew how.

Eventually, the bartender raised his head, picked up the pen and turned over what looked to be a letter. He scanned it, then grabbed some kind of financial sheet and cross-checked them.

"Damn it, I don't have a head for numbers."

Sterling, who definitely did have a head for numbers, leaned closer, trying to see what he was working on. The guy scribbled something else, and then rifled the papers.

He growled. "I know it's here somewhere."

Giving in to curiosity, Sterling asked, "What are you looking for?"

"My income sheet for the past month. I think I've got most of my incoming invoices here, but I'm having trouble with the outgoings."

Sterling's brows knitted together. "You own this place?"

The man nodded. "Sure do. Although my mother keeps us

stocked. I just pay the bills, handle maintenance, and work the bar." He held out a hand and Sterling shook it. "I'm Logan."

"Sterling. Pleasure to meet you." He nodded toward the papers. "You don't have a filing system?"

"A shoebox doesn't count?"

"I don't believe so."

Logan straightened. "Then no." He sighed. "This is a mess."

"Yes, it does seem to be," Sterling agreed.

Staring at him, Logan barked a laugh. "You don't pull any punches, do you?"

With a large swallow, Sterling finished his whiskey and set the glass down. He'd never understood when to beat around the bush and when to be direct, usually opting for the latter. "I suppose not."

Logan raked a hand through his wet, blond hair. "In addition to being blunt, you don't happen to know anything about finances and business paperwork, do you?"

The ground beneath Sterling's feet solidified. He was back on familiar ground. "As it happens, I do." It was only what he did all day, every day.

Logan laughed again. "Are you having me on?"

He frowned. "No, of course not. I'm the second in charge at my company, and I have a business degree."

"Well, hallelujah." Logan raised his palms to the ceiling and grinned. "Congratulations, you're my new best friend. Do you mind coming around here and helping me out?"

With trepidation, Sterling rounded the bar and looked over Logan's shoulder. "Tell me more about what's going on here."

Logan met his eyes. "Last summer, I started a second business, renting out gear for water sports and running a few surfing lessons. It was meant to be a hobby, but it's really taken off."

Sterling didn't see the problem. "That seems like a good thing."

"You'd think so. Except that I haven't been keeping a track of anything very well. Half my equipment needs maintenance, but I haven't got proper records of what's been done when, and I'm pretty sure I'm not turning a profit with the prices I'm charging."

"You're not certain?"

He shrugged helplessly. "What do you think? Everything I have is in this box—and that includes the paperwork for the bar. I don't even have a separate business account. Both companies go through my personal one."

Sterling winced. Separating costs and income at the end of the year would be a nightmare.

"I didn't start the watersports company to make a profit, but I can't afford to lose money on it, either. Especially not with how much of my time it's taking up."

At least most of the documents in the box were dated. Sorting out the finances would be tedious, but not difficult for someone with experience. As for everything else... Sterling was seeing a lot of room for improvement.

"Do you have an inventory?" he asked.

"Yes, thank God. I keep it up to date so I can make sure everything is being returned when it should be."

"Good." Sterling paused to look at a sheet outlining charges for different pieces of equipment. He didn't know much about recreational businesses, but he'd say Logan was undercharging. Significantly. If he were running this business, he'd research online to see what the norm was for comparative businesses and then adopt the median prices. Or perhaps more, depending on the state of Logan's equipment and his credentials.

Before he'd even given his brain permission, Sterling was firing through the dozens of ways he could improve Logan's business—the least of which was tidying his books. His veins thrummed with excitement. Business was in his blood, and the prospect of taking this chaos and making it into something profitable had his heart rate picking up and his palms sweating with anticipation.

But that wasn't his place. And besides, Logan hadn't asked. He just wanted help tidying things up. "You're absolutely correct that this isn't in great shape, but I think I can help, and it just so happens I have a free afternoon."

"Really?" Logan beamed. "You're a lifesaver. If you can help me with this…" He shook his head. "I'll keep you in free beers for a month."

"A month?" He wasn't planning to stay that long. "Make it whiskey, for a couple weeks, and you've got a deal."

They shook on it. For the next few hours, Sterling helped his new acquaintance wade through the mountain of papers and transform the information into something useful. By the time he realized he was starving, a fire had ignited in his belly. It had been a long time since he'd seen an opportunity like this, to take something okay and make it great. Before he left, he couldn't help but make an offer he never had before.

"Logan," he said as he prepared to leave. "I think you could make this business much stronger than it is. What you need is a plan, and I'd be happy to help you write one while I'm here. What do you say?"

Logan's eyebrows knitted together. "Seriously?"

"Yes."

A grin broke out over his face. "Forget our previous deal, you can have all the whiskey you can drink." His phone pinged and he checked it. "Damn, I have to prepare for a party that will be arriving soon, but you should come back later tonight. I play poker with the boys upstairs on Fridays. If you're keen to join, we could talk over options during the game."

"I'll be here," Sterling agreed. He excelled at card games

and was anxious to dive into his new pet project. "What time?"

"Around nine-ish. See you then."

Sterling headed out the door without saying goodbye, already organizing ideas in his mind.

KAT ADJUSTED the phone against her ear. "What would a typical session with you look like?" she asked Jack Farrelly, the owner of Seafaring Adventures, who she hoped to hire to take her guests on tours. She rested an elbow on the surface of the desk and doodled a repeating pattern of *koru* on her notepaper with her free hand.

"There's no such thing as a typical session with me," Jack rasped. "I change it up depending on who's in my group and what they want to get out of it. The one thing I guarantee is that they'll have fun, and an adventure."

Adventure was exactly what she wanted for her guests, but she wasn't convinced Jack was the best man for the job. He had a reputation for being unpredictable, and while she wanted her guests to have fun, she didn't want to risk them spending two unplanned nights in a cave on the side of a mountain, living off chocolate bars and melted snow.

"I'd need a certain amount of consistency," she told him. "Perhaps two or three different trips or activities you could rotate between? That way people know what to expect and can be prepared."

He scoffed. "Not knowing is half the fun."

That attitude was what she'd been afraid of. She was pondering which angle to take next when Sterling strode into the foyer, his legs eating up the short distance between the front door and the hall. He didn't raise his head, or even seem to notice her there. He was a man on a mission.

"Hang on a moment, Jack," she said, then laid the phone down. "Sterling," she called. "Where's the fire?"

He stopped abruptly and glanced around, finally seeing her. His eyes flared with warmth, and he hurried over, then came up short, his expression growing hesitant. She obliterated the space between them, drawing him in for a hug, and resting her cheek above his heart. Whether or not anything further happened between them, she didn't want him to doubt that the attraction was mutual. He'd put himself out on a ledge earlier by opening up about his feelings, and that deserved respect and recognition.

She pulled back, her lips curving as he pressed a swift kiss to them that ended far too soon. "Where are you off to in such a rush?"

He grinned, and it made him so blindingly handsome her pulse spiked. "I have a business plan to research."

"A business plan?" She frowned, wondering if he'd cracked. Perhaps their kiss, combined with yoga, and the surfing lesson, had been too much for him to handle. "What for?"

"Logan's side business. It's a complete nightmare." A fact he seemed inordinately pleased about. Kind of adorable, really. "I offered to help out, so I'm going back tonight and I need to learn a whole lot more about rental businesses and watersports."

She smiled. He'd offered to help one of the locals? Perhaps she was having more of an effect on him than she'd dared to hope. *Oh, but wait.* "Isn't Friday the boys'—"

"Poker night," he interrupted. "Yes, I'm invited." He glanced at her phone. "Are you on a call?"

"Oh, yes." She'd forgotten about Jack. "I'd better get back to that."

He nodded. "I'll see you later?"

"Sure thing."

With that, he turned and left. Kat stared after him,

bemused. Not only was he helping a local, but he was joining poker night, a longstanding tradition between the local men their age. The corner of her mouth twisted up. It was nice to see him excited about something, and especially sweet that he was allowing himself to become part of the bay's social scene.

For the first time since he'd arrived, it occurred to her that he was settling into local life with ease. Strange how that made her so nervous she felt like crawling out of her skin.

"Did I hear you talking about poker night?" Jack asked when she picked the phone back up.

"Yeah, it sounds like you've got a new addition tonight."

"Always a pleasure to have fresh blood." He sounded eager, like he was already counting the stacks of money he'd make.

"I wouldn't make a down payment on those new harnesses you want yet. Sterling is a corporate shark. I'd say he'll take you for all you're worth."

He chuckled. "No need to sound so pleased about it. I might start to think you don't like me."

She laughed. "You so sure I do?"

"Depends. Are you gonna hire me?"

Kat ran through her options. Having Jack do his adventure tours through Sanctuary would give her another way to attract people. On the other hand, it might be the nail in her coffin if he screwed up as he had last year.

"How about we give it a trial run?" she suggested.

"Okay," he agreed readily. "How often do you want me?"

She rolled her eyes at the double entendre. He'd made no secret of the fact he thought they'd be compatible, both of them liking the outdoors and preferring to keep busy, but she had no room in her life for a man. Especially not one who reminded her so much of Teddy, with his brash attitude and rough and tumble approach to life. It had become something of a running joke between them, and she suspected he wouldn't know what to do if she ever took him up on his offer.

"Say, two or three afternoons a week, to begin with."

"Can do."

"You'd need to be organized enough to be back by dinner or make sure Tione knows to save meals for later."

He sighed the sigh of the hard-done-by. "You're really putting a crimp in my style."

"Those are my conditions."

"Fine. Okay. You wanna be the fun police, that's all right with me. I accept your terms."

"Can you handle having people who aren't as fit as you, or who have injuries or chronic illnesses on your outings?" That was important to her, considering guests often opted to stay at Sanctuary while they recovered from illness or surgery.

"I'll do my best, but I want to know what I'm dealing with ahead of time and reserve the right to prevent someone from coming if I don't think they're up for it."

"That's reasonable. Can you start Monday?"

"Sure thing."

"Send me your plan for the first day by the end of the weekend and I'll circulate it round to see how many takers we get."

"Pleasure doing business with you."

"You, too." She paused, then added, "Play nice with Sterling. I don't think he gets out much."

"What's it worth to you?" he teased.

"Why don't you try it, and find out?"

"You're just teasing. I know you better than that." A click, and he'd hung up.

She heard a yell outside and glanced up in time to see Trevor playing tug-of-war with Betty, over her cardigan.

"Kat, will you lend me a hand?" Betty called.

Muffling a giggle, she went out to save the garment from the exuberant dog.

14

THAT NIGHT, Sterling stopped to ask for directions from the woman at the bar, who he presumed to be Logan's mother, then let himself through the door to the left. He passed a couple of storerooms and climbed the creaky wooden staircase.

"It's open," Logan called when he knocked.

"Hello," Sterling said, finding the other man in the kitchen, pouring nuts and chips into bowls. "Sorry I'm early. I wanted to run over some of my thoughts with you before anyone else arrived."

"No problem. Carry these out to the table while I mix up some dip, then I'm all yours."

Sterling put his papers aside, stacked the bowls and took them to the rectangular dining table, distributing them evenly along the center. A moment later, Logan followed with two bowls of onion dip.

"I can't believe you've already started looking into my business," he said, grasping Sterling's hand and clapping him on the shoulder. Was this how men communicated with each other in small towns? "I really appreciate it, man. You want a beer?"

"No, thanks." He retrieved his papers as Logan cracked the top off a bottle for himself, took a swig, and set it on the counter.

"What are you thinking?"

Sterling checked the first bullet point on his list. Pricing. "To start with, you're undercharging."

They worked through his list point by point, slowly migrating from the kitchen to the table, only pausing when a stocky guy with a mess of brown hair barreled into the apartment and helped himself to a handful of chips.

"What's this?" he asked, eying the papers spread between them.

Logan's eyes narrowed. "What's it look like, knucklehead? Business." He turned to Sterling. "This is Jack. He's got shit for brains. Don't pay attention to anything he says."

Sterling wondered whether it was appropriate to say, "Nice to meet you." Clearly, these two enjoyed some kind of banter he wasn't a part of.

"This from the guy with nothing but seawater between his ears?" Jack threw back, saving him the trouble of making a decision, then settling into a chair and peering over at the papers. "Seriously?" he said to Logan. "Is this guy an accountant or something?"

"I'm Sterling." He offered a hand, which Jack shook in a meaty fist. "I manage a business in Auckland and I'm helping Logan with some of his issues."

Logan collected the papers and passed them over. "Sterling could probably help you, too." To Sterling, he said, "Jack runs an adventure tour business, but he's got as much of a head for numbers as I do, and his organizational system is worse."

Worse? How could it possibly be worse?

Logan must have seen his dubious expression because he added, "Believe me, it's true. He keeps his paperwork in a backpack—when he bothers to print it out. Half of it never leaves the web."

"That's less than ideal."

"It's stupid," Jack grunted. "You can say it. I know I'm going to run into problems one day, but I really don't give a damn about dotting the I's and crossing the T's. I just want to take people caving and rafting and let someone else worry about the rest. So yeah, if you know your stuff and you're going to be in town for a while, I could probably use your help." His lips twisted wryly. "If you can be bothered with small fry like me."

A kernel of an idea began to form in Sterling's mind. More of an idea of an idea than an idea itself, but it tickled the back of his consciousness like a loose thread. One he wanted to pull so he could follow it back and see where it went.

"I've got a little free time on my hands," he said. "I'm staying at Sanctuary, so if you let me know when it suits, I'd be happy to look over your business plan with you."

"Business plan." Jack laughed. "Nice one. Tell you what. You give me your card and I'll call when I've tracked down and printed everything I can."

Sterling handed him a business card and he tucked it into his pocket. The door opened again, and a familiar face appeared. Just his luck. Logan was friends with Tione. He shouldn't be surprised. Haven Bay was small, and the men were of a similar age.

Tione's eyes widened when they alighted on him. "What are you doing here?"

"Playing poker."

His nostrils flared, indicating he didn't like the reply.

"I invited him," Logan cut in. "We have a problem?"

"No problem," Tione muttered, his jaw thrust aggressively forward.

"What's up with you?" Jack asked. "You eat a bad batch of seafood or something?"

Tione just glared.

Sterling frowned. "You mean that isn't his usual expression? It's the only one I've seen since I arrived."

"What did you do to him?" Logan asked. "Usually he's a surly S.O.B. but this is new, even for him."

Tione released a gusting sigh, straddled the chair beside Logan, and rested his forearms on its back. "He's sniffing around Kat."

Jack looked at him with renewed interest. "Wouldn't have figured she was your type."

Sterling shrugged. He didn't have an answer for that. Normally she wouldn't be, but he was learning there were advantages to being open-minded.

"You're too late, anyway," Logan told him. "Jack has dibs on Kat if she ever decides to move on from her tragic, doomed love affair with her husband."

Jack nodded, as though calling dibs on a person was a perfectly acceptable thing to do. He also didn't deny it. Something churned in the bottom of Sterling's gut, like a herd of gophers was rooting around in it. Suddenly, Jack didn't seem like such a friendly guy, and Sterling wanted to mop the floor with his smug face.

"Hate to break it to you, Jackie," Tione drawled, "but this guy's already light years ahead of you. He was lip-locked with her on the beach this morning."

"Get out of town," Jack exclaimed. "I don't believe you."

Sterling averted his eyes from their curious glances. It was none of their business what he did with Kat. They were consenting adults, with nothing to be ashamed of, and he'd repeat that kiss as soon as the opportunity arose.

"I think he's telling the truth," Logan said to the others.

"He is," Sterling confirmed. "I like Kat. A lot." Verbalizing it wasn't as difficult as he'd expected. "And she seems to like me, too."

"Good for you," Logan said, while Jack muttered under his breath and Tione scowled. "Just try not to get too attached to her. She doesn't date. She's still in love with her husband, and I don't think that will ever change."

Sterling blinked, surprised how much he ached inside at hearing those words. During his research, he'd discovered that Kat's husband had died in a car accident. It was the first thing to come up when he'd typed her name into Google. She'd been a world class rally driver who'd been behind the wheel when a drunk driver ran a red light and t-boned them. It had been big news, plastered over the papers, as had the ensuing court case. Then she'd disappeared off the radar. But that was three years ago. More than enough time for her to have moved on.

Apparently she hadn't, and he didn't want to think about what that meant.

She's still in love with her husband.

He couldn't blame her for that. It made sense, given what he knew of her loyalty, and it wasn't as if she'd divorced him. The love of her life had been taken from her by a reckless man who'd made poor decisions. Because of that, he'd been forever immortalized in her heart. How could Sterling possibly compete? Did he even want to?

He shook himself. There was no point mooning after Kat Hopa. In a short time, he'd be heading back to Auckland, and he wouldn't see her again, unless she decided to move to the city after selling Sanctuary.

Unlikely.

But possible, a voice in the back of his mind whispered.

"Thanks for the warning," he said, and was saved from having to add anything further when another man arrived. The latest attendee had shaggy brown hair that flopped as a bottle of sparkling water fell from beneath his arm and he ducked to catch it before it hit the floor. Awkwardly, he edged toward the table and deposited an armload of things. Sterling looked closer. He'd brought two containers of hummus and one of carrot sticks, as well as an assortment of fruit. His arms free, the man shrugged off a tweed jacket, yanked his collared shirt over his head to reveal a faded black t-shirt, and settled into a seat with a weary sigh.

"Mr. Walker," Jack greeted him. "Nice of you to show up."

"Had to feed the kids, wrangle Hunter into bed, and wait for Faith to arrive before I could leave," he said, then spotted Sterling and added, "The babysitter." He held out a hand. "Shane Walker. Nice to meet you."

"Sterling Knight."

"Ah." He nodded. "The guy who's trying to buy Kat's place." Sterling's eyebrows shot up, and Shane laughed. "Word travels fast around here. I teach at the school, so I hear gossip from the kids and their mums."

Jack jabbed an elbow into Shane's side and waggled his eyebrows suggestively. "Their mums, eh?"

"Leave off," Tione said. "It's harder than it seems, having all those gorgeous women throwing themselves at you."

"I'm ignoring you," Shane told them, then turned to Logan. "Are we expecting anyone else?"

"Not tonight."

Logan extracted a set of playing cards from his pocket and shuffled. Jack went to the kitchen and brought back a bag of M&Ms, explaining to Sterling that they used them for bets. Then Logan dealt, and the game began.

Sterling learned quickly that Tione, for all his talk of being ruthless, was a conservative player. Jack was unpredictable, bluffing wildly at times and folding quickly at others. Logan was unflappable and difficult to read, and behind Shane's rumpled professor façade was a clever mind and remorseless soul.

The men laughed. They teased, and mocked, and swore.

Alcohol flowed freely. However much Sterling drank, his glass seemed to magically refill. It was unlike any card game he'd played with his friends in Auckland, and to his surprise, he was enjoying himself. The game appealed to his competitive spirit and it wasn't long before he'd won Jack's entire stash of M&Ms. Shane took Tione apart, piece by piece, and Logan held his own, neither gaining nor losing many treats.

Finally, Sterling got a winner of a hand. A straight flush. He pushed his whole pile of M&Ms forward and said, "All in."

It was late, and Shane kept muffling yawns. Sterling had been counting on his weariness to make him less averse to risk. He'd been right. Shane called. Logan, apparently trusting Shane's read of the situation, did the same. Sterling laid down his hand. Logan stared. Jack roared with laughter. Shane rubbed his eyes and flipped over a pair of aces and a pair of eights.

"You win."

Sterling grinned, pumped beyond measure. These men might be different from his friends back home, but the outcome of the game had been the same. He collected his prize.

15

"STERLING?" Kat knocked on his bedroom door around ten the next morning. "You awake?"

She heard what might have been a groan. Slotting her master key into the lock, she let herself in. The room was still dark. Another low moan came from the direction of the bed, and she froze.

"Sterling?" she asked again.

"Whaddayou want?" came the reply.

She smiled. She knew that sound: a man who wanted to be left alone. He probably had a wicked hangover. Logan liked to ply newcomers with booze and wait to see what happened. It was a game to him, and Sterling appeared to have been his latest prey. Perhaps she should have warned him ahead of time, but he deserved to let loose a little and she trusted Logan not to go too far.

"It's DIY Saturday," she told him, perching on the edge of the bed. Her eyes had adjusted to the dimness and she could see the giant mound of blankets he hid beneath. "We'll be getting started in half an hour."

"DIY?" he asked, his head popping out of the end of the

blanket burrito. He blinked at her blearily. "As in, work on the lodge? Handyman work?"

"Exactly. There are a few people who come in regularly to polish up their skills. Like Shane, who you might have met last night. DIY Saturdays are his bonding day with his youngest son."

Sterling wriggled around until he freed a hand then massaged his temple, his eyes closed again. "Come back later. I'm not in the mood."

She laughed airily, amused by Hungover Sterling. "Feeling a little off-color, are you?"

"I'm tired. It's a weekend morning. I should be sleeping." He managed to speak in whole sentences, but his voice was strained.

"Here." She brought a couple of painkillers from her pocket and left them on the nightstand, beside his water bottle. "Have these. Drink some water, and shower. I'll make you dry toast, then I expect to see you in the west wing, raring to go."

"No." He pouted like a sullen child.

She did her best not to laugh. "If Shane can go to the same poker night you did, get his two boys up and ready, ship one of them off to cricket for the morning and bring the other here in time to start, you can drag your sorry butt out of that bed, clean yourself up and give it a go."

He scowled. "Don't bring my ego into it by comparing me to another man."

She smirked. "Don't make it so easy."

He came up on his elbows. "Fine, I'll be there in ten. But I want coffee."

"Done." Who said men were difficult to manage?

He dropped back to the bed and stared at the ceiling, looking so hard done by that she couldn't resist leaning over and dropping a kiss on his creased cheek. Then, before he could say a word, she bustled away. Maybe she was a wuss, but some things didn't need to be discussed.

STERLING'S TEMPLES WERE THROBBING, his mouth was dry, and there was a bad smell singeing his nostril hairs, which he couldn't seem to escape. He suspected the odor was him. How much had he drunk? He hadn't paid attention at the time because he'd still had his wits about him, but come to think of it, his cup had been full practically all night, and he wasn't sure how many times he'd emptied it.

With a great amount of effort, he wrestled free of the bedclothes and hoisted himself from the mattress. His head spun, and his stomach threatened mutiny. He downed the painkillers Kat had left, refilled his water bottle and chugged it, then turned the shower as hot as he could handle and scrubbed himself until he smelled like citrus-scented soap. He dried, then dressed in jeans and a faded t-shirt that usually only saw the light of day when he was in his apartment, alone, during the weekend.

As he was brushing his teeth, he caught sight of himself in the mirror. Transfixed, he stared. He barely recognized the scruffy fellow looking back at him. Red eyes, stubbly cheeks, messy hair, and none of the polished façade he usually cultivated. In fact, the man in the mirror looked so unlike Sterling Knight he could have sworn he was looking at a stranger.

The scariest part?

He wasn't sure he minded.

Was this who he really was? If he dropped the pretenses, stopped working seventy-hour weeks and went on a journey of self-discovery, as Kat seemed to think he needed, was this who he'd find at the end? Perhaps a better question would be: is this who he would have been if his mum hadn't died when she did, and if he hadn't vowed to never be powerless again?

But there was no point asking questions like that. He couldn't change the past.

He rinsed his toothbrush, and headed to the dining hall in search of the coffee he'd been promised. Ten minutes later, the coffee and painkillers had eased his queasiness enough that he was able to force down the dry toast. From the kitchen, Tione watched him struggle with barely disguised glee. Bastard.

When he finished, he wandered across the foyer into the west wing and immediately heard a cacophony of sounds that must have been blocked by the heavy door. Mechanical buzzing, people talking, and possibly an electric saw. The acrid smell of paint became stronger as he followed the noise to the end of the corridor and turned into the occupied room.

Just inside, Shane knelt at the skirting board, paint brush in hand, with a little boy next to him. The boy glanced up at Sterling, then averted his eyes. Sterling didn't blame him. He was a frightening sight. By the window, three old ladies were cutting lengths of wallpaper. They looked his way and started a low-pitched, fervent conversation, then as one, gave him the evil eye. The tallest of the three pointed two fingers at him in the universal gesture that meant "I'm watching you." He took a step back and wondered whether it was too late to escape. The old ladies were nuts. If he stayed, they'd find a way to hang him from the roof or use his head to decorate the walls.

But it was not to be. At that moment, Kat broke away from a young couple who were measuring a sheet of wood and approached him.

"You made it," she exclaimed. "Ready to try something new?"

He shrugged. "As ready as I'll ever be. And it's not totally new. I've been on a few work sites for my job."

"That's good. Let's get you going then."

His eyes narrowed suspiciously. "What do you have in mind?"

She didn't answer, instead tapping Shane's shoulder. "Shane, can you show Sterling where he can start?"

He grinned up at her, his dark fringe flopping over his forehead. "No worries, Kat." He stood and grasped Sterling's hand. "Good to see you again. I have to say, I'm surprised you're up and about after last night. Usually Logan knocks newcomers out of action for a good twelve hours."

Sterling winced. Had everyone known what Logan was up to except him? The possibility irked, although the fact he'd taken home the prize M&Ms made up for the damage to his ego.

"I'm made of sterner stuff than that."

Shane's grin slanted wryly. "Kat bullied you into it, didn't she?"

"Not at all."

The other man wasn't buying it. "Whatever you say, mate."

The little boy wrapped his arms around Shane's legs and stuck the same thumb Sterling had just watched him run over the floor in his mouth.

"Daddy?" the boy asked.

Shane ruffled his hair. "This is my son Hunter. Hunter, this is Sterling. He's staying with Kat."

"Oh." The boy didn't say anything else. Maybe he was shy. Sterling could relate. He'd been a socially awkward kid.

"Hello, Hunter," he said, hating how stiff he sounded. The trouble was, he never spent any time around children—with the exception of Eli's baby daughter—and he didn't know how to communicate with them. "It's nice to meet you."

"What do you say, Hunter?" Shane asked, tilting his son's face up. The boy mumbled something. "What's that? You need to speak up so we can hear you."

Sterling wanted to tell him that it wasn't a big deal if the kid didn't want to talk, but Hunter overcame his shyness and said, "Hi, mister."

Shane appeared pleased by this. He let the kid go and turned back to Sterling. "Have you done any DIY before?"

"Not personally, but I have some basic knowledge of the techniques involved."

"Okay." Shane thought for a moment and scratched his chin, which had too much scruffy facial hair to be considered stubble but too little to be called a beard. "You can finish painting the skirting board." He handed him a brush. "You can't really go wrong. Paint in lengthwise strokes along the grain of the wood, and try not to get too much of it on the wall and floorboards. It won't matter too much if you slip up because the wallpaper and carpet still need to be put in place."

"All right," he said, feeling like a student in one of Mr. Walker's classes.

"If you have any problems, let me know."

Sterling nodded. "You've been doing this for a while?"

"Yeah." Shane ran a hand through his messy hair, leaving a streak of white paint in it. "We started because I needed to grow some skills to renovate my house. It's an old villa and needs a lot of TLC. It's great practicing here because Kat is really patient if things go wrong, and we get the full experience rather than trying to learn using YouTube videos." He shook his head. "Trust me, that's far harder than people make it out to be. Anyway, DIY Saturday is Hunter's favorite part of the week. He'd throw an almighty tantrum if we didn't come."

Sterling looked over to where the boy was happily crawling along the floor, stopping every meter to check the level of the skirting board. "Unusual hobby for someone his age, isn't it?"

Shane laughed in disbelief. "Are you kidding? It's a rite of passage to play with daddy's toolbox."

Sterling blushed, reminding himself he couldn't have been expected to know that. If not for the fact that a baby couldn't be made without a contribution from a man, he would assume he didn't have a father. His mother had been his solo parent, and she'd done as well as she could, but she hadn't been in a position to spend the weekends mucking around playing Bob the Builder with him.

"You'd know better than me." He knelt where Shane had been and dipped the paint brush into the paint tin. Then, touching the tip of his tongue to the roof of his mouth, he concentrated on distributing the paint evenly. At some point, Shane moved away. As he worked, the drone of background noise faded out until all that remained was a distant hum. His back ached, but he hardly registered it. Before long, he'd painted the skirting board on one wall and moved around to the next. As he glanced back at where he'd been, a sense of achievement filled him. It looked neat. Not professional, but decent. By the time he came back for round two, he'd have mastered the technique.

"What's that silly grin for?"

He looked up at the sound of Kat's voice. "Nothing. Just, this isn't so bad."

Her eyes twinkled. "Fancy that."

She tucked her hair behind her ear, drawing it off the slender column of her throat, and heat punched him in the gut. He forgot about painting completely. A pulse throbbed beneath the skin at the base of her neck, and he wanted to latch onto it and suck. The urge was so unexpected he made a low humming noise. She tilted her head quizzically and her hair fell forward again, hiding the patch of skin he'd been staring at like a freak.

She drew in a breath that rattled past her lips, almost as though she were as shaken as he was. "Once you've finished the first coat, we can nail down the floorboards in the center of the room. Hine and Michael have nearly finished cutting them to size."

"Why is there a gaping hole in the middle of the floor?" he asked.

She rolled her eyes. "Long story. Suffice it to say, there was a large piece of rock, a crazy bull mastiff, and a well-intentioned member of the Bridge Club."

He winced, unsure whether he wanted to know any more details. "Oh."

"We had to do base repairs to the joists and supports beneath the floor first, and had to consult an engineer about it. That's why work has been going on around the edges of the room in the meantime."

"Fair enough." Though he didn't understand why they hadn't shifted to another room and come back to this one. "Hey, Kat," he said as she turned away.

"Yeah?"

This was the perfect opportunity to take another shot at persuading her to sell. Point out that she could live some-where without holes in the floor, crazy dogs, and scheming octogenarians. Suggest that she buy a modern stone building where she wouldn't need to host regular DIY sessions with amateurs to make the conditions livable. But he found that he couldn't. He had no enthusiasm for it anymore. His tongue stuck to the inside of his teeth.

He swallowed, and like a wimp, said, "You've got some-thing special here."

A winsome smile transformed her face. Her mouth relaxed, eyes crinkled, forehead smoothed. Being on the receiving end of that smile, he felt like he'd won the lottery, and he didn't regret delaying his next business move one bit.

"I know I do," she replied. "I appreciate it every single day."

He could tell she spoke the truth, and, just like that, he wished he had something he could be thankful for every day.

Sure, he had a great job, reasonable financial security, and two close friends, but when was the last time he'd woken in the morning feeling grateful for any of it? The fact was, his goal of becoming wealthy enough to never have to worry had lost its shine.

Huh.

Something else he'd learned about himself: he needed a new life goal. Without something to aim for, the earth might shift out from beneath him and send him into free fall.

16

"It's really coming along," Kat said, approaching Sterling from behind. He was standing in the doorway of the room they'd been working on earlier, deep in thought, and she'd made sure her footsteps had thudded on the wooden floor so he could hear her approach. She hadn't wanted to startle him.

"I can't believe you're renovating this whole place yourself," he said. "Finishing the east wing must have taken a long time."

"Yes and no."

He turned to face her fully, and raised an eyebrow, nonverbally asking for an explanation.

"It was hard going, and keep in mind I hadn't done anything like this before, but I didn't have guests or a business when I bought Sanctuary. I didn't know anyone in town and I had nothing but time on my hands, so it went faster than you might imagine."

She was glossing over the details, but he didn't need to know how angry she'd been at the world, or how she'd been unable to sleep and hammered through the nights. Or how she'd worked herself to exhaustion and fallen asleep on the floor, waking hours later, stiff and sore, only to drag herself to the toilet and throw up. She'd been lonely, confused, and belligerent to anyone brave enough to talk to her. Thank God for the persistently nosy people of Haven Bay who hadn't let her sequester herself in a crumbling building forever. She owed them all, and she always paid her debts.

"Why did you come here?" he asked. "If you didn't know anyone, and had no background in hospitality, why open a lodge?"

She looked away. "The answers to those questions are more complicated than you might think. The thing is, I never intended to open this place as accommodation. It just kind of happened. All I was looking for was a purpose. Something to fill my time and get me out of my head."

"Sounds like you were in a bad place."

She nodded. "Sanctuary was my escape. Hence its name."

"I always thought it an odd choice."

"Not when you know the back story. I'm heading up to the waterfall now. Would you like to come for a walk?"

He peered out the window at the darkening sky. "Is it far?"

"About twenty minutes or so. There's a trail behind Tione's cabin. It's still relatively warm outside and it'll stay light for a while yet." Not that being in the forest at nightfall bothered her. She found it oddly comforting. There was no one around who needed her attention, and nothing to do but listen to the rustle of the nocturnal creatures and wonder, once again, how she'd ended up here. The waterfall was her favorite place to sit and think. For some reason, she wanted to share it with him.

"You're on. I'll just get a jersey and sneakers."

Her heart pitter-pattered happily, and she tried to squash the excitement rising within her. This wasn't a date. It didn't mean anything, except that he was starting to open himself to new experiences.

"I'll meet you in the foyer," she told him.

While he went to his room, she fetched her jacket from behind the front counter and leaned against the wall to wait. In the garden, Tione spotted her, and lifted a hand. She did the same, but he didn't come over. The dogs would be waiting for their dinner, and the little darlings dictated his life.

Sterling stepped into the room, tugging a black jersey into place—one that hugged his chest in all the right places. "I'm ready."

"Great." Kat ignored the breathy quality of her voice, stopped ogling him, and opened the garden door. "Come on then, it's not getting any earlier."

She led him through the winding garden, explaining how it had been added to gradually over the past three years, which was why it sprawled with no apparent pattern. They passed Tione's cabin, and she checked furtively to make sure he hadn't seen them. No reason to give him anything to get his Calvin Kleins in a twist over.

She paced backward up the sloping lawn as they neared the edge of the forest so she could face him. "It's a bit steep," she said. "I hope you don't mind."

"I figured as much. The forest *is* on the side of a hill."

She couldn't make out his expression, but she thought he might have rolled his eyes. Smart-ass. Her lips quirked. He had a sense of humor, however dry it may be.

The trail weaving between the trees and native shrubs was perhaps three feet wide, but in good condition because she used it regularly and did routine maintenance. They hiked up the incline in silence. The scar tissue on her ankle pulled tight at times, but she was nearly immune to the twinges of pain by now. They were like an old, unwelcome friend. She listened to the sound of Sterling's breathing. She'd expected it to grow ragged after a while, but he

149

continued to exhale slowly and evenly. Whatever exercise he did in his other life, it kept him in shape.

Before long, the trail reached a flat ledge on the side of the hill and wound along it. She dropped back to walk behind Sterling, shaking her head at his questioning look. She wanted him to get an unimpeded view of the waterfall when he rounded the final bend. It was a breathtaking sight.

She knew the exact moment he saw it. He froze, his jaw dropped, and his face tilted up. She understood. The waterfall was somewhere between twenty and thirty meters high, a white ribbon rushing over the edge of a cliff and splashing into a spherical pool at the bottom. The cliff face itself was gray and craggy, starkly beautiful, but the growth fringing it was lush emerald green, almost ethereal, like something out of a fairy tale.

"I don't…" He didn't finish the sentence, taking a few steps toward the pool. Then he turned to her and she could have sworn his eyes were glittering with unshed tears.

Okay, so maybe that was her imagination taking a flight of fancy.

"I'm in awe," he said. "I can't comprehend that a place like this exists. If I couldn't see it with my own eyes…"

"I know," she whispered, joining him near the edge of the water. "It's magical."

He looked at her then, *really* looked at her, like he could see inside her whirring mind and knew all of her secrets.

I'm going crazy.

It wasn't a revelation. She'd suspected it would happen one day. But when he gazed at her in that all-seeing way, heat flaring in the depths of his eyes like blue fire, she had a vision of the two of them, naked and entwined beneath the waterfall, water beading on their skin as they moved together. She shivered, though the air temperature hadn't changed.

Whoa. Slow down, wahine. *You're only sightseeing. This isn't a seduction.*

Reaching down, she yanked off her shoes and stepped barefoot into the soft moss, treading over to immerse her feet in the water. Despite the pleasant evening, the water was cold. Her ardor cooled instantly.

"You look like a nymph," Sterling said, far closer than she'd thought he was.

And her libido was back.

There was nothing for it. She tugged off her jacket, tossed it aside, and pitched forward into the water, instantly dousing any remaining lust she might have felt. The pool was deep, several feet at least, and she sank down, then hit the bottom and pushed off, rushing upward. She broke the surface and gasped for air, flinging her wet hair from her face. Her eyes stung when she opened them, and water dripped off the end of her nose.

"Wow," she exclaimed when her chest had finished seizing from the cold and relaxed enough for her to speak. "That was refreshing."

"Are you completely nuts?" Sterling demanded, towering over her. "What on earth possessed you to do that?"

He looked shocked, appalled, and more than a little judgmental. She had the sudden and undeniable urge to ruffle him up. The man was far too self-contained. He needed to live in the moment for once.

Her teeth started to clash together, but she clenched her jaw and forced them to stop. Then she beamed up at him. "The water is lovely. You should join me."

He shook his head. "Now I know you've lost it."

You and me both, gorgeous.

"I'm serious," she said. "But you need to jump in all at once. It's much easier that way."

"No." He crossed his arms and looked down his nose. "Not going to happen."

"What?" she asked, rubbing her upper arms. "Are you too chicken?"

"Too smart. I'm not falling for that."

"Bawk bawk. Chicken."

"You can't peer—"

"Bawk bawk bawk," she interrupted. "Live a little. Would I still be in here if it were freezing?"

"You—"

"The old Sterling would never have done it, but I thought new Sterling was more daring."

That seemed to get him. He shrugged off his jersey, undid the laces on his shoes, and folded his jeans over a rock.

"I'll show you daring." Then he leapt up and bombed into the water. She shielded her eyes from the splash, wiped them dry, and waited for him to realize she'd tricked him. He surfaced, spluttering. When he'd caught his breath, he swore, the curse piercing the quiet around them.

She started to giggle, then clapped a hand to her mouth. He turned, slowly, until their eyes met. Her heart gave an extra thump for good measure. He looked like she'd killed his puppy—horrified and baffled at the same time. He was glaring, his sopping hair plastered to his face, his lips set in a thin line, nostrils flared.

"You…" he said, jabbing a finger in her direction. "You…"

She fluttered her eyelashes innocently. "Yes, me?"

"You…" He didn't seem capable of saying anything else.

She began to worry. Perhaps she'd broken him. "Are you—"

"I can't believe you did that!"

His expression was too much. He was bedraggled and utterly furious. She whooped with laughter. She couldn't stop. Not even when he dipped his hand into the water and sent it flying at her face. He was the funniest thing she'd seen in years.

152

IN THE FACE of Kat's laughter, Sterling's anger ebbed. He wanted to stay mad, but the truth was, she'd got him good, and he'd never seen her laugh like this before, with her whole heart and soul in it. Water streamed down her face and her eyes were tinged red, but that laughter made her the most irresistible woman he'd ever met. He adored it. Wanted to hear it tomorrow, and the day after that. Wished there was a way he could bottle her laugh and replay it over and over again. It wrapped around his heart like a hug, and he realized he didn't just adore her laugh, he was coming to adore her, too. Even the infuriating parts of her.

Still, she was laughing at him, and some things could not be tolerated. With a couple of strokes, he covered the distance between them, settled his hands on her waist and kissed her.

That put a stop to her laughter.

Her lips were cool beneath his and they responded sluggishly, but they did respond. She was kissing him back, hesitantly at first, then more eagerly. He was lucky they were in such frigid water or there'd be no mistaking how much he liked the taste of her and the sensation of her pebbled nipples against his chest. Her tongue flicked against his lips and he gasped. He hadn't expected her to take the role of aggressor. To be fair, he hadn't expected much of anything because he'd acted without thinking, and his brain was struggling to keep up.

She thrust him away and he tightened his grip on her waist, refusing to be dislodged.

"Sterling," she said impatiently. "We can't get out of the water if you won't let me go."

Oh.

He released her, watching while she hoisted herself onto a flat rock on the edge of the pool and climbed out, then he followed, feeling clumsy when he slipped and had to catch himself. When he stood on dry land, Kat grabbed the hem of her shirt and pulled it over her head. He heard her wringing the water from it, but he couldn't take his eyes off her exposed skin. The dusk light hid some parts of her while revealing others. Her skin glistened and her breasts were hidden by a functional black bra, but the deep shadow of her cleavage enticed him. Then she moved, and he noticed something on the side of her ribcage, black against the light brown of her skin.

"Is that a tattoo?" he asked.

She glanced down, as if to remind herself of what he was asking about. "Oh, yeah. I forget it's there sometimes. It's just a part of me now."

"What is it?"

She hesitated, gnawing on her lip, apparently weighing whether or not to tell him. He regretted asking.

"You don't have to say."

"It's a locked heart," she said. "I got it after my husband died, because that was how I felt. Like I should just lock up my heart and throw away the key."

Sorrow clawed at his chest. He didn't want to hear more, but he couldn't help wondering: did she still feel that way? Would she ever be willing, or able, to share her heart with another man? With him?

He reached out and traced the tattoo. Goosebumps rippled over her skin. He'd been ready to suggest they head back and each go to their respective rooms, but then he noticed her nipple peaking in response to his touch, through the wet fabric of her bra. Fascinated, he lowered the bra strap and caressed the side of her breast, edging around slowly until he reached the nipple, then rubbing it with the pad of his thumb.

Her warm breath gusted over his face as she exhaled shakily. He released her, but didn't back off, watching her intently to make sure they were both on the same page. Noting her eyes were dark with desire, he turned his attention to the side of her neck, brushing kisses along the length of it while his fingers ventured over to the smooth scar on the other side of her face. When he first touched it, she jerked away. She was skittish. About the scar, or about him? He couldn't tell, but he shifted his kisses to her mouth, not wanting to make her uncomfortable, or give her cause to push him away.

But then her hands gripped his upper arms and she did just that. His heart plummeted. Had he gone too far? Done something she didn't like?

"Take off your shirt," she said, and relief eased through him. She wasn't rejecting him. "If you get to see me, it's only fair if I get to see you, too."

He couldn't argue with that logic, but he hesitated. He wasn't golden all over like she was. Beneath his shirt, his skin was so pale he'd probably glow. He wasn't built as solidly as Tione, or from what he'd seen in his quick Google search, as her late husband. He was lean. A runner who ate well and took care of himself but could never be mistaken for a guy who lifted weights. He hoped that didn't put her off.

Fair was fair though, so he removed his shirt, crossed his arms over his chest, and shivered. His chill didn't last for long. She plastered herself to his front and kissed him. Perhaps she'd sensed his uncertainty, he didn't know, but he was grateful. Their damp bodies slid against each other, a delicious friction building as the kiss deepened. Unlike yesterday morning, it wasn't interrupted by a wave. Hands moved frantically and gasps escaped parted lips. As their tongues danced together and he clasped her bottom tighter to him, he thought he might go insane if he didn't get inside her soon. He wouldn't ask for anything she didn't want to give, but please God, let her be as desperate for him as he was for her.

"We need to get back," she muttered.

His heart sank.

"If I don't get you in a bed before long, I'm going to scream."

Hallelujah.

They each put their shoes on, donned their dry outer layers and hurried back down the sloping trail. Getting to the lodge took much less time than hiking to the waterfall had taken.

As they hurried across the garden, she said, "This is a one-night thing. Is that okay with you? Just one night."

He wasn't sure which of them she was trying to convince. One night wasn't what he wanted. But if that was all she could offer, he'd take it.

"Okay, one night."

He yanked open the door and she winced. "*Shh!*"

"Sorry." Apparently, she wanted to be sneaky. They tiptoed across the foyer and into the hall. The lodge had retained the warmth that had already faded outside. "Your room or mine?"

"Mine," she replied. "I've got a bigger bed."

He liked the way she thought. While she dragged him to the bedroom, he didn't see much of her small apartment. Just enough to know that she had an open plan lounge with a small kitchenette attached. She switched on a lamp and they both shed their clothes, then he snagged her by the waist and drew her close for a kiss. Her full breasts squished into his chest and he ran his hands down the sensual curve of her spine. Damn, he loved the shape of her. Soft in places, firm in others. Well-proportioned and athletic.

But something was missing. The kiss was nice, but now that they were both naked, she seemed more reserved than she had in the forest.

"You okay?" he asked. If she was uncomfortable, he'd leave right now, no matter how much he wanted her—and the hard shaft bumping against his lower belly proved just how very much he wanted her.

She ducked her head. "It's silly."

He propped two fingers beneath her chin and lifted it up. "I promise I won't laugh."

She squirmed, which didn't help the situation down south. "It's been a long time for me."

"Me, too."

"No, I mean a *really* long time."

Ah. "You haven't since your husband?"

She shook her head. "And the thing is, I haven't been naked with a man since I got all these scars." Her voice hitched on the last word, like she was afraid to draw his attention to them.

He knew how much it must have cost her to mention them. She wasn't by nature a self-conscious person, and he suspected she was upset at herself for giving into any kind of weakness, but how could she possibly believe he'd think less of her for the marks on her body that showed all she'd lived through?

"You don't have to worry about that," he told her softly. "Your scars are beautiful because they're a part of you. They show how strong you are. How much hardship you've overcome. You have absolutely nothing to be ashamed of."

She gave a strangled laugh. "Now I know you're just buttering me up."

"No, I mean it. You're perfect because you're you." He had never been one to compliment women extravagantly, and now that he wanted to, he hoped he wasn't botching it. "Do you know how much the last couple of days have meant to me?" he asked. "They've been really special, because of you." He dragged in a deep breath and took the plunge. "You have a beautiful soul, Katarina."

She stiffened and locked eyes with him.

He forced himself to continue. "If you want to stop now, or if you want to keep your shirt on so you feel more comfortable with yourself, that's absolutely fine with me."

For a second, he thought she might take him up on the easy out he'd given her, but then she practically threw herself at him, and he staggered backward, landing on the bed with her on top of him. They both laughed, and the tension dissipated.

She kissed him, taking the lead this time. She thoroughly took his mouth, then shimmied away and explored his body with her tongue and lips. He kept his eyes glued to her as she flicked his nipple with her tongue, then followed the groove at the top of his abdomen down to his navel, at which point she seemed to grow shy. She skimmed over his groin and started again at the inside of his knees.

"You have nice legs," she said.

He didn't think anyone had ever commented on the attractiveness of his legs before. "Uh, thanks. I run a lot."

She worked her way back up his body, this time peppering kisses over his upper thighs. Finally, he felt the warm wetness of her tongue dart over the tip of his erection. Any breath left in his lungs exited quickly.

"Again," he croaked.

She did. Her tongue danced on his tip in tight little circles, and she took him in her hand. Her dark head bent to welcome him between her lips, and he wasn't sure what was more erotic: the sight of her—naked and pleasuring him—or the sensation of her mouth like slippery silk around his hard length. He gripped the sheet and fought the urge to buck his hips.

Hell, it really *had* been a long time. *Please don't let me come without getting her there first.*

"Whoa," he groaned. "Slow down. Come up here so I can kiss you."

A mischievous grin crept over her face. "I've still got moves."

He laughed tightly. "Never doubted it."

When she was level with him, he cupped her cheeks

between his palms and kissed her, putting everything he felt into it, hoping she'd see how desperately he wanted her. She matched him kiss for kiss, touch for touch. Was it possible, he wondered, that she cared for him as much as he cared for her? Obviously she felt something for him, or they wouldn't be here. She wasn't the kind of woman to sleep with a man unless she liked and respected him. But was it possible she felt more than simple liking? Or was that wishful thinking? Had she used up her capacity to love during her marriage?

"Stop thinking," she ordered.

He tried. He slid his hand between them and dipped a finger into her core. The wetness he found there nearly undid him. He stroked through her folds and she shuddered, her hips jerking forward, seeking more. He gave it to her. Slipped one slick finger inside her and cupped his palm tightly against her body. She writhed and threw her head back, her eyes squeezed tightly shut. Shit, he wanted inside her. Needed inside her, or he was going to lose it.

"You want me?" he asked.

"*Yesss,*" she hissed.

"Now?"

"Now."

He slipped free of her and fumbled in his jacket pocket for his wallet, grabbing the condom from it and checking the date to make sure it was still good. *Thank God.* Then he unrolled it down his length and rejoined her on the bed. She lay on her back and he hovered over her, pressing slowly into her softness. Breath eased between his teeth and he bared them in a feral grin.

She stared up at him, panting. She was tight. "Like I said," she puffed, "it's been a while."

Finally, he was seated deep inside her. He claimed her lips with a hot kiss, giving her time to adjust. When she began to roll her hips beneath him, he started to move. As he thrust, she made sweet whimpering noises, and satisfaction surged within him. Satisfaction, and the blinding desire to keep this woman happy, sated, and safe. The desire was completely unexpected and would have knocked him for six if not for the increasingly urgent, all-consuming heat building between their bodies.

They moved together slowly at first, but it wasn't long before she gripped her thighs and lifted them, inviting him to pound into her harder and faster. He obliged, and they both moaned. His forearms rested on either side of her head and his lips didn't leave hers as their bodies slapped together rhythmically, carrying them higher and higher on a wave of delicious sensation until they reached a crescendo and both shook and trembled in release.

When he'd caught his breath and his brain was functioning again, he kissed her cheek, climbed off her and disposed of the condom. He returned, lay next to her and wrapped his arms around her. Warmth washed over him and he smiled. She was smiling, too. He touched his lips to hers in a light, affectionate kiss.

"Would you like—"

A shrill noise interrupted her, and it took a moment for his addled mind to recognize it as a ring tone.

She stiffened and her skin blanched. "It's Saturday," she whispered, then scuttled back from him, her face a mask of horror. "Oh, no."

17

HELL, shit, and damn. What had she done?

The shrill, alarm-like ringing blared through the otherwise silent room and paralyzed her. She stared at Sterling's naked body beside hers. This had been a mistake. A terrible, terrible mistake brought about by a moment of weakness and insanity. How could she possibly have forgotten about the phone call she received every Saturday night? Especially taking into account the significance of tomorrow's date. Shame flared hot. Her throat was thick. She couldn't speak. Her body curled in on itself, withdrawing from Sterling and the brief moment of abandon she'd found with him.

"Ignore it," he said. "Whoever it is, I doubt it's urgent. Stay with me."

Beyond all reason, she was tempted to do as he asked, bury her head in the sand and pretend the past hadn't happened. But she didn't have that luxury. She went to her phone, picked it up and did what she did every Saturday: watched the name on the screen, Amanda Hopa, until it stopped ringing and the icon popped up to say she'd missed a call. She pressed her lips together and tried not to cry.

Her mother-in-law made sure Kat didn't forget her

mistakes. She called every single Saturday to remind her. Every Saturday. Kat didn't answer, but she remembered. Remembered the way Amanda had gone to pieces when the doctors said they hadn't been able to save Teddy. Remembered the way Kat herself had screamed and cried and fought the nurses who'd tried to hold her still so she wouldn't worsen her injuries. Remembered the tortured expression on the driver of the other car, as he stopped by her room with nothing more than a few stitches and tried to apologize. She'd shut her eyes and pretended he wasn't there. The accident may have been his fault, but it wasn't his alone. She should have seen him coming. Should have been more careful. She'd been a professional driver, damn it, and she should have saved her husband. Instead, her carelessness had killed him.

"You need to leave," she said without looking up. Even to her own ears, her voice sounded cold.

"But—"

"Go!" she snapped. She couldn't look at his face. Didn't want to ruin what they'd shared, but should never have let it happen in the first place.

"Whatever it is—"

"We can't work through it," she interrupted, then rubbed her eyes, suddenly weary. "I'm sorry, Sterling. I didn't mean for this to happen, but you need to go now. Please."

"Fine." He sounded angry. "But at least have the decency to look me in the eyes and tell me why you're kicking me out. I know you enjoyed that as much as I did."

Meeting his eyes was one of the hardest things she'd ever done. "I did," she said quietly. "But I let myself get carried away and it was wrong. I'm sorry. I wish I could go back in time and undo it, but I can't."

"I wish you could, too," he said, and the words were like daggers sticking into her most vulnerable parts. "If I'd known how you'd react, I'd have saved us both the trouble."

And there he went, sliding the dagger deeper and twisting it around. Not that she could blame him. He'd be justified in thinking she'd used him for sex and kicked him to the curb after she got what she wanted.

Her eyes stung. Why did this have to be so hard? "Just go."

She wanted to be alone with her shame. How could she have forgotten Teddy, even for a second? She didn't deserve to forget, or to enjoy herself. She didn't deserve to have something—whatever it may be—with Sterling.

He started toward the door.

"Wait," she said. He turned around, brow raised. "I don't want you to think this has anything to do with you." She wrung her hands, hoping he could see she was telling the truth. "You're great, and what we just did... I mean, wow. But I killed my husband, and I don't deserve to have another man in my life."

He strode back to her, took her by the shoulders, and said, "You're the most deserving person I know."

Then he dipped his head, brushed her lips, and left without making a fuss.

STERLING WAS UP and about early. He ate breakfast, collected an extra croissant and a coffee, and went to Kat's bedroom door. He took a deep breath, then knocked and mentally crossed his fingers she'd feel differently this morning than she had last night. She'd needed some time to adjust and recover, but in the light of a new day, she might see how special the emotions growing between them were. He couldn't pinpoint exactly *what* they were yet, but he felt an eternal wellspring of tenderness toward her that he'd never felt for anyone else.

When she didn't answer the door, he shuffled the coffee and croissant around so he could try the handle. Locked.

Perhaps she was asleep. But she didn't usually sleep this late. It had been a difficult night, but worry niggled at the back of his mind.

"She's not there." Brooke stood in the hallway behind him, wearing glasses that magnified her eyes to twice their usual size, with a laptop tucked under her arm.

"Where is she?" Suddenly he was self-conscious, aware that he was standing outside a woman's bedroom early in the morning.

Brooke shrugged. "She headed out into the bush a while ago with a backpack. Said not to expect her back for a couple of days."

"She... what?" Of all the things he'd expected, an impromptu camping trip at the crack of dawn hadn't featured on the list. But all was not lost. He could join her. It would put him decidedly outside of his comfort zone, but she was worth it. "Do you know where she went?"

"No idea, sorry."

His frustration mounted. "You're telling me that she's somewhere in the massive forest out there—" he waved a hand toward the hills, "—and no one has a clue where?"

Brooke's lips quirked. She seemed to find him amusing. "Don't worry, Sterling," she said in the tone one might use with an agitated preschooler. "She does this sometimes, and she always comes back perfectly fine. She knows how to take care of herself."

"But anything could happen. A rockslide, a slip. She could twist her ankle and be stuck with no way out. There are thousands of variables outside of her control. Hundreds of things that could go wrong no matter how experienced or well-prepared she is."

And he doubted she was as well-prepared as Brooke might think. She'd been upset last night, and emotional people didn't make smart decisions.

"She has a locator beacon with her in case that happens."

After a moment's hesitation, she stepped forward and rubbed his arm soothingly. "Look, I think it's sweet that you're worried, but sometimes everything gets to be too much for Kat to deal with and she has to get away for a while. Especially at certain times of year. Dates that remind her of Teddy."

He frowned. "Her husband?"

"Yeah. Today would have been their wedding anniversary."

Immediately, things fell into place in his mind. Last night was the first time Kat had been with a man since her husband died, and it had happened on the eve of their anniversary. He wasn't an expert in love or grief, but that would be enough to tilt anyone's world off-axis. Especially if she held some sort of misplaced guilt over her husband's death.

He could understand guilt. When his mum died because they couldn't afford an experimental treatment, he felt like it had been his fault—that he'd failed to save her. But regardless of understanding Kat's feelings, his stomach squeezed at the thought of her, alone in the forest and wallowing in self-recrimination. His chest tightened with pain on her behalf. He wished he could have helped last night. Wished he'd been a different man, one who knew how to reach out to a woman who was suffering and lessen her load. But he'd never been particularly good at that.

"How do things work around here while she's away?" he asked.

"Tione and I keep things ticking along between us."

He nodded. "Let me know if there's anything I can do to help."

AN ENTIRE DAY and night passed with no sign of Kat. During lunch on Monday, Sterling suggested to Brooke that someone go looking for her. She laughed and assured him they had no reason to fear until she'd been gone for more than three nights, but her reassurances fell on deaf ears. He hadn't been this anxious over someone's wellbeing since his mother was alive, and he didn't like it.

In the afternoon, Logan called and invited him over to talk business. Relieved by the distraction, he agreed. To work off his nervous energy, he dressed in sports shorts and a t-shirt, and jogged the distance from Sanctuary to The Den. He nodded to Hugh MacAllister, who was cloistered in the corner with two men of a similar age, and dropped onto a stool at the bar beside Jack, who sat nursing a beer.

"How are you doing?" he asked.

Jack grabbed his hand and thumped him on the shoulder. "Hey, man. Good to see you. Hope you recovered from Friday all right."

"Nothing to recover from," he lied. "I can hold my liquor."

"Good for you, mate."

Logan served him a whiskey.

"Thanks," he said, before taking a sip.

"So, what's on the agenda?" he asked when Logan came around the bar to join them.

"I had a look at what you sent over," Logan said. "It's good stuff. I wasn't sure about some of the price recommendations or the additions you suggested, but I haven't ruled them out yet."

"Your prices are lower than the market average," Sterling told him, leaning forward on his elbows. "And if you look at the numbers, you'll see that hiring an enclosed trailer for your gear and storing it down by the pavilion makes good business sense. You want to keep your two businesses as separate as possible."

Logan nodded. "I'll think on it. The maintenance schedule

166

you wrote up will be helpful." He made a face. "Now I just need to remember to check it and do as it says."

"Not necessarily," Sterling said. "You could hire someone to take care of that for you."

Logan scoffed. "There's no one around here who does that kind of work."

Sterling pressed his lips together, annoyed by the setback to his otherwise good idea. He supposed living in a small town had some drawbacks, and he'd just found one of them.

"Anyway," Logan continued, "Jack had a look over it and he'd like you to do the same for him. He'd need something a bit different because of the different level of risk associated with his trips, but otherwise, his business is similar to mine."

"I have equipment that people use when I take them out on excursions," Jack said. "But I never loan it out the way Logan does. My business is also different in that I'm not directly teaching any skills. I'm more of a guide service."

"You run Seafaring Adventures?" He remembered seeing the place in the square on his first day in town.

"Yeah." Jack scratched his head, leaving a brown cowlick sticking up in the back. "But I need to rename and rebrand. I run boat trips and group kayaking sessions, but these days I spend more time taking people hiking, caving, rock climbing, and abseiling."

Sterling blinked. "Sounds extreme."

These adrenaline-driven businesses were a world away from what he'd become accustomed to in Auckland, and hearing the men discuss them like they were perfectly normal threw him for a loop. Yet he was excited by the prospect of taking the work on. Possibilities for ways he could improve Jack's business processes were already flitting through his mind.

"That's why I love it." Jack grinned devilishly. "Nothing beats the high you get from conquering a cliff face."

"Or jumping off the top of it," Logan added wryly.

"With a harness attached, of course," Jack agreed. "Or a parachute."

The mere thought had Sterling's skin prickling uncomfortably. But a few days ago, he wouldn't have thought he'd like surfing or kissing a woman in a cold pond after dark. His perspective was changing, and he wouldn't rule anything out.

"Do you have a pen and paper?" he asked Logan, who ducked around the bar and fished out an old notepad. "What ideas have you had so far?"

"How did your meeting with the boys go?"

Sterling glanced up from the spreadsheet on his laptop when Tione placed his dinner on the table, drew out the chair beside him, and sat. Sterling looked around. The dining room had emptied, except for him and Brooke, who was in a similar position with her laptop and an open textbook on the next table over. He frowned. He'd been so absorbed in work that he'd lost track of everything going on around him. In and of itself, that wasn't unusual, but having Tione interrupt him was.

"It went well," he said, turning back to finish the row he was working on before he forgot what he'd been doing. "I have a lot to do now, but I'm quite enjoying it."

As far as distractions went, having *carte blanche* to come up with whatever relevant plans or ideas he could think of for Jack's business was fairly effective.

"Good to hear it." Tione rolled up the pita bread he'd piled high with fillings and folded one end. "I'm glad you're taking the time to help. Gotta be honest, I expected you to thumb your big-city nose at them."

"A few months ago, I might have." Back before Eli started preaching the gospel of small towns, and before he found out for himself how pleasant they could be.

He felt Tione's stare. "Surprised you'd admit that."

"I'm not the kind of guy who bothers to lie just so people like me."

"Yeah, I can tell." Tione bit off a massive chunk of the wrap and the filling spilled onto his plate. Chewing, he contemplated something on the horizon. Sterling decided he'd been dismissed and went back to his spreadsheet. He worked in silence while Tione finished his wrap and wiped his chin with a napkin. Then the cook guzzled a glass of water and dragged his chair around to face Sterling.

"If you want Kat to open her heart again, you've got your hands full."

Sterling froze, his fingers on the keyboard, and looked over his shoulder, unable to believe that scowling, tattooed Tione had actually used the phrase "open her heart." Although come to think of it, Eli had used nearly the exact same expression the last time they'd spoken, in reference to his own heart. Was the universe trying to tell him something?

"Dude, don't look at me like that," Tione said. "It was hard enough to say the first time. I'm not going to repeat it, and don't worry, I won't sprout a vagina."

"Are you sure?"

He cracked a crooked grin. "Ninety percent."

Sterling closed his laptop. Despite the humor of the situation, his heart had started galloping. When had he become so transparent?

"Do you think it can be done?" he asked, accepting that there was no point denying his feelings for her when all and sundry seemed to know the truth. "Do you think she could ever get over her husband?"

Tione cocked his head and studied Sterling, his expression unreadable. "I don't know. I don't think it's so much a matter of getting over him as moving on. She'll never get

169

over losing him, but that doesn't mean she can't move on and be happy with someone else."

"That's remarkably insightful."

The man flushed. "I have my moments."

Sterling nodded, and resisted the urge to ask if Tione thought anyone could measure up to Teddy in Kat's eyes. He didn't want the other man to know how pathetically insecure he was about comparing unfavorably to a dead man.

"If you have any thoughts about how I could convince her to give me a chance, I'd love to hear them."

Tione cringed. "That sounds a little too much like being a double agent to me, but I want her to be happy, and I think you do too, so if anything springs to mind, I'll let you know."

"I appreciate that."

18

KAT EXTINGUISHED her mini gas cooker and stirred the oatmeal in her lightweight travel pot. She sprinkled a pinch of brown sugar over the top and waited for it to turn gooey, then used the bulkiest part of her pack as a seat while she ate breakfast. The oatmeal was warm, squishy, and not particularly appetizing, but it would fuel her for the long walk back to Sanctuary.

It was the third morning in a row when she'd woken to a morning breeze caressing her cheeks. She hadn't bothered to pack a tent because temperatures during summer rarely dipped low enough to warrant it. Instead, she'd spent the nights beneath an A-frame waterproof shelter that kept the dew off but was otherwise open to the forest.

When she finished her breakfast, she yanked the shelter pegs out of the ground, folded the cover and her bedroll, and packed them away. She chewed a minty teeth-cleaning tab, shoved a fistful of barley sugars into her pockets, filled her water bottle, and washed her face in the stream that ran past the campsite. The cool water soothed her puffy eyes, which were red and irritated from crying tears of grief, and tears of guilt. She'd spent the eve of her wedding anniversary in bed with a man who was not her husband. She'd accepted that, though she hated herself for it, and she'd voiced her apology to Teddy out here in the wild where no one would look at her like she was crazy.

Pressing her fingers firmly into her eyelids, she rubbed them. She hadn't finished apologizing yet. It was time to return and say sorry to Brooke and Tione—once again—for leaving them in the lurch. She supposed she owed Sterling an apology, too. He may have started things by kissing her at the waterfall, but she'd been the one to suggest they go back to her bedroom, then she freaked the hell out and sent him away.

The hike took the better part of nine hours, crossing saddles and traversing a rocky outcrop. When she went bush, she liked to get as far out of reach as possible. She maneuvered over the rugged terrain with care, and by the time she emerged into the garden beside Tione's cabin, she was blissfully exhausted. Edging around the garden, she circled the east end of the building rather than going directly inside, and let herself in through the discreet exterior door to her bedroom.

She dumped her bag on her living room floor, cranked up the shower, stripped off her clothes and laid out a fresh set, then stepped under the hot jet of water with a sigh of relief. For several long minutes, she simply stood there and enjoyed the sensation of water running over her body, easing her muscle aches and rinsing the sweat and filth from her skin. Then she slowly and methodically washed away every bit of the outdoors that lingered on her body, shampooed her hair, shaved her legs and armpits, and emerged feeling like a new person.

She chose the softest, fluffiest towel from the cupboard and dried herself, then moisturized, brushed her teeth, and dressed in shorts and a tank top she'd chosen earlier. Then she padded barefoot into her living room, then came up short. Sterling was sitting on her sofa, the coffee table in front of him laden with food.

"W-what's this?" she stammered. "How did you know I was back?"

His lips curved hesitantly, like he was unsure of his welcome. After what had happened on Saturday, his reaction was to be expected. "Tione told me. He saw you pass his cabin."

Huh. "Why didn't he say anything?"

Sterling scrutinized her like he was trying to read something in particular from her expression and body language. "He said you wouldn't want to see anyone until you felt human again."

"Fair call."

She waited for him to say something about how poorly she'd treated him, or ask why she'd run away, but all he said was, "I brought food and tea." He pointed to a massive chocolate muffin on the table, and a steaming bowl of pumpkin soup beside it. "I thought you might want something decent after living off granola bars and freeze-dried meals for a couple of days."

She stared, wondering what the catch was. Why was he being so sweet to her? She'd half expected to find him gone when she returned, perhaps having left one final offer to buy Sanctuary. Instead, here he was, on her sofa, in jeans and a t-shirt, with the beginnings of a beard softening his sharp jaw, and looking more at home with himself than she'd ever seen him.

She licked her lips. Damn, but he looked *good*. Like a chocolate bar after she'd been on a strict diet. Trouble was, like that chocolate bar, he was a forbidden pleasure. She couldn't go there again, no matter how much she might want to. It wouldn't be fair to either of them.

A powerful pang of yearning slugged her in the gut and she stumbled back a step. For a brief space of time, she wished she could be the woman Sterling Knight needed. That she could be someone who deserved to come home after a jaunt in the forest and expect to see him here, waiting and ready to comfort her. She closed her eyes, the emotions so disconcerting the room seemed to shift before her.

"Are you all right?" he asked.

"Fine," she choked, blinking her eyes open to see his forehead furrow with concern. "What are you doing here?"

The crease deepened. "Like I said, I stopped by with food and herbal tea." He stood and went over to her, laying a hand on her bare forearm. It seemed to burn her skin and she flinched. "Are you sure you're okay?"

She nodded and hurried over to the sofa. "Just need to sit down. Exhausted, you know. Done a lot of walking."

"How far did you go?"

She shrugged. "Hard to say."

She hadn't really paid attention. Just walked and known that if she left markers along the way, she'd be able to find the path back.

He returned to the sofa and sat next to her. "Have a muffin. Tione says they're chocolate with a caramel center."

Her mouth watered. It had been a while since she'd enjoyed a sweet dessert. She reached for the muffin, and was struck by the absurdity of the combination of things he'd brought her and had to laugh. Soup, cake, and tea.

"This is the most confused meal tray I've ever seen."

He looked affronted. "Soup is comfort food, and so are muffins. I know you like herbal tea, but I wasn't sure what else you liked and I didn't want to bring you something you'd feel obligated to have and not enjoy."

She shook her head. "You're misunderstanding me." Chuckling, she broke off a chunk of muffin and offered it to him. "I think it's adorable. You're very sweet. Thank you."

His upper lip curled, like he wasn't sure whether to be pleased or annoyed by the fact she'd called him adorable. She dipped a chunk of cake into the oozy caramel center and closed her eyes in bliss as she chewed it. She wasn't always a big fan of sweet food, but at this very moment, the sugary goodness was exactly what she needed.

Sterling stayed silent while she ate, and when she glanced over, she saw he'd picked up an interior design magazine from the shelf beneath the coffee table and was flipping through it. She had dozens of them around her apartment as a source of inspiration and ideas for the lodge renovations.

"You don't have to stay here," she said. "I'm okay. Cross my heart."

"I know," he said, looking up and smiling. "But I want to, if you don't mind. I enjoy your company."

Well, what could she say to that?

Somehow, over the past week and a half, he'd morphed from coldly handsome businessman to knicker-twistingly sexy friend, and it was largely thanks to her poking and prodding him into relaxing and letting his guard down.

Good work, wahine.

She'd just have to pull herself together and deal with his company, while keeping in mind what she deserved, and what she didn't.

"I like you being here," she told him. "But seriously, don't feel like you have to stay. I'm not about to go off the deep end."

He set the magazine aside and took her hand. "Let me be here, Kat. If not for you, then for me. It will make me feel better if I can pretend I'm helping you, even a little bit."

———

STERLING'S HEART was in his mouth as he waited for a response. He was still weak-kneed from the rush of relief he'd felt when Tione knocked on his door and said she'd returned. He wanted to take care of her, but he didn't know

175

how to do that other than making sure her physical needs were met, and being present in case she needed him.

"Okay," she said softly. "Stay."

He released the breath he'd been holding. "Thank you."

She quirked a brow.

"For not sending me away," he explained.

Her eyes filled with an emotion he couldn't put his finger on. Not pity, but something close. Like she'd guessed how hard it was for him to be in a position where he was trying to help someone without being able to give them what they most needed. He couldn't bring her husband back from the dead, and despite his good intentions, he wasn't sure he wanted to. Perhaps it was selfish, but more than anything— more, even, than he wanted to buy Sanctuary and get back to his structured life in Auckland—he wanted to be the man she turned to in her moment of need.

This intense emotion coupled with helplessness reminded him too much of those last weeks with his mum. The difference was that Kat wasn't dying and he could help her. He didn't have to sit back and watch as everything went to shit, as he had with his mother.

"No," Kat said, so quietly he almost didn't hear. She set the muffin aside and took his hands. "Thank *you*. No one has cared for me like this in a long time. You don't know how much it helps to have you here."

"Is there anything I can get you?"

"No. All I need right now is you."

The bottom fell out of his stomach, and his grip tightened. He was flying. Soaring above the clouds, her words unlocking the shackles of guilt and loss that had held him prisoner for all the years since his mum died. How was it that such a simple statement could have that effect? After years of feeling like he wasn't worth anything unless he had the resources to provide for loved ones and ensure their continued health and safety, this wonderful woman had shown him that he did have something to offer other than money.

God, he loved her. He *loved* her.

He wouldn't have thought it possible after such a short time, but his heart didn't need to wait the socially acceptable length of time to recognize the truth, and having seen his two best friends be felled by love in short order, he didn't doubt it was possible to love Kat after only knowing her for as long as he had. Forget flying, he felt weightless enough to shoot right up through the ceiling and land on the moon.

Love.

Who'd have thought it? He released her hands and pulled her into a firm embrace, resting his cheek on her shoulder and breathing in the scent of shampoo on her damp hair.

"I was worried about you," he admitted. "I missed you so much I thought I was going crazy."

"I'm sorry."

"Don't be." He squeezed her tighter, then slipped his hands beneath her and dragged her onto his lap so he could loop his arms around her properly. "I understand why you needed to get away."

She gave a breathless laugh. "What are you doing? I'm too big to sit on you. I'll crush you."

He scoffed. "Don't be ridiculous. You weigh less than I do, and even if you didn't, I'd still want you here."

Close to me. Just like that, tears welled up in his eyes and started rolling down his cheeks. *Well, that's embarrassing.*

Kat collected one on the tip of her finger. "What's the matter? It's all right, I'm here."

He shook his head. "I don't know. I'm not upset." He reached around her and wiped his eyes on the back of his hand. "I haven't cried since Mum died. God, what the hell is wrong with me?"

"The last time you cried was when your mum died?" she asked.

"Yeah."

"When was that?"

"About fifteen years ago."

"Damn." Her eyes turned watery. "That's just sad." She sniffed. "Now look what you've done. You've set me off again."

Sterling chuckled, and rested his forehead against the side of her face. His throat constricted. "I'm sorry, I can't seem to stop."

For a while, they held each other and sniffled intermittently. Finally, Sterling straightened, his eyes dry, and Kat dabbed hers on his shirt.

"What a pair we are," she said.

I love you.

He didn't say the words. Just nodded. "It's getting late—should we get you into bed? You must be tired."

She smiled. "Yeah, that's a good idea, but…" She trailed off awkwardly.

"I'm not inviting myself to join you," he assured her. "Unless you want me to. But would you mind terribly if I grabbed a spare blanket and slept on the sofa?"

"So you can keep an eye on me?"

"So I can be here if you need me," he corrected.

He thought she might turn him down. She was Kat-the-Independent, after all. But she searched his eyes for a long moment, and all she said was, "Go for your life."

19

TIPTOEING into the living room so as not to wake Sterling, Kat looked over at the sofa, where she'd left him sleeping. She needed to think about what to do next. She'd found herself in an unusual situation, and she struggled to stay objective when he was awake. He was too adept at seducing her with sweet sentiment delivered in an awkward parcel.

But he wasn't on the sofa. A wool blanket was folded on the arm, and there was no sign of him. She glanced around to see if his shoes were there, or if the bathroom door was closed. Huh. It looked like he'd left. How the heck was she supposed to mull things over properly when he wasn't cooperating?

She poured coffee, went to her room to dress, and padded out into the hall, taking her mug with her. Sanctuary was quiet this time of morning—with the exception of the foyer—where, if she wasn't mistaken, the yoga class would be in session. She opened the hall door and slipped in. The class was busy, with at least ten guests and a couple of locals present. There, on a mat in the center, was Sterling, battling to hold warrior two pose while the elderly lady next to him peppered him with encouragements. He followed her directions, and his legs stopped shaking. He thanked her. Then he looked straight over at Kat and smiled.

Bam!

That smile hit her like a smack in the heart, zapping through all of her defenses and making her fizz on the inside. Thankfully, he became absorbed in the yoga once again, and she leaned on the door frame to watch. The change in him was unreal. She could scarcely believe that the laid-back guy with scruffy blonde whiskers was the same businessman who'd had an iron rod up his spine when he arrived in the bay.

For the first time since she'd woken, she smiled. Sterling looked comfortable in his own skin and she liked to think she was partially responsible for that. With one last glance at him, she headed to breakfast. The dining hall was empty, so she went straight to the kitchen.

"Hey, Tione," she said, edging inside in case a pan or other metal object flew at her head. Sometimes her friend didn't take her unscheduled vacations well. "Thanks for holding down the fort while I was away."

He was standing at the oven, in front of an omelet, and didn't turn when she spoke. He grabbed the pan handle, flipped the omelet in the air, and caught it neatly.

"It wasn't a problem," he said in a neutral tone that made her nervous. "Everyone behaved. No large groups turned up unexpectedly. We were fine."

"Okay, that's good." She waited for the other shoe to drop.

"How was your camping trip?"

She set her cup down and crossed her arms over her chest, bracing for whatever shitstorm was about to come her way. "Same as usual. I walked, I cried, and now I'm better."

"Your city boy was worried about you."

And there it was. Her stomach dropped. She didn't want to consider that Sterling might have feelings for her beyond

180

attraction and friendly affection. That only complicated an already complex situation.

"He's not *my* city boy."

Tione looked over his shoulder and raised a brow. "Are you sure about that?"

"Yeah." She sounded surer than she felt.

Tione dumped the omelet on a plate, then poured another batch of mixture into the pan and came over to her while it cooked. "Then I suggest you let him down now. You don't want to lead him on. He cares for you, Kat. Wouldn't have thought it was possible with how far he had that stick shoved up his ass, but he's a decent guy and he's into you. I don't want to see him make a fool of himself or get hurt."

Her shoulders slumped. Tione was right, and she knew it. She just didn't want to accept that she needed to pull the rip cord on the beautiful thing growing between them. "I'll say something to him today."

"Good." Tione handed her an omelet. "Eat up. You'll need your strength."

WHEN THEY FINISHED SAVASANA, or corpse pose, Sterling blinked slowly and rubbed his eyes.

"You did so well," Christine, the lady beside him, said, tidying her short white hair with one hand. "I could see how much you improved during the session."

"Thank you. It was all because of your help."

She flushed with pleasure. "How are you enjoying your stay?"

"It's been life-changing," he told her. "I might just stay forever."

He was completely serious, but she laughed anyway. "Me, too. The atmosphere is lovely, and the sea air is doing wonders for my sister." She leaned closer and lowered her voice. "Emmaline had cancer, but she's in remission. It's the second time, and she seems to be recovering. I'm cautiously optimistic."

"That's wonderful. I'm glad for you and Emmaline." He stretched toward the ceiling, then released a contented sigh. "Sanctuary is pretty great."

"It really is."

He rolled up his yoga mat and packed it away. Last night he'd come to the realization that he couldn't be involved in anything that would shut down the lodge. Earning professional kudos wasn't worth it. He'd passed some of the happiest days of his life here, and it needed to stay exactly the way it was. He'd also decided that he wanted to stay for a while longer and explore both the place and the way it made him feel. He didn't have a plan yet, just a few loose wisps of one floating around in his mind. Before he firmed them up, he wanted to tell Kat. After all, without her, he might have been fifty years old and still never have known that he liked surfing, or that laughing at himself could actually make him feel better.

He found her in the kitchen with Tione. Both looked tense. He wondered if they'd fought about the way she'd left without warning.

"Morning," he said.

"*Ata marie*," Tione greeted him in Maori.

"Kat, I'm heading down to the beach for a walk. Would you like to come with me?"

She and Tione exchanged glances and she seemed to hunch in on herself. "Sure thing."

"Great. I'll just put some shoes on. Meet you in the foyer?"

She nodded, and he went to grab his footwear. He'd only brought one pair of sneakers and one pair of work shoes. If he was going to stay, he'd need to invest in sandals so he could feel the sand between his toes. As he met Kat and crossed the parking lot with her, he felt positively buoyant. The air seemed crisper, the sun warmer, the shrubs greener.

"You're in a good mood," she observed as they reached the sand.

He grinned. "I am. I've figured out some important things over the last few days, and that tends to brighten a man's outlook."

The smile she sent his way seemed forced, and that was his first inkling that something wasn't right, but he decided to ask about it after he'd shared his good news. He simply couldn't wait another minute.

"I don't want to buy Sanctuary anymore."

Her jaw dropped. "What?"

He laughed at her stunned expression. "You were right. Staying here changed my perspective, and my life. I want you to keep on doing what you're doing. I'm officially withdrawing my offer."

Finally, her face relaxed and her lips curved up. "Thank you. You have no idea how good it is to hear that."

"I mean it, one hundred percent," he said, gaining confidence. "The time I've spent here—with you—has meant so much to me that I've decided to stay in Haven Bay for a while."

Her smile froze in place. "You what?"

Nerves niggled at the inside of his gut. This wasn't the reaction he'd hoped for. But he was being brave, putting himself out there, and he'd say what he needed to if it killed him. He stopped walking, reached down and took her hands in his. They were limp, and strangely cold despite the mild temperature.

"I have more than three months of vacation time. I'm going to take an extended leave and investigate the possibility of opening a business here. There are a number of people who would benefit from employing a consultant to improve their processes and oversee things at a high level so they can focus on the day-to-day operations."

Her brows knitted together. "You've really thought about this, haven't you?"

"I suppose so." That fact took him by surprise. He hadn't realized he'd been idly turning over the possibility ever since meeting Logan. Even then, it seemed he'd subconsciously known he was happier here, doing his own thing, than back in Auckland, managing a successful multi-million dollar company for someone else. "You've helped me see that there are things more important than money."

He stared into her chocolate brown eyes and everything else ceased to exist, the two of them caught in a bubble of solitude and emotion, cut off from the lodge behind them, and from the seagulls that soared overhead and the waves that nipped at their toes. He shored up his courage. Though it wouldn't be easy for him, she needed to hear how he felt. To know how important she was to others, and that she was worth so much more than she thought.

"Katarina, you're beginning to mean the world to me."

Her eyes shuttered faster than a sprinter racing off the mark. She dropped his hands and backed away, palms facing him like she was using them as a shield. She may as well have screamed, *I don't feel the same way.*

"S-Sterling," she stuttered, then looked around as if hoping someone would materialize to save her. When no one did, she said, "I'm happy for you. I think what you're planning is brilliant, but I'm sorry, I won't be able to spend time with you anymore."

He'd known he risked rejection. Had prepared himself to hear her say these very words. Or so he'd thought. But nothing he'd imagined could compare to the actual sensation of her plunging a dagger of ice into his heart and wriggling it around, leaving the beating center a cold, empty mess. His hand came up to his chest, as if to hold it in.

Why was she doing this? He knew she had feelings for him, at least to some extent. If she didn't, she'd never have slept with him—the first time she'd been with a man since her husband. Not to mention that she'd have sent him on his way when he turned up with food last night.

"I—"

"Stop," she interrupted. "I can't bear to listen to you." Cradling her head in her hands, she rocked back onto her heels. "I'm sorry. You're a great guy—"

Ouch.

"—and I really like you, but I had a man in my life, and I killed him. I don't deserve another chance at happiness because Teddy will never have one. Thanks to me, he's gone, and I'm going to spend the rest of my life alone."

"His death was an accident. It wasn't your fault." Just like his mum's death hadn't been his fault. He accepted that now. He'd only been a teenager, the situation out of his control.

Kat's arms dropped to her sides and he could see she'd started crying. Her tears struck him harder than her rejection had. He stepped toward her, desperate to hold her, but she evaded him.

"It *was!*" she cried. "The other driver ran a red light, but I was a *professional*, I should have been paying attention. I should have seen him coming and gotten the hell out of the way, but I was stupid and complacent and Teddy paid the price." Her shoulders rose and fell, and her chest heaved as she tried to regain control of her breathing. "I wish you all the best, and I hope you get the success and happiness you deserve, but it won't be with me."

When she started to walk away, he followed, but she picked up the pace, and then she was running across the beach—away from him. He stopped chasing her, sank to the ground and stared out at the water.

What was he supposed to do now?

Just fifteen minutes ago, a world of possibilities had been

open to him. His expectations of life had expanded beyond the edge of his known universe and he'd been ready for whatever came his way. He picked up a pebble and tossed it at the sea. It landed with barely a splash.

What a difference fifteen minutes could make.

He'd ruined everything, and Kat had left him. Not that they were ever really together, except for in a beautiful fantasy he'd concocted. He felt bereft. He'd found what he'd been looking for all his life, only to have it snatched away because of misplaced guilt. Or was her guilt just a convenient excuse? Could she truly never fathom loving anyone other than her late husband?

He wasn't sure he wanted to know the answer. He lowered his forehead to his knees and groaned. What good was it to finally know what he wanted from life if he didn't have her to share it with?

20

KAT STARED at the sheet of numbers she was working her way through. They blurred in front of her eyes as she pictured Sterling's face, and the way he'd looked like the sky was crashing down when she'd left him on the beach.

No. Focus on work.

She checked the computer screen, then went on to the next page, doggedly wading through the dreaded finances and bookings until her head ached and she felt ready to scream. She headed to her room, warmed a facecloth under the hot tap and covered her eyes until the throbbing in her head receded. Then she sought out Susan, the cleaner, who was servicing the occupied rooms.

"Tell me how I can help," she said. "I need to be busy."

Susan, a fit woman in her fifties, nodded, her fluffy hair bouncing. She was used to Kat's occasionally erratic behavior. "The room to the left of Brooke's is empty. The couple left ten minutes ago. Do you want to make a start in there?"

"Yes, thank you." Kat went to the room, pulled the sheets from the bed, folded the duvet, emptied the rubbish bins, washed the dishes, wiped down the sink, and was cleaning the bathroom when she heard Susan come in behind her to collect the laundry and vacuum the floor. The physical work was a blessing, but it was over far too soon.

"Where next?" she asked.

"No one else has checked out yet," Susan said. "I'm going to make a start on the foyer, but that's a one-woman job. Why don't you rest, Kat? You look terrible."

"I'm fine. Put me to work."

Susan raised her palms. "I'd love to, but I've got nothing for you. Perhaps you can help Tione with lunch."

"Yes," Kat exclaimed. "Good thinking."

But Tione didn't want her help either.

"I've already prepared pizzas," he said. "All I need to do is put them in the oven."

"What about dinner?"

He crossed his arms. "I'm not even thinking about that for a few hours yet. I'm heading out to run the dogs on the beach. You should think about getting outside and burning off some energy. You're going to wear a hole in the floor with your pacing."

She stopped pacing. She hadn't even noticed she'd been doing it. "You're right."

"I'm always right." He cracked a crooked grin. "I *am* a certified genius. So what's all this about? Did you talk to Sterling like we discussed?"

"Yeah." She banded her arms around herself, suddenly feeling fragile. "I did, and I know it was the right thing to do, but now I can't stop thinking about him."

His expression softened. "I'm sorry, Kat." He opened his arms, and she walked into them, welcoming his big bear hug. "You want to come with me and the dogs?"

Releasing him, she stepped back. "Nah, I'll be fine. I just need something to do. Go run your mutts, brain-boy."

"Okay." He hesitated, then added, "I'm here if you need to, uh, talk about it or something."

At this, Kat managed to smile. If she needed someone to

empathize with her, she certainly wouldn't choose Tione, but she appreciated the sentiment. "Thanks for the offer. Now, go." She waved a hand, and he left with one final glance over his shoulder.

She fixed herself another coffee, eyed it, then poured it down the sink. More caffeine wasn't what she needed. She was high-strung and fidgety enough as it was. Maybe she could surf for a couple of hours. The waves had been good that morning and the onshore breeze was mild. But no, she'd left Sterling on the beach. What if he was still there? She didn't want to encounter him right now. But if she stayed in the lodge, she may see him when he returned for lunch, or to work on his laptop in the living area.

Her office was safe. She went there immediately, shut the door, and flopped into her chair, burying her face in her hands. How had she ended up in this situation? All she'd wanted to do was help Sterling get some much needed rest and relaxation, and maybe rack up a personal win. She'd never meant to make him love Sanctuary or the bay so much he wanted to live there.

God, what a mess.

Looking around the desk for something to do, her gaze fell on a scrap of paper with Jack's name and a few notes jotted on it. She grabbed her phone and called him.

"Hey, Kat," he said when he answered. "How are you keeping?"

"I'm good." The falsehood tasted bitter in her mouth. "Are you free now? I wanted to continue our discussion about hiring you to do trips for my guests."

"No can do, sorry. I need a bit more time. Sterling is helping me write a business plan, and I want that in place before we finalize anything."

Sterling. Damn, she couldn't escape the man. He'd thoroughly infiltrated Haven Bay, and her life here.

"Okay," she said quickly. "I've got to go. Call me when

you're ready to talk." Hanging up, she took a long, shaky breath. She needed to get out. She went and retrieved her bike from its usual spot, then hopped on it, aimed it toward town, and started peddling. She bounced over the gravel, crossed the bridge and passed onto the smooth road. Then she worked her legs as hard as she could until she'd passed through town and reached the end of the street, stopping outside the mansion where Anderson Gray, an ex-Holly-wood-starlet-turned-temperamental-recluse, lived. Not in the mood to be yelled at, she turned around and headed back toward the town square, and Bex's gym for a workout. Hopefully the exercise would help clear her mind.

STERLING WANDERED AIMLESSLY along the beach until he realized he'd walked so far he'd reached the pavilion. It was occupied by tourists who, like him, didn't need to be at work midway through the day. He strolled into The Shack, bought a carrot cake and cream cheese flavored ice cream from the quirky redhead who insisted on calling him Alexander, then crossed the street and dawdled in the town square. When he'd finished the ice cream, he went into The Den and greeted Logan, who poured him a finger of whiskey.

"What's the news?" Logan asked, leaning against the bar.

"I'm staying in Haven Bay," Sterling replied, the words rolling off his tongue easier than he expected. The decision hadn't come easily, especially with Kat's rejection so fresh, but he'd spent a long time thinking it through before he broached the subject with her, and while she'd weighed heavily into his choice, his reasons for staying were still valid. He wasn't ready to give up the new way of life he'd only just begun to embrace, and it was past time for him to strike out on his own in the business world. He also wasn't giving up on Kat. Not just yet.

"That so? For how long?"

He shrugged. "At least a couple of months. Maybe permanently."

Logan nodded, and the tips of his hair dripped on his shoulders. Presumably he'd been out surfing. "Good for you. And good for this town. We could use someone a little more…"

"Uptight," Sterling suggested.

"Efficient," Logan amended with a wink, "around here."

"Kat doesn't seem to think so."

"Oh, really? She tell you that?"

He sighed and stared at the amber contents of his glass. "I told her I cared about her, and she told me she won't be able to see me anymore."

Logan winced. "That sucks, man. Sorry to hear it. Maybe she'll come around."

"You probably know her better than I do." Though admitting as much hurt. "Do you think she will?"

He waved a hand noncommittally. "Hard to say. She's a stubborn woman. Still hasn't driven anywhere since she's been in town. Not even in the passenger seat."

"She never drives *anywhere*?" Sterling let that sink in. If it were true, that meant she literally never left the bay. He tried to recall seeing her in a vehicle—surely she'd been in one at some point during his stay—but came up empty. She only ever traveled on her bike or on foot, and insisted he not drive her anywhere, either. "Whoa."

"Intense, right? The point is that Kat doesn't do anything she doesn't want to. If she wants to move on and be with you, she'll find a way to make it happen, but if she wants to cling to the past, there's nothing you can do about it." He shrugged. "Accept it, bro. The ball is out of your court."

"You're right." Relief washed over Sterling, lifting the dark cloud that had lingered above him since he and Kat parted ways. There was nothing he could do. Whatever happened next, it was out of his control, and coming to terms with that felt fantastic. He felt like announcing to everyone around: *My name is Sterling Knight, and I'm a recovering control freak.*

"I need to make a call," he said.

Logan nodded, and Sterling stepped away from the bar, pacing to the back of the room and dialing Eli's work phone.

"Aren't you supposed to be on holiday?" Eli asked upon answering.

"I am," he replied. "That's what I'm calling about." He was much surer of himself than he'd expected to be. He owed Eli a debt of gratitude, or at least, he'd always believed he did. Not because Eli had said as much, but because his friend had chosen him over older and more experienced candidates to bring into his new business, back when he'd started it fresh out of university. Now, he realized he owed Eli nothing. He appreciated the opportunity he'd been given, and relished the challenges he'd been able to sink his teeth into, but he'd proved his worth a dozen times over. He'd been a good investment, and he was under no obligation to stay at Lock-wood Holdings.

"Did you seal the deal?" Eli asked.

"No, I'm afraid not."

A moment of silence demonstrated Eli's shock more effectively than any words could. Finally, his friend ventured to say, "That's not like you."

"I know. But here's how it is. I'm not certain that the 'me' I've been for the past few years is really all the 'me' there is." He sighed, frustrated by his inability to express himself. "That came out wrong. I don't know how to explain it. This place has me second-guessing everything I thought I knew about myself."

"Just the town?"

"Perhaps the people, too. One in particular."

Eli's voice was soft when he said, "I'm happy for you."

Sterling scraped a hand over his cheek. "Might be a bit

early for that, but thanks. What I called to say is, I'm cashing in my leave. All of it."

"You're leaving the company."

It was a statement, not a question, and Sterling respected Eli enough to give him the truth. "Most likely. It's not certain yet, but I'm investigating my options."

Eli sighed. "I'm disappointed to hear that, but I'm not surprised. I've always thought you had too much potential to stay as my 2IC when you could be doing your own thing. Frankly, I didn't expect it to take so long for you to reach the same conclusion."

"I'm grateful for all the opportunities I've had at Lockwood's."

His friend snorted. "Don't act like I did you a favor, Sterling. You've always been more like my business partner than my employee. If you decide to strike out on your own, you'll be damned successful."

"Thanks." Sterling swallowed, humbled by Eli's belief in him. "I'll help you find a replacement."

"I'd expect nothing less."

He hesitated. There was one more thing he wanted from Eli. Advice. But asking for help wasn't exactly in his nature.

"There's something else?" Eli asked. "You're thinking so loudly I can hear you all the way from Itirangi."

How to phrase this? "When Aria was pregnant and didn't want anything to do with you—" His voice cracked. "How did you get through it?"

"Oh, man. Are you doing all right?"

"I will be. Eventually." A couple of men in their sixties entered the pub and Sterling turned to the corner for privacy. "It's just a rough patch. I'm waiting her out."

"What's her name?"

"Kat." Even to his own ears, his voice sounded different when he said her name. Warmer. She brought that out in him. Brought out the best side, the one he hadn't known he possessed. "You're going to laugh so hard when you meet her. She's not the type of woman I thought I'd end up with."

"Isn't that always the way? Who'd have thought I'd end up with a nosey journalist, or that Mark would make an honest man of himself with someone in the wedding business?"

"Mark's lucky." Sterling had a lot of admiration for his live-in girlfriend, Clarissa. "So are you." He gazed out the window, at the surfer statue, and a memory drifted into his mind. One of a similar phone call, not so long ago. "Remember when you said to keep an open heart? I didn't know what you meant at the time, but I'm beginning to understand. I didn't see any of this coming. Not Kat, or the way this place would change me, but somehow, I think it's exactly what I've always needed."

"That's great," Eli said. "And don't worry, you'll be as happy as me and Mark before long. You just need to get on with life and refuse to give up on her."

"Thanks, I'll do that. She needs time, but I'll make sure I'm waiting when she's ready. I appreciate your advice. I'll call you when I can and let you know what my plans are."

"Take as long as you need to think everything through. There's no rush."

They exchanged farewells and hung up.

"Logan," Sterling called. The man had vanished into the back, leaving his customers unattended.

He stuck his head through the doorway. "Yeah?"

"Do you mind if I sleep on your sofa for a couple of nights, until I get my own place sorted?"

Logan grinned, and emerged fully into the bar. "I can do you one better. I have a spare room. You're welcome to it."

"Thanks." He smiled back. Things were beginning to fall into place. "I'll pay board."

Logan shook his head. "Don't be ridiculous. You've already done several hours of unpaid work for me. I'm willing to bet your charge-out rate would be more than enough to cover it. Let's call it even."

Sterling hadn't helped Logan because he wanted to get anything out of it for himself, and was about to protest, but the other man reached over and clapped him on the shoulder. "Tit for tat, that's how we operate around here. If you're staying, you'd best get used to it."

So instead of arguing, he accepted the offer. Then he finished his drink and walked back to Sanctuary with renewed purpose. After packing his bag, he sought out Brooke. He found her sitting cross-legged on an armchair in the communal living area with a thick tome on her lap.

She glanced up when he approached, took a look at his bag, and asked, "You're leaving?"

"Yeah. I'm moving into Logan's spare room. Could you let Kat know I'm gone? She has my card details, and can charge whatever costs I've accumulated to it."

"Oookay." Brooke's forehead wrinkled, and her brows drew together questioningly. "Is everything all right?"

"Never been better." He shifted the bag and shuffled from foot to foot. "You'll pass on the message?"

"Of course."

"Thank you." He lifted his hand. "I'll see you around."

21

THE BUSTLE of people outside the apartment woke Sterling the next morning. He sat up, stretched, and blinked the sleep from his eyes. He'd grown accustomed to a certain level of noise at Sanctuary, but Logan's place, which was situated in the center of town, was much louder. Especially because Sterling's bedroom fronted onto the square. He climbed out of bed, pulled on a t-shirt, found a pair of shorts, and drew back the curtains for a spectacular view over town. Unlatching the window, he breathed in a lungful of fresh, salty air and smiled.

For the first time since he'd finished high school, he didn't have the next five years mapped out. Half of his life was at loose ends, but he didn't feel the crushing sense of failure he'd always worried he would if this day ever came. He wasn't a rudderless boat, or a ship without an anchor, or any other suitably nautical metaphor.

What he felt was *free*.

He was starting from scratch. He could do or be anything he desired.

Well, he amended, *anything within reason*. He wasn't about to up and become a go-go dancer.

Was this how other people felt every day? People who didn't have everything figured out, but were happy to be along for the ride? If so, he'd been missing out.

The smell of something delicious tickled his nostrils, the scent carried on the breeze. He grabbed the key Logan had given him yesterday, left through The Den's back exit, and followed the smell of freshly baked cinnamon rolls to Cafe Oasis. He bought two, waved hello to Jack, who was opening his store on the opposite side of the square, and returned to the apartment. Sitting at the table, he pulled apart a steaming roll and bit into the buttery goodness, before licking his fingers clean. He made a coffee, then used the internet to research the steps he needed to take to start a business.

As he ate, he compiled a to-do list. Register a company, set up a website, separate the business finances from his personal finances, find an accountant, write a business plan, decide if he was going to rent an office space, look for clients, hire a graphic designer to make a logo and business cards. The list went on. And the more things he added, the more concrete the idea became in his mind, and the more excited he grew.

He was actually going to do this. Or at least, give it a damn good shot. If the business didn't take off, he was reasonably confident he could go back to working with Eli or pick up a well-paid position elsewhere. The thing was, he no longer wanted to make money for someone else. He wanted a new dream for himself, and admitting that felt so very good. He was so absorbed in his research that when the door swung open and Logan strode in, he jumped an inch off his seat.

"Sorry, man," Logan said, grinning. "Didn't mean to scare the crap out of you." He went to the bathroom and returned with a towel slung around his shoulders, his eyes slightly bloodshot from saltwater. "What are you working on?"

"I've been going through some ideas," he replied. "I'm

thinking of starting my own business, working as a consultant to improve other businesses' practices or managing the operational parts the owners can't be bothered with."

Logan nodded. "Like what you're doing for Jack and me."

"Exactly. What do you think? Would you like someone to take care of that part of your business permanently?"

Logan tilted his head. "Are you kidding?"

Sterling's stomach somersaulted. For a moment, he thought he'd badly miscalculated, but then Logan finished his thought.

"Hell, yeah, I'd be into that."

Sterling breathed out. "Thank God. You had me worried."

Logan clapped him on the shoulder and offered a hand, which Sterling shook. "You're hired."

"But I haven't even told you what my charging schedule is yet." Because he hadn't figured it out for himself.

Logan pulled out a chair and sat. "Don't care. If you're willing to do my dirty work, I'll pay whatever price you're asking, as long as it's within my budget. But hey, you'd know more about what's in my budget than I do at this point."

Sterling's lips twitched. "You can afford me. Do you think any other business owners in town would be interested?"

"No doubt about it."

Opening an empty document, Sterling slid the laptop over to him. "Any chance you could make a list, and I'll approach them over the next few days?"

"No problem." Logan started typing, hitting one key at the time, his movements clumsy and unpracticed. Sterling would guess he didn't sit in front of a computer often. His shoebox full of papers supported this theory, too.

While Logan was busy, Sterling looked up the local real estate agency in the newspaper and booked an appointment to look at offices and rental homes. He didn't want to stay in Logan's spare room for longer than needed, but he also wasn't ready to commit to shopping for a forever home yet. Though to be completely honest, he wasn't far off.

KAT'S ARMS ached as she scrubbed the tiled surface of the bathroom floor. The workout hadn't distracted her the way she'd hoped, so she'd decided to channel her energy into a thorough cleaning session instead. She cleaned her own apartment, because it hardly seemed fair to ask Susan to do it when it wasn't technically part of the lodge's accommodation quarters. She rinsed off the scrubbing brush, dipped it in her bucket of floor cleaner, and moved to the other side of the room.

"Kat."

She stiffened at the sound of her name.

"I've been looking for you everywhere."

Getting to her feet, she turned to face Brooke. "Here I am. What do you need me for?"

Brooke frowned. "You haven't been answering my calls."

"Sorry, my phone died."

Brooke pointed to a power outlet in the corner. "You didn't think to charge it?"

"Must have slipped my mind." Yeah, she wasn't fooling anyone. Her phone was dead because she'd been both hoping Sterling would call, and praying he didn't. In the end, she'd decided she couldn't handle the suspense.

"Take a break," Brooke said. "I'll make us a hot drink. Tea, coffee, hot chocolate?"

Kat didn't want a hot drink. She wanted to be left alone to wallow. But the firm line of Brooke's lips told her she wouldn't be allowed to wallow any time soon. Her young friend may be the quiet, studious type, but she possessed a singularly stubborn streak and would dig her heels in if challenged.

"Coffee with a spoonful of drinking chocolate added?"

Brooke nodded. "One homemade mocha, coming right up." She looked Kat up and down. "You might want to change your shirt before you leave the apartment."

Kat cringed. She was wearing an old, comfortable t-shirt that had been one of Teddy's favorites, and which now was so thin it was translucent. "Thanks for the advice."

"No worries, chick." Brooke padded away, her bare feet nearly silent on the carpet. Kat mopped the soap suds off the section of floor she'd scrubbed and went out into the living room. She'd just taken a seat on the sofa when Brooke returned with a steaming mug in each hand, and set the larger of the two in front of Kat, keeping the other for herself.

"So, Sterling left the lodge yesterday," Brooke said, getting straight to the point. "He said to let you know he'd gone. I heard he's staying at Logan's place."

"Thanks for letting me know." She'd assumed he'd either left or was taking pains to avoid her. Neither option appealed.

For a while, they didn't speak, and Kat began to wonder if that was all Brooke had come to say, but it seemed she'd just been summoning the courage to continue.

"Why did he go?" she asked. "What happened between you?" When Kat began to blow her off, Brooke touched her arm softly and stopped her. "Don't lie to me. Or to yourself. Anyone with eyes could see you liked him."

Kat laughed bitterly. *Liked* him? As if he were nothing more than a high school crush. As though she wasn't a woman in her thirties with a dead husband and a wealth of life experience behind her. What did Brooke, with her sheltered life and unbroken heart, know about *liking* people?

"You don't know anything about it," she snapped.

Brooke flinched, reproach in her azure blue eyes, and guilt twisted Kat's gut. "Because you won't tell me," she said.

"How am I supposed to know anything if you clam up and keep it all to yourself?"

"You're not supposed to, that's the point. It's not anyone's business except mine."

Brooke leaned forward and took her hand. "Please, talk to me. I'm your friend, Kat. I want to help."

"You *can't* help." The words wrenched a sob from somewhere deep in her chest. "No one can. It's my fault Teddy is gone, and I don't deserve to have another chance with someone else—especially someone like Sterling, who wants to go all in. I can't offer him the same. I don't have a whole heart to give him, only scraps of what was left behind after the crash. He should have better than me."

"But what if you're all he wants?" The question was asked quietly, like she was unsure how Kat might react. "What if the scraps of your love are enough for him? Sterling doesn't strike me as a guy who says or does anything without thinking it through and meaning it one hundred percent. If he said he wants you, maybe you should take him at his word."

Kat buried her face in her hands. "It's not that easy."

"Maybe it could be. I know you're scared, but you can't let fear hold you back. If I stayed away from things that might hurt me, I'd be shut inside an empty, padded room all day. Actually, forget the pads. They'd hold dust. It'd have to be an empty concrete box."

"At least you'd be safe."

They both chuckled, although Kat's was tearful.

"It's not just fear," she said. "The truth is, I don't deserve to have a second chance at love. I had my turn, and I screwed it up. The universe doesn't give do-overs to people like me."

"You're a good person, Kat. Look what you've done for me and Tione and the other people who come to stay at Sanctuary. You've given us a home when we didn't fit in anywhere else."

Brooke's voice had thickened, and when Kat glanced up, her eyes were glistening. Kat's own throat tightened in response. The past few days had been a constant stream of emotion, and she wasn't sure how much more of it she could take.

"If anyone deserves to have good things happen to them, it's you," Brooke continued. "You've paid your penance, and no amount of scrubbing floors or pushing men away will bring Teddy back. He's gone, and he'd want you to at least try to be happy."

"You don't know that," Kat whispered, digging her nails into her palms to ground herself.

"But I do," Brooke said kindly. "Because you loved him, and any man you loved would be decent enough to want the best for you."

Kat's heart cracked in two, because Brooke was right. Teddy wouldn't want her living in some kind of limbo of guilt and grief. He'd want her to be the best she could be. That was the type of relationship they'd had.

"Thank you, Brookie," she sniffed, as tears flooded her eyes. Her chest heaved and then she was ugly crying, loud sobs that came from deep within her soul and wracked her entire body. Brooke's arms came around her and she murmured comforting nothings in her ear.

When she finally finished crying, Kat felt cleansed.

22

"HAVE YOU HEARD THE NEWS?" Betty asked as she and Nell bustled inside carrying paper bags bulging with baked goods, with the Cafe Oasis logo printed on them.

Kat looked up from the invoice she was entering into her laptop on the desk in the foyer. "Hi Betty, Nell. What news is that?"

Nell flattened her gray hair, which was standing on end because of the strong breeze outside, and handed Kat one of the bags. She opened it and grinned. A spinach, cream cheese, and chili roll. Delicious.

"That nice boy who was staying with you has rented the office above Cafe Oasis," Nell said. "Just yesterday, apparently."

Whoa. Kat drew in a slow breath. "Do you mean Sterling?"

One couldn't jump to conclusions when he'd been the devil incarnate as far as they were concerned until a matter of days ago.

"Yes, that's the one," Betty said. "My, he's performed an about-face, and it's all your doing."

Kat ducked her head, embarrassed. "I don't know about that."

"Pish." Nell waved her free hand. "He as good as told us."

Her heart flopped like a landed fish. "You saw him?"

All of a sudden, she wanted to know how he was, whether he was struggling as much as she was, how he was settling in, and whether he regretted his decision to stay. Or, possibly, whether he was rethinking it. If he left, it would certainly make her life easier. She may have accepted that Teddy would have wanted her happy, but that didn't mean she was ready for a relationship, and seeing him around town would drive her to distraction.

"When we went there for breakfast. He's rented a house in town as well." Betty's expression turned sly. "He's looking very handsome." She fanned herself. "Must be the sea air. I always say the men in this town are more attractive than your average bloke."

Kat bit her tongue. Hard. She wished she could stick her fingers in her ears and drown them out. She didn't want to hear that he was flourishing. She wished him the best, but she also… well, she missed him, damn it, and it'd be nice if he missed her, too.

"Mavis is already collecting bets," Nell said.

"Bets?" Kat echoed, uncomprehending.

"On which young lady will snatch him up first," Betty explained. "We don't get too many young men moving to the area. I don't suppose it'll take long for the sharks to start circling. I've got money on Bex."

"Bex?" She was beginning to feel like an idiot. What, exactly, was going on here?

"Yes," Nell said, snapping her fingers in front of Kat's face to catch her attention. "Is something wrong with your hearing today? You don't seem yourself."

"Just a headache." It wasn't a total lie, since a steady pounding was developing behind her temples and her left eyelid was spasming. "Why would Bex want to snatch up Sterling?"

Betty sighed with all the flair of a seasoned soap-opera actress. "Why do you think? Rebecca is a pretty, single mother, struggling to get by. Sterling is a successful, good-looking man of a similar age, and while he comes across as cold, he's not at all. He's a man with stepfather potential."

Kat felt sick. Her gut churned and she actually thought she might throw up. Would she have to sit by and watch while her close friend got together with the only man she'd cared for romantically since Teddy had died, and formed a ready-made family?

"You don't see it?" Nell asked. "Neither do I. I think Brooke is more his style."

"B-Brooke," she stuttered, clutching her temples. God, could this conversation get any worse?

"They're both reserved and very clever," Nell added. "Plus Brooke doesn't come with the same level of baggage that Rebecca does."

And there they went, making it worse. Kat had more baggage than either Bex or Brooke. Was she a hopeless case? And why had none of them considered her as a prospect when they were matchmaking?

Wait a minute—did she *want* to be included? God, this was a nightmare.

"Do you want in on the action?" Betty asked. "Ten dollars gets you one entry. If you want to choose someone who's already on the board, the buy-in price is double."

This was crazy. Completely bonkers. Kat gaped at them for a long moment, then, with effort, snapped her jaw shut and said, "It's wrong to gamble on people's personal lives. I won't be a part of it. You should be ashamed of yourselves."

She sounded snooty, even to herself. Betty and Nell both drew back, regarding her with identical expressions of censure. Then they stuck their noses in the air and walked off. Nell paused, then came back and grabbed the paper bag she'd given Kat earlier. Kat watched it vanish, disappointed that her temper had ruined her morning tea.

THAT AFTERNOON, Kat was searching the kitchen fridge for a snack when footsteps heralded Tione's arrival.

"There's a mini bacon and egg pie in the warmer beneath the oven," he said.

She immediately headed over to collect it. "You're a life-saver." She took a bite. The pie was warm and hearty and fill-ing. "Everything set for dinner?"

"As much as it can be." He backed her to the counter, resting his palms on either side of her body, and stared down into her eyes. If another man had done this, she might think it was a come-on, but this was just Tione trying to figure out what was going on in her head. Good luck to him. She didn't know herself. "Are you sure you'll be all right if I leave for the evening? I don't mind hanging around to keep you company."

"I'll be okay," she replied with a half-hearted laugh. "Go and swindle Logan's money out of him."

"Yeah, about that." He moved away and looked uncom-fortable. "I think I'll be the one getting swindled. Logan invited the city boy to join poker night on a regular basis."

Kat pressed her lips together and stared at a dirty spot on the wall over his shoulder. Why did everyone insist on telling her about Sterling freaking Knight?

"You all good?" he asked, cautious.

"Fine," she bit out.

"Uh-oh."

"No, really." She dialed the intensity back. "Good for you. Maybe you'll be conned out of some of that stash of money you keep in the bank."

His eyes glinted. "Dream on, Hopa. You're just jealous you're not invited."

She sauntered to the door. "I wouldn't want to come anyway."

Especially not now that Sterling would be there. That didn't stop her palms from sweating or her heart from pounding more violently than a jackhammer at the realization that Sterling really wasn't going anywhere.

He was here to stay.

FOR THE SECOND Friday in a row, Sterling sat around a table with Logan, Tione, Jack and Shane. Logan's younger brother Kyle had also joined them. He wondered if this was how it would be for the foreseeable future, ending every week with a friendly game of poker before walking the short distance to his new home. He'd rented a place beside The Refuge, which was the quirky name for the retirement community, and he'd learned it was also the base of operations for the Bridge Club.

"This week, I'm the only one who refills my glass," he said, eyeballing the other men.

Shane had the grace to look guilty. Tione, Logan and Jack just exchanged conspiratorial grins.

"Don't tell me Logan pulled his usual trick on you," Kyle said.

"If by that you mean my smooth induction of newbies into the bachelor's club of Haven Bay, yes," Logan replied. "Yes, I did."

"And I missed it?" Kyle sighed and ran a hand over his golden buzz cut. "Damn."

Jack shuffled the cards, cut the deck, and dealt. Shane and Sterling ponied up the big and little blinds, and the first hand started.

"How's the website coming along?" Logan asked, refer- ring to the site Kyle had been designing, with Sterling's guid- ance, for the better part of the day. It turned out that in addition to being the local librarian, Kyle had a background in IT. The two of them had been working together at the library, with brief interruptions when customers needed assistance.

"It's looking great," Sterling told him. "Kyle is better than some of the pros I've worked with."

Kyle's cheeks reddened. Sterling had already discovered that the librarian, though built like a tank with a military- style haircut, was shy and didn't like attention.

"He has his moments," Jack agreed. "He did my website as well, although it'll need an update once you've finished over- hauling my business plan."

Kyle turned even redder. "I'm happy to help, but you guys do remember that Tione actually is a web designer, right?"

Tione grunted. "Not anymore. Been there, done that, not going back. You're it, I'm afraid."

Sterling's curiosity piqued. "If you're a qualified web designer, why do you work as a cook?"

"Because I want to," he replied shortly.

"Which is the only reason Tee does anything," Jack added. "What I'm interested in, is what happened with you and Kat. Spill your guts, man. We're all dying to know."

"Excuse me?" Sterling had been reaching for his glass but Jack's comment startled him and he knocked it. Whiskey sloshed over the rim and splashed his cards.

"Don't pry," Shane scolded. "It's not our business."

Something squeezed in his stomach. It had been a full-on week, and he felt emotionally wrung out. "Are you all wondering?" Now that Jack had mentioned it, he caught the undercurrent of curiosity. "It's not a very interesting story."

"You don't have to tell us," Kyle said.

"Shh," Logan hissed at his brother. "We want to know."

"I don't mind sharing." Telling people he was a goner as far as Katarina Hopa was concerned wouldn't change the fact she didn't feel the same way. Or at least, that she wouldn't admit to it. "The truth is, I care about Kat a lot and I want a relationship with her, but she isn't ready for that because she hasn't forgiven herself for her husband's death. She needs to come to terms with that on her own. There's nothing I can do about it."

For a moment, they were all silent, and then Logan cleared his throat. "That was deep."

"I've spent a lot of time thinking about it." Stewing over it, more like.

"Great," Shane said. "We've cleared out the elephant in the room. Can we play poker now?"

They all hastened to do just that.

23

STERLING ROSE bright and early the morning after poker to jog along the beach, then looped around to visit the house he'd rented but not yet moved into. He paused outside to admire the clean lines of the white stone building and the lush lawn running right up to the fence. It had no garden, except for a collection of rocks and shrubs near the drive-way. He may be turning over a new leaf, but he also knew his limitations. A lawn was more than enough for him to maintain.

The house was vacant, so he wandered up to it and peered in a window, reminding himself what the interior looked like. Living in a house, as opposed to an apartment, would be a massive change, both in terms of atmosphere and the sheer size of the place. He'd planned a trip back to Auck-land this afternoon to pick up his furniture and collect a few more of his things, but not everything he owned. He'd give his new business a three-month trial run before he officially told his Auckland landlord that he was moving out and handed in his notice at Lockwood Holdings.

He continued jogging, a smile on his face, nodding to the people he passed and greeting a few by name. When he got

210

back to The Den, he showered and dressed. Then he visited the minimart to restock Logan's fridge since he'd done a fair job of emptying it over the past few days. He grabbed a basket and added a selection of fresh produce, milk, coffee, and a bag of trail mix to snack on during his drive to Auckland. He was at the counter and had just finished paying the cashier when a voice behind him caught his attention.

"Hello, Sterling."

Closing his eyes briefly, he clenched his fists around his wallet, then pulled himself together, pasted a smile on, and turned. "Hi, Kat. How are you doing?"

He had to double-take at the sight of her. She looked wrecked. Dark smudges shadowed her eyes, her hair was piled haphazardly on her head, and she was washed out, her usual vitality absent. It seemed that the days since they'd parted had been rough on her, and his heart ached on her behalf. He wished he could take away her pain and guilt, but only she had that power.

Her lips pursed, and she sighed. "I've been better, but I'm hanging in there." Her dark eyes searched his. "How about you?"

"I'm all right." He paused to take his bags from the cashier, and moved aside to allow Kat's groceries to be scanned and packed into a bag. "I'm making progress with my business."

"I heard." She smiled at him, swiped her card, and grabbed her bag. Then they walked outside together and stopped in the square. "You rented the space above Cafe Oasis, right?"

She'd been keeping tabs on him.

He nodded. "Yes, and I've rented a house on Elizabeth Street. I'm heading back to Auckland to pick up some things later today."

She smiled, her teeth gleaming white between plum-colored lips. "Good for you. You're going to do well, I just know it."

She laid her bag down on the cobblestone sidewalk and

rested her palm on his arm. Awareness zinged through him, strong enough he could have sworn his hair stood on end and his toes curled up.

"I'm so proud of you," she said. "I know how brave you have to be to take a risk on something new."

He appreciated the sentiment, but couldn't help wishing that she'd be brave enough to take a similar risk.

"So far, everything is going well," he told her. "Everyone has been supportive, including my boss."

"That's great." He knew she meant it, but her enthusiasm was forced. In fact, she sounded worn out. "I'm happy for you."

"Thank you." He hesitated, then added, "I hope you're taking care of yourself."

She rolled her eyes. "Don't worry, if I wasn't, Tee and Brooke would tie me to a bed until I promised to do better. I know I look like shit. I'm just not sleeping well."

He could guess why, and he wanted to let her know she didn't need to beat herself up over it. "About what happened between us—"

"I'm sorry," she broke in, then glanced down at the ground, followed by the statue—at anything other than him. "If I hurt you, I mean."

He placed his bags beside hers and pulled her into a hug, his heartache irrelevant because she needed him. Needed reassurance. If nothing else, he could give her that.

"No hard feelings," he murmured beside her ear. "I promise. You're an amazing woman. I'm grateful for everything I learned from you, and I hope that one day you can forgive yourself."

She snuggled into his chest and for a wonderful moment, he soaked up the feeling of being near her again. If only he could truly comfort her, erase her sadness, and replace it with all the love and joy he had to offer. If only he could give her the self-forgiveness she needed. He hoped with all his heart that she'd take his words on board and try to find peace.

When she extricated herself, he kissed her cheek, then lifted his bags so his hands were occupied. Otherwise he might reach for her before he could stop himself. Bidding her farewell, he returned to The Den, longing for her to be walking by his side.

UNLIKE LAST SATURDAY, this time Kat was ready when the phone call from her mother-in-law came. She watched the number blink on her screen and held her breath, her thumb hovering over the answer button. She chewed on her lower lip. She needed to do this. She owed it to Amanda, and to herself. She needed to front up to what she'd done, and try to move on. On the ninth ring, just before it went to voicemail, she accepted the call.

"H-hello." Her voice shook when she spoke. She heard an intake of breath through the speaker but for a long time, no one said anything. "Amanda?" she asked. "Is that you?"

A hiccupping sob came down the line, loud and clear, then a series of sniffles. Her mother-in-law was crying. Kat's gut wrenched. This was why she'd never answered.

"I'm sorry," she whispered. "It was a mistake to pick up. I didn't mean to cause you any more pain. I should go…"

"No!" Amanda exclaimed. "No, don't go. They're tears of relief, Kat, because I didn't think I'd ever get to talk to you again. It's so good to hear your voice, *tamahine*. I've missed you."

"You what?" The room spun. Kat sank onto the sofa in case her trembling knees gave out, and her breath wheezed unevenly past her teeth. "But I thought you blamed me," she said, dumbstruck. "It's my fault Teddy is gone."

"No, darling. No, no, no," Amanda gushed. "I was worried

you might believe that. Why do you think I keep calling? It was an accident. Just a stupid accident. There was nothing you could have done about it."

Her vision blurred. "I was driving."

"I know, darling. I'm putting you on speaker phone. Motu is here with me."

"Katarina," Teddy's father said in his husky smoker's voice. "Someone else t-boned you. He was a drunk asshole who ran a red light. That's on him, not you."

She squeezed her eyes shut, formed a fist with her empty hand and bit her knuckles so hard it hurt. The pain grounded her. "I should have seen him coming. I should have been able to prevent it."

"Oh, baby," Amanda crooned, like she was a scared kid. "You've got to let go of the hurt. No one could have saved Teddy. Not the way it played out."

"You don't know that." She heard how pathetic and self-pitying she sounded, but could do nothing to stop it.

"Pull yourself up by your bootstraps," Motu ordered. "That drunk served time. He got what was coming to him. The crash wasn't your fault, and we would have told you that in person, but you vanished and we didn't know where you'd gone."

Kat clutched the fabric of her shorts and asked the question she most dreaded hearing the answer to. "Do you think you could ever forgive me?"

Amanda laughed a watery laugh. "You're not listening to us, darling. You don't need our forgiveness because you did nothing wrong. We miss Teddy every day, but nothing you could have done would have saved him."

Kat rolled onto her side, rested her head on the arm of the couch and curled into a ball, trying to hold in all of the emotions unfurling within her. The room seemed to shake around her, and she realized it wasn't the room that was moving, it was her. Her entire body was trembling uncontrollably.

"You need to let yourself off the hook," Amanda said. "We don't hold you accountable, and our son wouldn't want you hurting yourself the way you have been. He adored you, and he would have wanted you to let yourself be happy."

Kat's chin wobbled. "I miss him. He always made everything seem better than it was."

"Nothing ever shook that boy," Motu said. "Funny, the things you remember."

"And the things you forget," Kat murmured. She needed to think. "I'm glad I talked to you both. I'm sorry I've ignored your calls for so long. I was afraid. I didn't want to hear what you had to say."

"There's nothing to apologize for," Amanda said. "But if it eases your conscience, we'd really like to visit sometime."

Kat nodded. That might be okay. "I'll text you the address. Just let me know if you decide to come."

Amanda hesitated. "Please don't shut us out again, Kat. When you and Teddy were married, we loved you like our own daughter. When Teddy died, it felt like we lost both our *tamariki* at once. All we wanted to do was to keep you close and give you all our love. Our *aroha.* To grieve with you. We know you had no choice but to miss the *tangi* since you were in hospital with your injuries, and I hate thinking that you've bottled everything up all that time."

"I won't shut you out," Kat said. "I promise. If you call this time next weekend, I'll answer." She hesitated. "It would be —" she considered her word choice, "—nice to have you in my life again."

"We'll talk later," Amanda replied. "Goodnight, darling."

They hung up, and Kat dropped her phone to the floor and buried her face in a cushion. She screamed, the sound muffled so much she doubted anyone outside the room heard. The weight of the world should have been lifted from her shoulders, but it hadn't. And she thought she knew why.

Sterling had been right. Amanda and Motu, too. It wasn't their forgiveness she needed. It was her own. A thing that should be simple, but somehow seemed an impossible task.

Curling into a ball, Kat fell into an exhausted slumber on the sofa.

24

KAT WOKE WITH RENEWED PURPOSE, marched down the hall to Brooke's room, and knocked on the door. It cracked open, and Brooke's bespectacled face appeared in the gap.

"*Morena*," Kat said. "I hope I didn't wake you."

"No, you didn't. I'm studying." Stepping back, Brooke opened the door wider, revealing the laptop and textbook on her bed. A steaming mug of coffee sat on the cabinet and faint music played from the headphones hooked around her neck. Her hair was collected in a messy bun and she wore faded pajamas that read: *Woman. Noun. Wuh-Man. Equal to a man, only cuter*.

"Am I interrupting?" Kat asked.

Brooke smiled. "I could use a break. Why don't you come in and snuggle up with me?" She returned to her bed and climbed in.

Kat joined her, pulling up the blankets. "What are you working on?"

"I'm writing an essay comparing nudes as painted by men and women artists between the 16th and 17th centuries. It's for the New Zealand Journal of Art History." She sighed. "Part of my doctoral program is that I have to get four articles accepted for publication in national or international journals."

Kat nodded. "What number is this?"

"Two."

She searched her memory. "The first was the one about the interpretation of Mary Magdalene in renaissance art?"

Brooke beamed. "I can't believe you remember that."

Kat laughed. "Of course I remember. You do know you're my best friend, Brookie? I keep tabs on what you're up to."

Brooke put her cheek on Kat's shoulder and wrapped an arm around her waist. "It's never mattered to me whether I'm your best friend, because you're mine."

Kat hugged her tightly. "I need a favor," she said, when they let go of each other. "It might take up most of your day, is that all right? I can ask someone else if you're busy."

Brooke clasped Kat's hands in hers. "Whatever you need, I'm your girl. If I have to read another word about the objectification of women's bodies, I might hit someone."

Kat rolled her eyes. Though Brooke was a staunch feminist and sassy as hell, she didn't know anyone less likely to hit a person. "Sure, sure. Here's the thing. I need you to drive me to the cemetery where Teddy is buried. It's about two hours away."

Brooke gasped. "You're asking me to *drive* you? Are you sure? I know what a big deal that is."

Every part of Kat resisted the thought of getting into a metal death trap, but it was necessary if she wanted to visit Teddy. Walking or biking would take days, and even she knew that would be taking things too far.

"I'm sure," she said, praying that she didn't freak out and make a fool of herself. "I'll manage."

"You know you don't have to prove anything to anyone."

"But I do," Kat argued. "I need to prove to myself that I can do it. It's been nearly three years since the bus dropped me off in the square, and I haven't been in a vehicle since.

Maybe it's not something I want to do all the time, but I need to know that I'm capable of it. I trust you to get me there and back safely."

"Then of course I will," Brooke said. "I'm honored you trust me." She slipped a bookmark into her textbook and closed it. "Do you want to make a start now and get it over with sooner?"

That would be too easy. Besides, Kat was still feeling fragile. She needed a while to build up the courage to endure the trip. But only a few hours, she promised herself, nothing more. She wouldn't put off being in a car for any longer.

"Let's get breakfast first. I could use a good coffee and a muffin. Want me to bring something back and we can eat in bed and watch an episode of Star Trek?" The show was one of Brooke's favorites.

Her friend grinned. "Absolutely. I might have a shower and freshen up before we leave." She glanced down at herself. "I can't go anywhere looking like this."

"It's a plan." Kat kissed Brooke's cheek and climbed out of bed. "I need to do the same, then I'll be back with *kai*."

"Bring me something sweet!" Brooke called after her.

WHEN THEY REACHED Brooke's little white Nissan, doubt assailed Kat. What had she been thinking? What if she couldn't do it? Her feet rooted to the ground and she stared at the car like the Grim Reaper was emblazoned on the passenger door. Suddenly, the memories were all too close. The almighty smash of metal against metal, the squeal of rubber on the road, the scent of petrol and burning.

She shuddered. "I-I…"

Seeing her dilemma, Brooke came around and opened the passenger door wide, so all she needed to do was slide into the seat and buckle up. "You can do it, Kitty Kat. I believe in you."

Her faith was all Kat needed to take the first step, then the second. She bent at the knees mechanically and got in. As she looked through the windshield, a pair of headlights appeared in her vision, careering toward them. Her blood pressure spiked, her head spun and she squeezed her eyes shut, throwing her hands up to protect herself. But nothing happened.

"Easy." A hand landed on her thigh and a soothing voice spoke near her ear. "You're okay. You did it. You're in."

Kat opened her eyes again. There was no other car. She'd imagined it. They were sitting, motionless, on the edge of Sanctuary's gravel parking lot in broad daylight. She cringed. "Sorry, I thought I saw…" She trailed off.

"No need to explain anything to me," Brooke said. "I'm here to support you, okay?"

"Okay," she whispered, then pulled the door shut and clicked the belt into place. The tiny click seemed to echo ominously through the car. When Brooke turned the key in the ignition and the engine roared to life, Kat tensed.

"You all good?" Brooke asked.

"Yeah. Just drive."

They crawled forward, a stark contrast to the days when Kat had been one of the fastest women on four wheels, but no less terrifying for it. She clung to the edge of her seat so hard her knuckles turned white.

"Remember to breathe," Brooke urged.

"I can't," she choked. "I feel like I'm going to—" She slammed her hands over her mouth as bile rose up the back of her throat. Brooke stopped, and Kat undid her seat belt, threw the door open, stumbled out, and wretched up the contents of her stomach all over the grass bordering the driveway. A hand stroked her lower back, and she closed her eyes. "I'm sorry, I didn't know that was coming."

"Shush. Stop apologizing."

Something pressed into her hand. A water bottle. She

gulped greedily, swirling water around the inside of her mouth and spitting it out. "Thanks."

"No problem. Now get back in the car, and let's keep going."

Brooke was a hard taskmaster, and Kat did as she was told. Twice more they had to stop for her to empty her stomach, but each time, she rinsed her mouth, wiped her clammy forehead on her sleeve, and got back into the car. It wasn't as if she had any choice. She couldn't exactly walk home.

They stopped for lunch in Tauranga, and the sheer volume of traffic and quantity of pedestrians unnerved Kat, given she hadn't left Haven Bay in years. She watched people pass as they sat in the window of a cafe and ate. Neither of them spoke much. When they'd finished, Kat gave Brooke directions to the cemetery and asked her to wait near the exit. This was something she had to do alone.

It took nearly fifteen minutes to find Teddy's grave. The nondescript black headstone was decorated with artificial flowers, which looked like they'd been delivered recently. Amanda and Motu must have come by, or one of Teddy's friends. He'd had many. He was that kind of guy.

The stone read:

Edward Hopa
1987-2017
Beloved husband and son.
You will be missed.

Kat's eyes watered. The simple words did nothing to describe the impact Teddy had had on the lives of those around him, but they were perfect all the same. Sinking to the ground above the spot where he lay buried, she touched a finger to one of her cheeks and realized they were wet. A sob wracked her body.

"I'm so sorry," she said to Teddy's headstone. "*Aroha mai nui*. I'm sorry about the crash. I wish you were still here. I miss you like crazy. You were the glue that held me together."

She fell silent, gathering herself. A fantail swooped from a tree and landed nearby, watching her with beady black eyes. It hopped closer, and in that moment, she felt that she wasn't alone. The sun warmed the back of her neck, as though Teddy was reaching down from the heavens to comfort her.

"I have to move on with my life," she said, hoping that wherever he was, he could hear her and understand. "Your *whaea* told me that's what you'd want." The fantail took off, and she watched it flit over rows of graves and into the blue horizon. "I love you, with all my heart. *Aroha tino nui ki a koe.* In a little pocket of my heart, I'll always love you. But your parents are right. It's time for me to be brave and try to be happy again." Her throat thickened and she hardly managed to get the last words out. "So, I guess this is goodbye." Her eyes prickled with fresh tears and she sniffed. "I hope wherever you are, you forgive me."

"I think he does, love."

She looked over her shoulder. A wizened old man was laying flowers on the grave behind her. She'd been so absorbed in her own sorrow, she hadn't heard him approach. He came closer, and she noticed his eyes shining with tears. She glanced at the grave he'd left.

Ada Marie Nelson
Wife, mother, and friend to all.
May you fly with the angels.

The dates indicated that Ada Marie would have been in her seventies when she passed away. His wife, she assumed. This man was as familiar with grief as she was.

"Your young man is up in heaven with my Ada, and I'm sure he forgives you for whatever happened. I'm tearing up myself, just listening to you."

She blinked rapidly. "Thank you, that's very kind of you." She swallowed past a lump. "You know what? I think he forgives me, too. And so do I. Finally." Clearing her throat, she gestured to the headstone across from her. "I'm sorry about your Ada."

"So am I, love, but she's in a better place now."

Kat smiled and left him there, heading back to Brooke. She climbed into the car and repressed the instinctive urge to shield herself as the engine started.

"You okay, Kitty-Kat?" Brooke asked, touching her arm.

Kat turned, meeting her friend's worried gaze. "I am. Thank you for bringing me here. I needed closure, and you've helped me with that."

"You're so welcome. I'm glad I could help even a fraction as much as you've helped me." They hugged across the gap between the seats. When they separated, Brooke put the car into gear and steered it onto the road.

Kat stared out of the window, her heart lighter than it had been since the accident. The oppressive weight that had been smothering her for so long had finally lifted, and she felt like she could float out of her seat and soar across the sky the same way the fantail had. Even though it had been years since she'd experienced it, she knew what this feeling was. *Freedom.*

25

STERLING CHECKED off another item on the inventory of Logan's equipment he was wading through. He sat at the desk in his new office, facing the window that overlooked the town square. He'd had to shut the office door to block out the mouthwatering smell of pastries wafting up from Cafe Oasis. If he wasn't careful, he'd gain ten pounds from snacking on the delicious fare below. A knock on his door drew his attention and he turned and straightened, stretching his arms above his head, the muscles between his shoulder blades pulling tight.

"Come in," he called.

The door opened, and Kat stepped inside. His breath caught. She'd undergone a transformation since he'd seen her on Saturday. The shadows beneath her eyes had faded, her complexion was back to its usual tawny hue, and the corners of her mouth hitched up. It wasn't quite a smile, but it was a dramatic improvement. She looked happier, and years younger. His heart kicked up a gear. He didn't want to get ahead of himself, but her presence made him hopeful.

"Hi, Kat," he said, warmth filling him from the inside and

diffusing out. God, he loved the effect she had on him. It made him feel like a new man. "It's great to see you."

She glanced at the papers on his desk. "Can you spare a moment to talk?"

"For you, always." He spun the chair around so he was facing her fully, and gestured for her to take the seat he'd bought for clients to use.

She sat, fidgeting with something in her palm, hidden from his view. "I owe you," she said. "Thanks to you, I was finally able to see myself clearly."

His chest felt too tight to contain his rapidly swelling heart. He clutched handfuls of his jeans. Where was this going? And where did he want it to go? "You're welcome."

"You were right," she continued, staring at her lap like she couldn't quite bring herself to meet his gaze. "I needed to forgive myself. Teddy wouldn't have wanted me to keep going on like I was."

He suppressed the stab of pain brought on by the mention of her late husband's name. *He was a part of her life*, he reminded himself. *A very important part, that made her who she is today.*

"I talked to my in-laws over the weekend."

"That was a big step for you." He was inordinately proud that he'd been able to contribute to her getting there in some small way.

She took a deep breath and lifted her head, her dark eyes locking on his. "It was, but I'm really glad I did it. We cleared up a lot of misunderstandings." Her fists squeezed together as she went on. "I also visited Teddy's grave."

"You did?" Then the implication hit him. "You drove?"

"Brooke drove me," she corrected.

"Still, that's massive. I'm so proud of you." He wished he could have been there to hold her hand and talk her through it. Regardless, he was pleased she'd had Brooke. He'd have to buy the other woman flowers and pay her a visit. "How do you feel now?"

"So much better." The smile accompanying the statement loosened the knot of complicated emotions in the pit of his stomach. His optimism grew. This was actually happening. She was really here, in his office, telling him she was moving on. He hardly dared to hope she might be ready to acknowledge the feelings between them.

"I have something for you." She opened her hand and offered him a small velvet pouch, the type one might find at a jeweler's. He stared at it, both intrigued and afraid of what might be inside. "Go on," she urged. "Open it."

His fingers fumbled with the tiny drawstrings, and he slipped his thumb and forefinger inside. They brushed a small item wrapped in tissue paper. He drew it out, his brow crinkled in thought. It was weightier than he'd expected, and an odd shape. He had no idea what it could be. Lifting the sticker that sealed the paper together, he unwrapped it. When he'd finished, a key lay on the center of the tissue, shiny enough to be new despite its old-fashioned style.

"What's this?" he asked, confused.

Kat took it from him and held it up. "It's the key to Sanctuary," she said. "Dual-purpose. It unlocks both the front door and my apartment."

He swallowed. His throat had become dry and scratchy. "Why are you giving this to me?"

She pressed it into his palm. "I cleared space for you, in case you want to stay permanently." She lowered her gaze, tugged at the hem of her shorts, and added, "If not, I hope you'll come by whenever you want to see me, or anyone else. Treat it like your second home, because as far as I'm concerned, it is."

He was touched. He wondered if she could possibly know how much this gesture meant to him. Since his mother had died, he'd never had a home. A place where he was always welcome, no matter what. A place where he could be himself. The backs of his eyes prickled and he swallowed a lump of emotion. To him, home had become as much about the people as about the place. Sanctuary was home.

Kat was home.

"Thank you." He grasped the key so hard it bit into his fingers. "This means a lot to me." He blinked quickly and chewed on his tongue to suppress the rising tide of love and affection from spilling over and emerging as tears, or, God forbid, words.

"There's something else," she said, shifting awkwardly. "Another thing I need to show you."

DAMN, this was much harder than Kat had expected. She must be keeping it together better than she thought though, because if she'd looked half as edgy as she felt, Sterling wouldn't be staring at her with that steady, thoughtful gaze. He'd have already called a shrink or a paramedic. Fortunately, her fear was accompanied by an equal level of excitement because—finally—she was embracing life again. She was putting herself out there, going out on a limb, and it felt great. Better than great. Like a real turning point.

She stood, aware of his watchful gaze upon her, then slowly raised her shirt until she'd bared the left side of her torso. The addition to her tattoo was still hot to the touch because it had only been made yesterday, and last time she'd checked, it had been slightly red. It was fitting, she thought, to mark this major turning point on her body. There was no going back now. She'd firmly closed the door on the last chapter of her life and locked it behind her.

"I added to my tattoo," she said unnecessarily, fearing her heart might leap out of her throat while she waited for a response from him. He came over and knelt by her side, examining the fresh black ink.

"A key," he said wonderingly, tracing the outside of the shape with the tip of his finger, so softly she scarcely felt it. "You added a key to the lock on your heart."

She nodded.

He looked up. "Why?"

She tried to remember the speech she'd rehearsed earlier, but it fled her mind. "I don't really know how to explain it."

"Try." If she hadn't known him as well as she did, she might have found this abrupt, but she could see the patience in his expression, and the genuine desire to know and to understand her.

Her eyelids fluttered closed. It was easier to think if she couldn't see the sharp angles of his handsome face, or the sincere emotion in his deep blue eyes. "Because of you, I realized I don't have to lock my heart away." She fought the urge to pull the shirt down and hide both the tattoo and the multitude of scars that crisscrossed her body. Difficult as it may be, she wanted to reveal herself to him. To show him everything. "You were the key to learning how to open my heart to love again."

His fingers brushed her skin again, and they trembled. "The key is for me?" he asked softly.

"It is," she whispered, grateful he understood.

"What are you trying to tell me?" His lips touched the inflamed skin so tenderly she thought she might weep. "Are you saying what I think you are?"

She dropped her shirt, opened her eyes and pulled him to his feet. Then she squared her shoulders, summoned her last drop of courage, and said, "I want to make a life with you. I'm ready for that now, if you still want me."

His jaw worked, but he didn't say anything. His Adam's apple bobbed. She held her ground, feeling remarkably like she'd tiptoed out onto a ledge above a hundred-foot drop, and was waiting for someone to throw her a lifeline. Then he smiled, and it was the most wonderful thing she'd ever seen.

"Nothing would make me happier."

He took her hand and pressed it to his cheek, then leaned forward and kissed her ever-so-sweetly. Once, twice, a third time. She was breathless. She'd tumbled off the ledge only to find it was two feet high, and had a layer of pillows ready to cushion her fall. She couldn't recall the last time she'd been this truly happy.

And then he said, "I love you, Katarina," and her soul took flight.

"You do?" she whispered.

The corners of his eyes crinkled with laughter. *This.* This was the expression she wanted to see on his face every day for the rest of her life.

"I do," he confirmed. "You opened my heart, too. I'd never realized how much possibility was out there until you came along. I love you."

"That's a relief," she told him, "because I love you, too. Sorry it took me a while to figure it out."

He cupped her face in his palms and peppered her cheeks and forehead with kisses. "I would have waited longer if I'd needed to." Gathering her in his arms, he hugged her tight. She sighed happily, and rested her cheek on his chest, feeling safe and secure and all those glorious things she'd never believed she'd experience again. "Would you rather I move in with you now, or wait for a while?" he asked. "I don't mind either way. Whatever you're comfortable with."

She looped her arms around his lower back and squeezed. "You're welcome at Sanctuary whenever you're ready. I'd be happy for you to move in today if that's what you want."

"Really?"

She could tell he was battling some insecurities of his own. Insecurities she never wanted him to feel again. "Absolutely. I'd love to have you there, but I know you have your own place now, which might complicate things."

"Then yes," he said. "Let's do it. I've never been more ready. As far as my new place goes, it's not home. Not the way Sanctuary is. I'll keep it for a while until we sort out our living situation properly, but the landlord won't have a problem finding a new tenant."

Her hands slipped down to grab his butt. "Oh, really?"

He groaned. "What say we get out of here? I have the sudden urge to go home."

She loved the way he said "home," and the pleasure that passed over his face at being able to do so. She stretched onto her toes and kissed him. "Take me home," she murmured.

They joined hands and hurried down the stairs. When they entered the square together, both flushed, hands still intertwined, a few of the locals clapped and catcalled.

"Shall we run?" Sterling asked, catching her gaze. Her heart flipped over at the emotion he no longer made any effort to hide from her.

She nodded. "I don't want to talk to anyone right now."

"About time!" Logan yelled from The Den.

Jack, drawn out by the cacophony, wolf-whistled as they ran past, and the tourists, always down for a bit of fun, applauded around the square. Kat knew her face must be beet red, but she couldn't bring herself to care. Together, they sprinted around the corner and out of sight, slowing to a walk once they reached the beach.

"I don't remember the last time I had so much fun," Sterling said, laughing.

"Neither." She stopped and grabbed both of his hands in hers. He smiled down at her, eyes twinkling, chest rapidly rising and falling. God, she loved this man. "But I promise you, we're going to have fun every day from now on. Just you and me."

"I like the sound of that."

The gleam in his eye turned dark and speculative, and whatever else she'd been about to say vanished from her mind. She twined her arms around his neck and drew him down for an intensely thorough kiss. The kind of kiss that wasn't an ending, but rather the beginning of something new. Something built to last. When it finished, they walked arm in arm along the beach toward Sanctuary, where their home, and their future, awaited.

THE END

TWO OF A KIND EXCERPT

Jack Farrelly wished, not for the first time, that he wasn't such great friends with Logan Pride. If not for his loyalty to Logan, he'd have packed a tent and headed into the wilderness for a bit of R and R. Instead, the cherry on top of his shit-cake of a day was attending the annual New Year's Eve costume party Logan hosted at his pub, The Den.

"What are you supposed to be?" his friend demanded as he arrived, sauntering over in a pair of red swimming trunks and nothing else. The theme this year was, 'dress as your favorite fictional character', but Jack hadn't had the energy after running into his ex earlier—which had thrown him out of whack—so he'd rocked up in his usual.

"Bear Grylls."

Logan rolled his eyes, and swept his tousled blond hair off his forehead. "Not a fictional character. Come on, man. Make an effort."

Jack looked pointedly at him. "You're a fine one to talk. You look like you just rolled in off the beach." Logan had been a professional surfer in a previous life, and now taught surfing classes when he wasn't busy at The Den. "Who are you supposed to be?"

He gestured down at himself. "Isn't it obvious? I'm Mitch Buchannon from Baywatch."

"Is that the show with Pamela Anderson in her golden days?"

Logan grinned, the edges of his eyes crinkling. "Now you're getting it." He jostled Jack with his elbow. "Come on. Grab a beer. First one's on me." As they made their way through the throng, navigating between the bar leaners that ran from the door to the classic old-school counter, where the drinks menu was scrawled across a surfboard—Logan's personal touch—he asked, "So, what's up with you?"

Jack grunted. "Claudia is in town."

Logan pulled a face like he'd tasted something bad. "She staying long?"

"God, I hope not." He hadn't asked, had just gotten away from her as quickly as possible. Since they'd broken up two years ago, he seen neither hide nor hair of her, and that was the way he preferred it.

Logan rounded the bar, filled a pint glass, and pushed it over. Jack took a healthy swig then set it down to scan the room and pick out familiar faces. Logan's brother Kyle sat in the corner with their mutual friend Tione, but Shane—the other man in their circle—was notably absent, most likely because he hadn't been able to find a babysitter.

A customer called Logan's name, and he shuffled along the bar to serve them. Beer in hand, Jack headed for the corner table to join his friends. He was halfway there when the door opened and a woman appeared, silhouetted against the dim evening.

His heart stuttered. The woman—she must have been a tourist because there was no way he'd have forgotten a face like hers—surveyed the room, her chin raised, very much the queen she'd come dressed as. He took a moment to appreciate her outfit, as did every other heterosexual man present. Khaleesi Daenerys Targaryen, the mother of dragons. Her eyes, a glorious blue, passed over him, then flicked back, resting on his face. He met her gaze and held it. Of their own accord, his feet carried him to her side.

Khaleesi's blonde hair fell over her shoulders in pale waves, and she wore her iconic battle costume, a fitted black leather dress with a cape attached. Her lips were baby pink and glossy. Jack wanted to capture that mouth with his own and devour her. He'd never been a big Game of Thrones fan, but Khaleesi was the woman of his dreams. Gorgeous, strong, take-no-prisoners. This woman, with her shoulders thrown back and her face tilted up, gave every impression of having walked directly out of his fantasies.

"Khaleesi," he rumbled, his voice gravelly and rough. "Do you have a date?"

She raised an imperious eyebrow. "Why is that any of your business?"

He put his hand to his heart. "Because if you don't, I'd like to rectify a terrible wrong by buying you a drink."

The corners of her glossy lips lifted, and a bolt of arousal shot straight to his groin. He shifted, and remembered Kyle and Tione, who were no doubt watching him from the corner. He couldn't get an awkward boner in front of his friends.

"As it happens," she said, "I don't."

"Excellent." He cupped her elbow and escorted her past the partygoers, many of whom turned to stare, into a private room out the back. Logan wouldn't mind him using it. Not under these circumstances. When Khaleesi gave him a questioning look, he said, "I have an in with the owner."

They sank onto the couch, and she gave him a cheeky little smile that sent a pulse of heat due south. "So, handsome man with an 'in'," she said, the tip of her finger tracing a line down his chest. "Who are you playing today?"

He willed his eager dick to play it cool. "Bear Grylls." His voice emerged even raspier than before. Being turned on tended to do that to him.

She nodded thoughtfully. "I see that. Manly, outdoorsy, hot as hell."

Her caress drifted lower, and his abdominals quivered in response. He clenched his jaw, trying to figure out how she'd managed to get him rearing to go with no more than a gentle touch. "You think I'm hot?"

She cocked her head and grinned at him, her lower lip caught between her teeth. "Eh, you're not bad."

"Not bad." He huffed. "I'll show you not bad."

With that, he reached over and dragged her onto his lap, enjoying the soft exhale that proved he'd caught her by surprise. She settled onto him, and he looped his arm around her waist, holding her close. Those glistening lips parted, taunting him.

He grinned at her. "What do you say to that?"

"I say Bear Grylls better kiss me before I tell him off for taking liberties with my body."

Taking liberties with her body? Who talked like that?

He wondered what part of New Zealand she came from; he couldn't pick up her accent or way of speaking. Then his brain refocused on the pertinent word—*kiss*. She wanted him to kiss her. His erection leaped gleefully beneath her bottom. Whoever she was, and wherever she was from, tonight his Khaleesi was up for some fun, and he was more than willing to assist.

———

Brooke couldn't believe this was actually happening. After making goo-goo eyes at Jack Farrelly for two years, he'd finally noticed her. All it took was an inch of makeup, eyelash extensions, and a first-rate costume she'd been waiting for the perfect opportunity to show off.

A little effort, a few flirty words, and here she was, in his lap.

Oh, happy days.

His big, calloused hand went to the back of her head, and she reveled in the feel of it. He was such a vital guy, almost larger than life. Brooke wasn't one to play the role of delicate, wilting flower, but she was overwhelmed by his presence. His hand smoothed down her hair, and his face angled toward hers. Her breath caught, then she released a happy sigh as their lips touched.

He groaned against her mouth. "God, that sound is sexy. I bet you'd be loud with me inside you."

Heat flushed her neck, but she didn't have it in her to be embarrassed. Not when the evidence of her effect on him throbbed hot and steely beneath her. She drew his mouth back to hers and kissed him again, tasting a hint of beer on his breath. His hold on her waist tightened, and she moaned, loving the sensation of his muscled arm banding around her body.

"Fuck," he murmured, burying his face in the crook of her neck, lips moving against her skin, sending shivers of pleasure creeping down her spine. "What spell have you cast on me, Khaleesi? I'm so damn hard for you, it hurts."

In that moment, Brooke felt as powerful as the queen she was pretending to be. She'd never have guessed Jack liked to talk dirty, but hell *yes*, she could get behind it. She wanted to hear more, particularly as he stripped the clothes from her body, kissed every inch of exposed skin, and thrust into her. She'd bet *all* of him was big and solid. When she wriggled her butt against him, he shuddered, his fingers clenching fistfuls of her hair.

"You tease," he hissed from between gritted teeth.

She started to grin, but then he flicked his wrist and spanked the side of her ass. Her core throbbed in response, and her underwear dampened with her arousal. *Oh, boy.* Her lips parted in shock. She'd never have guessed she liked to be spanked, but she suspected that wasn't the only thing Jack could teach her about herself.

Her head fell back, and he latched onto her neck, kissing the length of it, sucking her pulse point, nipping it with his teeth. Then he raised his head to study his work, his lips curling in a smirk. "Yeah, that's more like it."

"Did you leave a hickey?" she demanded, far less annoyed than she ought to be—secretly thrilled that he'd want to mark her in such a way.

"Mmhmm." He kissed the spot tenderly. "You don't have a problem with that, do you?"

His tongue darted out to lap her skin, and she gasped. "I'll only have a problem if you stop."

He made his way back to her mouth, and their gazes clashed, his dark with intent. "I don't plan to stop until you're screaming, honey."

Hearing that remark, her mind whirred frantically, chaotic thoughts buzzing through it. Did she want that? How far was she prepared to go before she slowed things down?

Her body begged her to go however far Jack wanted, because she'd been craving him for so long, but her brain suggested they get to know each other better before progressing to the bedroom.

Their lips reconnected, and she sighed again. He was kissing her boneless, which didn't help her clarity of thought, nor did his fingers venturing beneath her dress. Their lips clung, then separated, tongues tasting, breath coming in pants. She fisted her hands in his t-shirt and fully committed to the kiss.

Crash!

The door flew open, and a couple stumbled into the room. Brooke and Jack jerked apart, staring at the intruders.

Flipping his scruffy blond hair out of his eyes, Logan

winked at them. "Sorry guys, the owner needs this room now."

The woman accompanying him hid her face in his chest and giggled. Brooke's sense flooded back. She was sitting on a man's lap, her dress hitched up around her thighs, love bites marring her neck, completely prepared to go to bed with someone who'd never given any indication he even knew she existed before today.

What was she thinking?

Shooting to her feet, she yanked her dress down, stumbled, then righted herself, and raced out of the room. Jack's voice echoed after her, but she didn't stop, and the absence of footsteps behind her indicated he hadn't given chase. Perhaps he didn't want to cause a scene. She was beyond caring.

On the way out, she passed her friend Kyle, who took in her red face and stricken expression and immediately ushered her into the square.

"What's wrong?" he asked, concern evident in his gray eyes.

"Nothing. Just get me out of here—fast."

Kyle led her to his car, which was parked outside the library. When they reached her place, he escorted her as far as the bedroom door, where he gave her a hug and promised to call to check on her. Fifteen minutes later, she was in her pajamas, her face scrubbed clean, lying in bed, and replaying the scene in her mind over and over as she stared at the ceiling, wondering if her stolen moments with Jack had been a one-off, or the start of something special. Only time would tell.

ALSO BY ALEXA RIVERS

Haven Bay
Then There Was You
Two of a Kind
Safe in His Arms
If Only You Knew
Pretend to Be Yours
Begin Again With You
Let Me Love You

Little Sky Romance
Accidentally Yours
From Now Until Forever
It Was Always You
Dreaming of You

Little Sky Romance Novellas
Midnight Kisses
Second Chance Christmas

Destiny Falls

Stay With You
Come Back to You
Always Been Yours

Blue Collar Romance
A Place to Belong

ACKNOWLEDGMENTS

The list of people who have encouraged me on my writing and publishing journey is endless. I've encountered so many wonderful and supportive people, both in my personal life, and amongst my colleagues. But to begin with, I'd like to thank you—yes *you*, the person reading this book. Thank you for reading my words and trusting me to give you the happily ever after you want. Without you, none of this would have been possible, and it's an honor to share the stories in my head with you.

An especially big thank you to my beta readers and review team, whose help and kind words have kept me going every time I wondered where on earth I was going with my stories, and if I'd ever get there. Thank you to my husband, who is my number one supporter, and has always believed in me even at times when I doubted myself. You have no idea how much your unwavering confidence means to me. Likewise, thank you to Mum, who religiously reads every one of my books each time it comes back from the proofreader to check for anything that's been missed. You're the best. XX.

Thank you to everyone who helped in the production of this book. Kate S, who helped shape the story into something beautiful, and Serena C, who polished it until it sparkled. To the crew at Deranged Doctor Design, the cover you made me took my breath away.

Lastly, thanks to my dog, Ella, without whom this story likely would have been finished much faster. Regardless of your interruptions, we got here, and your company is much appreciated.

ABOUT THE AUTHOR

Alexa Rivers writes about genuine characters living messy, imperfect lives and earning hard-won happily ever afters. Most of her books are set in small towns, and she lives in one of these herself. She shares a house with a neurotic dog and a husband who thinks he's hilarious.

When she's not writing, she enjoys traveling, baking, eating too much chocolate, cuddling fluffy animals, drinking excessive amounts of tea, and absorbing herself in fictional worlds.

Made in the USA
Columbia, SC
13 January 2023

10283028R00152